Melidora

Ryan Z. Dawson

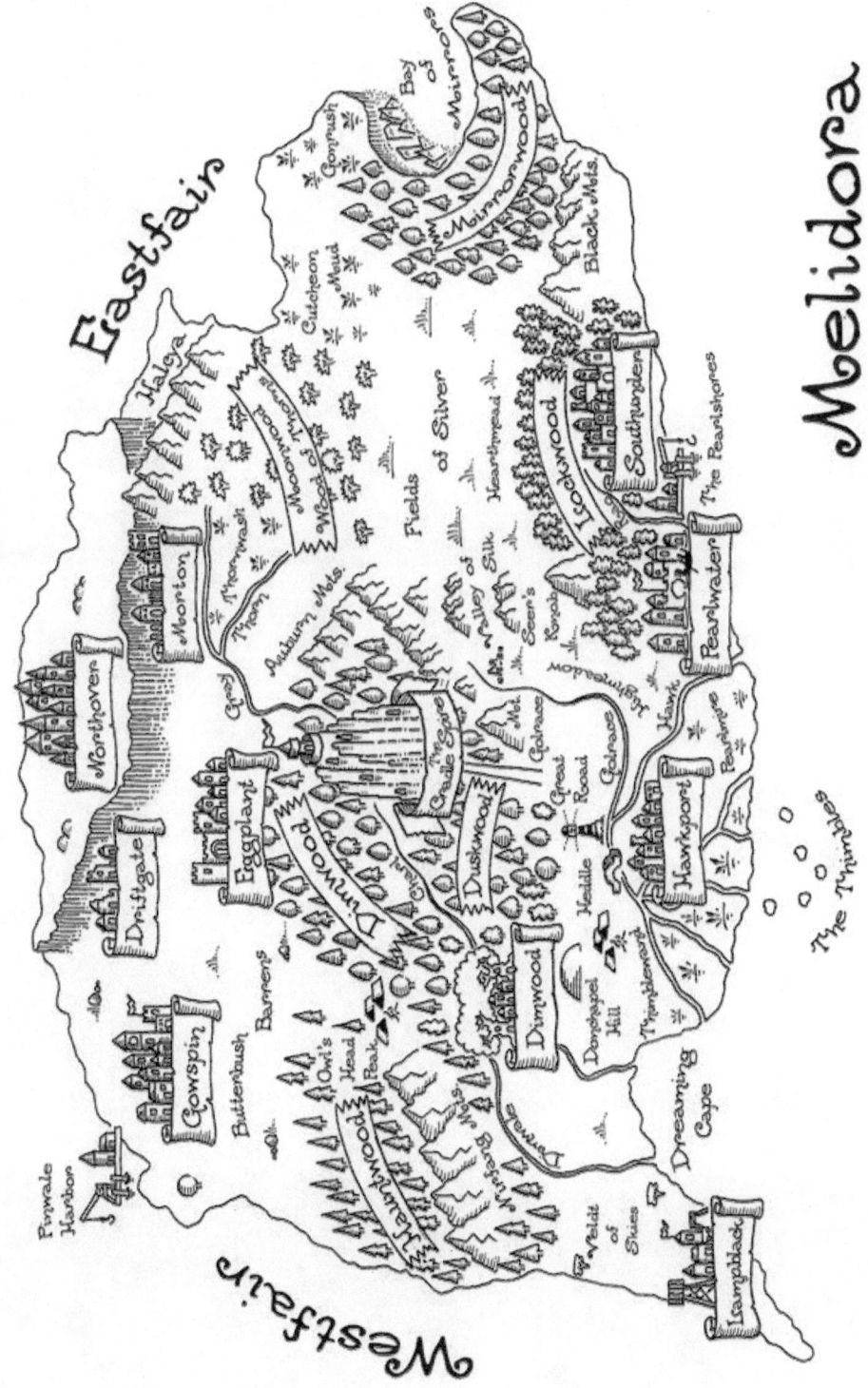

Melidora

by
Ryan Z. Dawson

Edited by
Michelle Lovi
Dara Rochlin

Cover art by
Ryan Valle

Inner illustration by
Jorge Cristino

First Edition: 2014

ISBN 978-0-9907920-2-4

Dire Ninja Media
Live Oak, CA 95953

www.direninja.com

For Lisa and for Rainbow

Acknowledgements

I'd like to acknowledge the help and support of Lisa Dawson, Zack Dawson, Ryan Valle, Jorge Cristino, Buddy Wagner, Michelle Lovi, Robin Bev Connelly, and Dara Rochlin. There are no small contributions. Thank you all.

ᏒᎬᏒᏒᎬᎦᎥ ᏁᎬᎯᎦᎯᎦ ᎰᎦᏒ ᏒᎥᏒᏒᏒᎦᎯᎦ. ᏊᏒᎦᎦᎥ
ᏁᎬ'ᎦᎥ ᏁᎬ ᏁᎦᏒᎦᏡ ᏕᎦ ᎦᏁᎦᎦᎦᎦᎦᏁᎦᎦᎦᎦᏒᎦᏁᏒᎬ
ᎦᎦᏁᎦᎬᎥ ᏁᎬ ᎦᎦᎠᏒᎥ.

Everybody needs his memories. They keep the wolf of insignificance from the door.
-Saul Bellow

One

Arrival

She awoke on the beach, drenched to the bone and choking. In the pouring surf, she rolled to her hands and knees and retched. Her throat burned and she convulsed, eyes bulging wide as she fought to disgorge a bellyful of seawater. At last, she vomited, and the surf pounded her clean as she struggled to stand. Too weak, she collapsed.

The whole weight and rage of the sea were on her back. Light moved behind her eyelids, pulsing, burning a warning through long spells of seizures. Then the tide slipped out, and the last of the worst paroxysms passed. She sat up and opened her eyes.

There was something cold and smooth beneath her. She looked down and was horrified for a moment: a face gaped up at her, gaunt and desperate with pain, its eyes framed by black bruises. Its tattered lips curled back over small, even teeth. She sucked a difficult breath and began to remember the world of form. She was seeing her own face in a large mirror.

With swash flowing foamy over her and black tendrils of seaweed wrapped around every limb, she paused to consider her reflection. She remembered that she was a girl and that stinging weight in her bones was deep cold. She remembered pain, and she remembered fear, and she forced herself to her feet in spite of both. She attempted a weary march up the beach, limbs like solid ice. She fell forward a good way past the strandline and lay for some time listening to the wailing of seabirds.

Breathing hard into the sand, she tried to piece her mind back together. The sun rose, and she turned over to watch the sky brighten. She was still struggling when it went down again. There were huge pieces of her missing. It was as if she was flying through thick mist with peaks rising slowly around her. She grasped for them, frustrated, but the mist swallowed them up continually. Who was she? How had she come here? She searched even into her dreams, but these were distorted by nightmares of suffocation.

As the sun rose again, she coughed awake and turned to spit up more brine. Her head hurt so badly that she thought her eyes might pop out. She felt thin and frail, but her strength began to return as the sun warmed her. She finally got up when birds started to peck at the seaweed in her hair.

Noon was passing. She turned and looked out at the ocean and the mirror that must have carried her to safety. There were still gaps in her memory. She couldn't remember how people managed to cross such vast expanses of water, but she could recall that they did. The names of the little birds that skipped through the surf were beyond her reach – as her own name still was. But she remembered, with unshakeable certainty, that she did have one. She was someone, had come from somewhere, and now she was lost.

The ocean pulsed against the shore, caressing the sand in susurrus longing. It was as deep and as blue as a gem. She peeled the seaweed from her body and threw it away in wads. The white birds that crowded over those green-black piles were called kittiwakes; she remembered this because of their piercing calls. She was in a bay, and there was a cape to her right protruding into the halcyon distance. There she saw great flocks of kittiwakes roosting. By turns, they would brave the sea in reckless dives or land upon the beach to chase crabs.

On her left, the beach curved wide, and she was surprised to see mirrors stuck in the ground on that side. Most were further inland, standing right at the tree line. A few of them were anchored entirely in sand, and many of these tilted, dangerously close to falling over. Fewer still were right in the surf. It was to one of these that she went first, and the sun crawled down into the west again while she moved among the mirrors.

She tarried longest before the mirrors that showed her reflection. She was thin and small and virtually nude; whatever she had been wearing before the sea spit her out was not much like clothing anymore. Her eyes were gem-blue like the ocean, her cheeks were lightly freckled, and her hair was long and brown and wavy. She ran her fingers through it, arranging it as best she could. Her scalp itched painfully from sand and salt. She frowned in one mirror, deciding that she didn't like having brown hair. But in the gloaming light, she began to see that it was not brown after all. It was actually red – as red as the rays of the setting sun – and she smiled. Red was pretty. It was much prettier than brown, and it suited her milky skin tone.

She remembered that there were taller people. Older people. She thought she must be very young. Behind one mirror, she found a piece of gray cloth and a rope with which to cinch it around her waist. It was tattered and shapeless, but she grew to like it as she looked at herself wearing it. At some point, she realized that it must have been a dress at one time. Now it was her dress, and it wasn't gray after all; it was seaweed green and the rope was gold. The longer she spent with her nose pressed against reflecting glass, the more she remembered about what it meant to be a physical thing, a part of the world, and subject to rules. She remembered more and more about memory itself, and she began to feel safer in her own skin.

In some of the mirrors, her reflection was distorted: she appeared tall and sapling-thin or short and round as a dumpling. In some, she was very old and her hair was white, and in others, her facial features seemed misaligned. Still other mirrors refused to show her reflection at all. Instead, they showed mountains and canyons, or hills and forests, or bridges over rushing rivers. One showed something that didn't look like anything, and she found she couldn't stare at it for too long without her stomach churning. She felt dizzy as she left this mirror behind, and she was about to sit down when a terrible cry erupted from the kittiwakes on the beach. The birds nesting on the craggy shoulders of the cape answered this, and in a great chaos of noise and motion the flocks left their roosting perches and disappeared into the darkling sky.

An awful sound came bubbling out of the water, and she knew she could not stay on the beach anymore. The tide was clawing the sand. It was coughing something up. Seized with horror, she pushed herself to run from the bay of mirrors. She charged blindly as far as she could into the bush, and when it became too thick for her to advance any further she dropped into a ball, hugged her knees, and waited in fear to see if the things from the sea would come as far as the forest.

There, she fell into a fearful sleep, and she had one nightmare after another, but the sea-things did not come into the woods that night. When she woke, the sun was up and she was safe in a patch of yellow flowers at the base of a tree. Its boughs arched over her like a roof. Quite by accident, she had found the perfect spot to hide.

She might have stayed there long into the afternoon if a flutter of butterflies had not descended upon her flower patch. She watched in wonder as they danced from bloom to bloom, and she giggled when they landed on her shoulders. The sound of her laughter startled her briefly, but then a smile spread huge across her face. The butterflies moved off and she rose to follow them, barely noticing as the forest opened to let her pass.

She followed the butterflies all morning. The flutter went deep into the woods, moving among clumps of yellow flowers along the remains of a path. They would light in her hair to stroke her cheeks with their cobalt wings. Last night's pain was finally ebbing away, flowing from her muscles to make way for renewed lightness and strength. The flutter stopped in a neat little clearing to crowd about a pedestal that stood in its center, and she lay down there on a pile of leaves and grass and went to sleep. When she woke, the butterflies were gone and noon had passed. She could still smell the sea and hear the babbling of the kittiwakes, though it appeared she had traveled quite far in a short time. Unfortunately, she was no less lost than before.

She stood and took stock of her surroundings. The trees in this glade were birches, alders, and sycamore maples. And here was an elm, tall and strong, its winged seeds falling in languid spirals, and at its broad feet was another patch of yellow flowers. She picked a small handful of these, wound a few into her hair, and was pleased to find no more sand behind her ears. Then she turned to inspect the pedestal. It was covered with intricately carved figures. Flowering vines curled around it, and there was sweet smelling moss growing in feathery patches at its base. Engraved around its top were symbols in an alphabet that looked vaguely familiar.

ꞯꙆꞀꝹꙄꙄꙆ ꙄꙄꙆꞢꞮꙄ ꞮꞀꙆꙄꙄꙆ

She crouched to run her fingers over them, tracing the odd lines. She might have been able to decipher the symbols if she had spent more time examining them, but she was more interested in the large jewel that sat on top of the pedestal.

Now she stood. The pedestal was almost as tall as she was, and the jewel was just below the level of her widening eyes. It glowed brightly even in the light, rose-pink and roughly round, and there was a black cord wrapped around it. She reached out to pick it up and found herself hesitant to touch it; it was so vivid and perfect that she wondered if it might not be an illusion. She took up the cord instead, and as she lifted the gem from the pedestal she was surprised by how light it was. It was like lifting a butterfly. The gem hadn't a single scratch or fracture, and she could see almost completely through it. It was dazzling, and she was left blinking as it caught the light of the sun. Without thinking, she put the cord over her head, and it fit perfectly around her neck. The gem lay upon her breast like a lingering kiss. Light and healing warmth poured endlessly from it, and at last she touched it to find it as soft as a petal in her hand. She realized that it was as much like a bloom as it was like a jewel. She knew the color of this stone, and she searched her mind for its name, but that part of her memory was still wrapped in shadow.

She was turning the jewel in her hand and running the pad of one finger over its silken surface when the sky darkened and rain began whispering down around her. Clutching the pendant gem as if to protect it, she left the clearing for the safety of the big elm. The rain turned to sleet as night came on, and she fell asleep in the warmth of the gem with the huge elm's spreading branches shielding her. She slept peacefully, dreaming of colors and feather-light touches and sounds like singing. When she woke again, stretching, it was the middle of the night and the gem was blazing like a star on her breast.

She stared into the jewel. It cast strange shadows on her face. It was painfully bright, but she could neither blink nor look away. The light burned into her, and some veil within her was torn aside. The sleet had turned to rain again, and it pounded down in sheets of stinging drops. She shivered, wrapped now in the cold embrace of the wailing wind. She remembered walking the docks in the dark with her father, his rough hand enveloping hers, his pipe smoke sweet and acrid. She remembered her mother's irrational fear of storms. A great homesickness overwhelmed her, though she still could not remember where her home was. She worried for those that must miss her, but there was greater suffering to come. She began to remember secrets and lies that she had told herself. She remembered erasing whole parts of her history, leaving chasms that crawled with shapes of shame and disgust.

There were things she could not allow herself to admit even then, with her mind hemorrhaging memories.

The elm no longer protected her. It beat the air with its branches, its great trunk creaking, seeds cascading down to be blown to shreds in the gale. Gripping the jewel, she got to her feet. Tears were freezing on her cheeks. As she fought against a deluge of memories that left her sobbing, she fell against the bole of the elm and stared into the jewel's fiery heart. It was now hot in her hand. Rays of light spread out from it, and as she watched they began to converge. She turned, and the rays split again. Now there came a horrible cracking sound from above, and she looked up to see the top of the elm tree bending at a dangerous angle. Lashed by the wind and the rain and tormented by an equally violent storm of remembrance, she left the elm and the little clearing behind and ran headlong into the forest. She cut her feet on rocks and jutting roots. Brambles pulled at her dress and clawed her arms. Again and again, she found her path blocked. Eventually, she came back to the clearing, having succeeded only in making a full circle, and then she fell to her knees in dismay and frustration.

The storm worsened. She heard panicked animals crashing through the woods, rushing for shelter. Some of them sounded very large and very close. The top of the elm snapped with a tremendous noise, and it crushed a sapling into a woody mess as it fell. Only the glow of the jewel brought her back to her senses. It pierced her fear, shrouded her physical pain in heat and growing light, and finally stemmed the horrible flood in her mind.

She caught her breath and stood, shivering like the shattered elm. She could not stop the tremor in her bottom lip. But the gem's light put everything behind her, seeming to pull her out of the storming world a little way, and as she looked into the jewel she was able to focus. The rays of light converged again; the single beam they formed was like the needle of a compass. What could she do but follow that light?

She was sweating, her jaw ached terribly, her feet were pricked and scratched and swollen, but she went back into the woods with the light of the gem to guide her. She walked for a long time, and when she finally found shelter from the storm in a cave at the base of a cliff, she was too tired to stay up thinking about what had happened. Her last thought as she curled up beneath the roof of stone was of a mirror in a bedroom. Perhaps it had been her father's. She remembered that most

- 14 -

little girls had fathers. But it may have been her grandmother's mirror. That she could not remember. She had stood before it once in her nightgown and imagined that she was the captain of a pirate ship sailing the sea. She took this into her dreams, and she slept on the cave floor for a full day. When she woke, she found she was not alone.

Two

Michael

The cave mouth was wide and deep, and the floor fell into a pit near the back. There, the voice of the wind came moaning up from the deep walking passages below. Speleothems in thick clusters and fifteen-foot gypsum chandeliers hung from the ceiling of the cave entrance. A little curtain of rainwater spilled over the lip, falling across the entrance, and it was the gentle slapping of this stream upon the stone that finally woke her.

She opened rheumy eyes and stretched. She ached all over, and her vision was bleary, but she was neither cold nor wet. She was in a downy bedroll that was only partially closed with a red-tasseled drawstring. As she pushed her way out of it, a cramp seized her stomach, and she let out a little whine. Someone was cooking; wonderful smells were wafting into the cave mouth. Was it bacon and onions? She stood up to look and was shocked by what she saw outside the cave.

Sitting on a collapsible stool was a weasel in a high-necked waistcoat. Its fur was rusty brown, its right ear pierced with a crystal stud, and its black-dipped tail was curled up into a shape like a question mark. It wore a mitt and was holding a skillet over a fire, and this is where the wonderful cooking smells were coming from. The weasel must have heard her then, because it turned around and looked at her, its eyes like drops of tar. Its nose twitched, its whiskers bristled, and it hurried over, walking upright like a person.

"You're awake!" It chirped. "Please, Empress. Allow me." It reached out to her. It was a good deal taller than she was, and she cowed away from it.

"Stay back!" she cried, and the sound of her own voice made her jump. "Who are you?"

"It's Michael," said the weasel, looking perplexed for a moment. "Lord Underbridge."

"You're a weasel!" She found herself clutching the stone to her chest. She still had it, then. At least the weasel hadn't robbed her.

"Not the bad kind," Michael replied.

"I wasn't aware there *was* any other kind!"

Now he smiled, though he still looked sad. "You've forgotten me. I've been looking for you for weeks! They said you had come. Washed up in The Bay of Mirrors. I'm sorry it took me so long to find you, Empress." He hung his head. "It's the Forgetting. It's fallen upon everyone – even me. I couldn't remember whether to go east or west from Dimwood, you know. But it came to me. And I've found you! It's good to see you again, Your Majesty." Here he dipped a bow. "Don't be afraid. Look at me. I won't hurt you! I tucked you into the bedroll last night. You were dead asleep; you hardly even moved. I'm here to help. There's bacon and onions cooking, and I have eggs, too. Please, Empress. Come down and eat, and you'll feel better."

She made a face and backed away another foot. "I don't like eggs."

"But you always did before," Michael said. He looked exasperated.

At last, she released her grip on the jewel. She approached Michael cautiously, her fear slowly fading. The gem seemed to burn with the growing intensity of her curiosity. It pulsed, warm and soft upon her thorn-ripped dress.

"Did you say 'Lord'?" she asked.

Michael's face moved strangely, but his expressions were still recognizable enough. He added a wrinkle of his slender snout and a twitch of his whiskers to a patient smile.

"Yes," he replied. "Lord Underbridge of Dimwood. It was a long time ago that you gave me that title, and in jest at first, but it stuck. I was a member of your court. See?" He held out his right paw. On the second of four clawed fingers, he wore a large signet ring with a rose-pink stone. The emblem engraved upon it was intricate and beautiful, and in a circle at its center were letters in the strange language she had seen on the pedestal in the clearing.

"The Seal of Melidora. *Your* seal, Empress."

And now a great stillness came over her. For a long moment she stood in deep peace, hearing the water falling over the cave's mouth and smelling Michael's campfire burning nearby. She breathed, and it was as if she inhaled the light of the jewel. She began to remember – to really remember - and when she looked back at Michael she felt painfully close to complete. She smiled and put her hand on his shoulder. His fur was coarse and still dew-wet.

"Ruby," she said. Her voice seemed to come from a deep place.

"Yes," Michael beamed. "Yes, that's your name, Empress."

"I remember." All her fear of the storm, all her simple bliss in the company of the butterflies, coalesced into a real identity, and Ruby remembered all at once what it meant to be herself. "In Dimwood. You were fishing alone on the river Charl under an ivory bridge." Now the light of the jewel seemed to be everywhere. The world took on a supernal brilliance, with colors so rich and real and sensations so intense that Ruby briefly thought she might be overwhelmed. The forest canopy was loud with birds. The sky was as deep as the sea. "Michael Underbridge. Bard, scholar, priest. You would come, of course."

"And I have," said Michael. He stood out against the rest of the world as if traced in thick lines of light. "I knew you would return! I never doubted. Never! I'm only sorry that no one else has come."

Ruby frowned. She took Michael by the paw and began to lead him back toward his fire. She was not whole yet.

"Thank you, Michael. I've been kept away for a long time. There's still a lot to remember. When I arrived, I couldn't remember anything. Not who, not where, and not even what I was. I'm finally at a real beginning again, but I can feel the Forgetting you mentioned. It's like a cover of cloud obscuring the sun, or a weight on my memory, pressing it down. But while we're together, I think we can fight back against it. Together, I think, we can remember ourselves again. Tell me what's happened while I've been gone."

Ruby and Michael ate and talked all morning, and she found that her taste for eggs was indeed gone. They drank butterbush sap, which flowed like water but was sweeter and more restorative, and when the sun was high they put out the fire. They spoke of their memories, and Ruby described her vision of flying over peaks that loomed now and again from milk-thick mist.

"My mind," Michael explained, "is like a land with many rivers. Over most of the rivers, there are bridges. But some of the bridges are out, and I don't know how to rebuild them. That is what the Forgetting has done: it has left me unable to reconstruct the past. I feel so helpless against it, but I am one of the lucky ones. Others have lost themselves entirely."

Michael was pleasant and glad to be in Ruby's company, but he was also clearly troubled and distracted. Several times, as he spoke of the way the Forgetting had come to Dimwood, he came very near to tears. But he would not weep, he told her.

"Because there is so much still to be thankful for."

They packed up the campsite and began to head west through the forest, following the light of Ruby's red jewel. Of course it was hers; it had always been hers. The Tidestone, he called it, and she remembered when it had been hewn from the mines of Lampblack.

"A religious relic," Michael explained. "Made in honor of the Halcyon, who calms the sea."

They shared much, filling in memories, building bridges. They reached peaks together. But Ruby kept some things from Michael. The Forgetting was a force she was still learning to feel and to cope with. She did not ask him where she was from, where Melidora was, or how it had come to be. There was still a great fog in her mind, and she was reluctant to reveal how terrified she was of it.

"The Forgetting is only a symptom," he said. They were deep in the woods, surrounded by a flutter of blue butterflies. Michael was holding her hand tightly. She could feel his claws pressing on her flesh. His paw was calloused. In his other paw, he held a long dagger. He had no weapon for her, he had been sorry to say. Not yet. It was just as well; Ruby wasn't sure how much help she would be in a fight, armed or not.

"The Empress is the sickness," Michael continued. "The new one. When you left, we had peace for many years. My cousin took the throne. Or it may have been my uncle. Whoever he was, his name was Alexander, and as far as anyone remembers anymore he was a good and kind emperor. But Melidora has begun to fade, and many things are changing. One day, Alexander was gone, and the Empress was in his place. Dark times followed, but now you are here. You will bring the light once again. We're all sure of it." He was silent for a moment while he helped Ruby up an embankment. At the top, the woods opened out. Ahead, just within sight, they dwindled into a rolling prairie. "Do you remember the *gagwan*? The Nixies?"

Ruby stopped at the top of the embankment and put her hands on her knees. She breathed hard, head down, and mopped sweat from her brow. She was still weak. Fatigue was setting in, though they had only been walking for two hours and the going had been easy. She sipped from a canteen and pushed her hair back behind her ears. Michael produced a length of ribbon from his waistcoat pocket, and she used it to tie her auburn locks into a precarious ponytail.

"Nixies?" She panted. The word conjured nothing in her mind. She grasped, frustrated.

"The Children of Nix," Michael said. "Great beasts made of steel and dirt and oil. Clanking, mindless things. Hateful machines. The new Empress commands them. She has declared herself the Empress of Nix."

Ruby began to nod. She felt the light of recollection. Peaks soaring from the mist. But the word felt artificial. Its associations were nearly hollow. Perhaps that was appropriate.

"Mindless machines," she replied. "Yes. I can see them. Black and dirty, bronze and brass, marching from Nixieland." She suddenly saw a terrible connection. This memory was tied to something dark – something she had tried to hide away from herself. She decided that she didn't want to remember any more about the Nixies. She felt herself giving in to the Forgetting then, and the sensation turned her stomach.

"The Lay of the Nixians," Michael said. "I haven't thought of it in a very long time. I believe I must have begun to forget it even while Alejandro was Emperor. Or was it Arthur?"

Now Michael sipped from his own canteen. He was strong, lean, and lithe. Their short journey from the cave hadn't taken much out of him so far, that was obvious. Ruby smiled up at him. She had thought him repulsive at first. Now she saw that he was dashing. She put her head down for another deep breath.

"Ahead are the Fields of Silver. We shall be crossing the western bounds of the Nixies' patrol soon, I suppose," Michael went on. "The Empress has mobilized them in a way we've never seen before. They are the Nixian Army now, and they patrol in pairs. Stay beside me, Empress, as we step out into the open."

Three

Hearthmeade

They stopped to rest at the edge of the wood, where the butterflies left them. The sun stayed longer in the sky than it had the day before. Time was expanding, Michael explained. It was stretching out and growing thin; sometimes you could see right through one day to the beginning of the next. Some nights, the moon would barely rise above the trees.

"Leora looks down on us now with disdain, tired of her nightly journey," Michael told her. "She goes about unveiled and without nearly as many of her sidereal retinue. But she still shines, and that gives us hope."

When they finally left the forest behind, a long twilight was beginning. It was cool and breezy. The ground was soft under Ruby's hurting feet. As she and Michael emerged from a little linden hollow and were descending onto the plain, the Tidestone's guiding gleam began to point northwest.

"We can't turn that way just yet," Michael said. "Those roads are being watched. We have to go the long way around."

So they went on, and the Tidestone's rays slowly began to dim and separate again.

The Fields of Silver ran west from the Mirrorwood to the foothills of the Auburn Mountains. From there, they followed the Golrace River south to become a great floodplain, and beyond that was the Dimwood, where Michael had come from. He sang of his home as they walked, and his voice was sweet, and the lilt of those old melodies brought some of Ruby's memories back. They were returning at a measured pace now, and she felt better equipped to understand them and to place them correctly. She told Michael about the night she washed ashore, and he apologized again for not being there. Then she spoke of the Cradle, and of their days riding arthewags up Donchapel Hill.

"Mostly Nixie country now," Michael sighed. "I've not been up the Hill in what must have been three years. Perhaps longer. The arthewags have all moved north into the cold, and they've grown great shaggy coats. We rarely see them in the lowlands anymore."

Leora hung reluctant in the purpling sky, accompanied by a single pinprick of starlight. The whole plain seemed to undulate as the dry south wind combed across it. The low hills were dotted with stands of sugar maple – islands in a whispering sea of silver-green. Ruby wanted to walk until nightfall, but pain and fatigue caught up with her at last. Her feet were cramping, and when she began to limp, Michael helped her into the expanding shade of a weeping birch, where he made camp.

"No fire," he said, "because of the fountain grass. And it might draw unwanted attention. But we have pemmican and plenty of butterbush sap, and I'll rub your feet with salve."

Ruby fell asleep with her wounds wrapped and her muscles aching. Michael sat singing with his dagger out and his back to her. She dreamed of dark waters seizing her body, closing her tight in a drowning grip, and of the cries of the kittiwakes ringing out in sadness far above the heart of the deep.

Midmorning, Ruby slipped from the bedroll and saw Michael not far away talking with a hooded stranger. She hunkered in the bluestem watching them, and she could not make out whether the stranger was male or female – human or otherwise. Tall, thin, and wrapped in robes that seemed unnaturally black, the stranger nodded as Michael spoke. Ruby could not make out what Michael was saying, but the tone of his voice was grave and determined. The stranger handed Michael a bundle, they appeared to say their goodbyes, and then the dark-robed figure turned west and disappeared over the shoulder of a hill.

Ruby swallowed, suddenly heartsick, and for a moment she felt her own essence beyond her, watching her knowingly like a winking conspirator. She stood up as Michael approached, pretending that she was only just waking, but she knew he saw through her ruse.

"We had a visitor last night," he said. He held up the bundle. "Or we nearly did. Scouts say a Nixie patrol came within a mile of us. We were lucky."

"Scouts?"

Michael looked at Ruby with something that was not unlike condescension. She might have bristled, but she didn't have the energy. Out of the corner of her eye, she was still watching the spot where the stranger had disappeared.

"I didn't leave Dimwood without telling anyone where I was going," Michael explained. "When word of your arrival reached me there, I left as soon as I could, but I had affairs to put in order first. I had to leave my home in trustworthy paws." He indicated the field behind him. "That was Ketha, from Hawkport. You don't need to worry about him. He's watching out for us."

He unwrapped the bundle and presented Ruby with its contents: a pair of sturdy moccasins. They were chocolate brown and silky on the inside, with embroidered uppers and beaded catgut laces.

"We have a lot of walking to do yet," he continued. "But not as much as we might've had. There's an outpost near Southunder; Ketha says that a pair of horses will be waiting for us there. Word travels slowly through the east these days. We'll head there, and then we can ride to Pearlwater."

"South?' Ruby repeated. "But we can't go south. The Tidestone is leading us northwest." The Tidestone's light had dimmed considerably as they had continued west into the fields, but she didn't need that guiding ray anymore. The stone had been whispering into her mind, using her own inner voice.

"The Tidestone lead you to me," Michael replied. "And now I am here to protect you. To *guide* you. Trust me, Empress. Everything north of Cutcheon Mud is hostile now. There are big things going on. Great things. In your name!" He sighed, his slim shoulders rising and falling in an exaggerated motion. "Melidora is at war, Majesty. Pearlwater and Dimwood are where the resistance is starting. Pearlwater is waiting for Dimwood, and Dimwood is waiting for you – waiting and praying. We won't ignore the Tidestone's urgings. I promise! But we must make a stop or two first to prepare. Nothing will happen without you."

Ruby nodded. She still felt a little far away.

"I trust you," she said, and she put her small white hand on his arm. "We'll go to Southunder, and then to Pearlwater. There, we'll decide what do next."

At this, Michael bowed. Then he packed up the bedroll while Ruby slipped on her new moccasins. They were light, and they fit her perfectly. She sighed happily as she strode about in them.

"Ketha said you were unlikely to find anything softer," Michael grinned.

They stood for a while and chewed pemmican while they tried to remember which way south was. The sun's position was unreliable. Ruby felt unreliable, too. Finally, Michael remembered that south was to the left if one was facing away from Mirrorwood, and they started across the field again in the burgeoning heat of a long and windless day.

Heading south, the Fields of Silver sloped gently up into thinning scrublands dotted with flowering yucca, chemise, and prodigious clumps of deerweed. Small flocks of red-beaked parrots flitted between stands of Islay, chattering and fighting for cherries. Over the balding crest of a hill, the fields sank into a glen overhung with Muller oaks and apricots. As Ruby and Michael descended into this long valley to follow the trickle of water carving across its woody floor, the sun finally hauled itself to its apex, where it seemed content to stay and rest a while.

The leaves had begun to change. Amid the evergreens burned the perfervid fire of new autumn – gold and orange and stunning blood-crimson – and the air was heavy with the smells of earth and smoke. Ruby had been weakening, her personhood seeming to bleed away as she worried over the failures of her memory. The Forgetting tortured her, allowing her brief glimpses of her true self as if in a mirror; but most of the time she felt as though she were only a reflection. But the new colors of the leaves lifted her spirits. Autumn had always been her favorite season. She kicked through the scrim of fallen leaves and laughed while Michael sang, or she twined leaves into her hair while he spoke of the armies of Pearlwater and Dimwood.

"We are small," he told her. "But we'll move together with great speed and force. We've been preparing for a very long time."

"Preparing for what?" Ruby asked, chewing on a water-root and holding on to Michael's paw.

"Hawkport will fall," he replied, "and Southunder is practically in Nixian hands now. I've long anticipated a battle on those two fronts."

Sometimes he would carry her on his back, and she would wrap her spindly limbs around him and sleep with her face pressed into his fur. Once, they found a deep impression in the mud that Michael said was a Nixie's track. After that, they walked in careful silence for three days, but they never saw a Nixie in the valley. When then they were almost to Lockwood, the trees turned to quaking aspens. Some of the aspen leaves were blue, and some of them glowed late at night. Sometimes, Ruby could remember that this wasn't quite right, and other times she only goggled childishly at them, accepting.

On the Hearthmeade, the broad, green lawn at the northward edge of Lockwood, Michael made camp. He dug a pit and used his bow drill to start a fire. They were just beyond the edge of the Nixies' south-eastern patrol route. They would have hot food for the first time in weeks. Ruby stood nearby to block the wind, looking north up the valley toward the Fields of Silver waving in the distance. The sky was as dull as brass. She was amazed at how far they had come. The Bay of Mirrors was far away; the night she'd spent coughing on the beach seemed almost like a dream. But Michael said that distance was changing, too.

Now she looked west across the plain toward the Auburn Mountains and Mount Golrace. A whispering breeze came sweeping up the lawn from that direction, carrying the faintest hint of burning coal beneath the pleasant smells of black sage and milfoil.

"I don't think we're too far from the outpost," Michael told her. The fire was small. He fed it with punk wood and shoe polish, and as it grew he added larger kindling. "Kasha will meet us here…or Ketta. Oh Ketha! Damn this confusion! I am foggy tonight, Empress. Forgive me.

I believe Ketha's plan was to meet us in the forest. The outpost was newly established, it seems. It's in Lockwood, but I don't know exactly how far outside Southunder it is."

With the fire nearly roaring now and sparks swirling up on a column of smoke, Michael came to Ruby's side and pointed south. Rising against the backdrop of a distant mountain ridge was a tiered tower. Large birds circled it or sat roosting in its eaves, and all around it little wisps of white were rising from the yellowing forest.

"The Black Mountains," Michael said. "I know of no pass over them. And Southunder before them. That tower was a Halcyon pagoda; now it's the watchtower at Aaron's Door. Southunder still resists Nixian occupation, but they are on friendly terms with the Empress of Nix. One of the wonders of the south it was – a great center of industry. Its technology rivals that of even the Cradle. The first flying machines were built there, but no one builds them anymore. The Empress outlawed them. Southunder was ruled by Aaron the Younger, who hated the Empress. But he was killed on a boar hunt and was succeeded by his nephew. Some hero or another was born there. I don't remember his name, but there are statues of him in Southunder still."

"Bratcher," Ruby said. "Dallie Bratcher, the Hand of the South."

Michael nodded. "You would remember."

"It's luck," she replied. "I can't believe how much I've forgotten. I haven't felt like myself of late."

"Who *have* you felt like?"

"I don't know," Ruby sighed. She sat down beside the fire, and Michael joined her. "Someone else." She took up a handful of stones and started throwing them into the fire to knock embers off the largest burning log. "Do you ever feel old, Michael?"

"Yes," Michael said after a pause. "But then I *am* old. I remember when Southunder was being built, when Pinwale Harbor was just a dock with a dinghy tied to it, and when the crystal foundries of Lampblack were mining camps built by gnomes coming south from the ice. I wonder how many years I've lived."

"Do you remember who built the Cradle?"

Michael shook his head. His voice dropped almost to a whisper.

"No," he said. "No one remembers that."

They waited for Ketha until dark, unsure of whether he was to meet them in the woods or there on the lawn, but he never came. They ate a small supper of potato soup, hard bread, and butterbush sap, and then Ruby curled up in the bedroll while Michael sang to her. This was a sad song, and he stopped and started many times at first. The later verses he remembered well, and Ruby listened in silence to the haunting melody. It was a song about Leora, the moon, and how she came to Melidora to bathe in crystal pools in the northern forest. Tragedy befell her, and that forest was called Moonwood ever after. When it rained there, the song said, the drops were like crystals with hearts of blood. Ruby watched Leora rise over the Fields of Silver and hang low, looking tired and old. There was a shadow upon her face, but her light was as bright as ever. That light, Ruby thought, for all Leora's sadness, was unquenchable. It was the source of her beauty, and as it fell on Lockwood it left a few shivering leaves glowing as blue as gems.

Four

Lockwood

Ruby was toeing the verge of sleep when a sound made her sit bolt upright. It was a long howl coming from far across the lawn, and it sent her heart pulsing into her mouth. From a throaty bellow, it rose into a shriek and then trailed off stuttering, and as it died away there came an answering call from Lockwood Forest. Ruby's blood turned to cold lead. Her shoulders bunched into knots. She gathered the bedroll up around her chin and tucked her knees against her chest, her eyes wide with fear. She looked for Michael, and he was there with his dagger out, standing before the fire with his shadow falling huge behind him.

"Barghests," he said, the fur on the back of his neck bristling. "Dire-dogs." A third howl went up, this one nearby, and the two animals they'd previously heard began baying over one another. "It's all right. I don't think they like fire. Usually."

Ruby took a few deep breaths. The howling rang to silence at last, but she stared west down the lawn long after the last echo.

"There've been more of them lately," Michael explained. "They come east from the Mountains of Nirfang and the Veldt of Skies, driven out by Nixies at Owl's Head Peak. They cross the Charl and enter Dimwood, where we hunt them down. Those that escape flee to cross the Golrace into the Pearlmire, and from there they move up into Lockwood and slowly make their way north, in search of food. It must be lean times now for even those foul things. Only the strongest and smartest make it all the way here from the Westfair."

After a few long moments of silence during which Ruby held her breath, there was a tremendous commotion in Lockwood Forest. It sounded like a team of horses crashing through the trees. After that, there was no more howling. Michael came to sit beside Ruby. He turned his dagger over in his paws, back arched and tense, his keen eyes narrowed.

Finally, Ruby slipped down into the bedroll again. She reached out to touch his arm.

"Tell me a story," she said. She remembered that her mother had never told her stories at bedtime. This certainly wasn't because Ruby had never asked for them; her mother simply wasn't the kind of person who kept stories.

"You?" Michael laughed, turning to look at her. His tar-drop eyes seemed to sparkle. She suddenly realized that they had brown irises. Of course they did. "Tell *you* a story? You are the storyteller, Empress. Not I!" Now he put his dagger in his lap and patted her hand. "But if you wish, I'll see if I can remember one all the way through right now. Close your eyes and relax."

"I do wish." Ruby closed her eyes. She was still a little shaken. "There. Go on! You have a soothing voice."

Michael gave this a little chuckle. Then he cleared his throat and began.

"Once there was a blind king of the sea. He was temperamental and extremely vain. He was also hideously ugly, but his many wives and daughters told him that he was handsome to appease his pride. He sat on the throne for most of his life, but his power was gradually taken away from him through treachery; eventually, he was a ruler in name only. His family and his courtiers lied to him, cozening, raving about how popular he was, and he believed them for many years after all his kingly duties were stripped away. But the king was not stupid – not terribly stupid, at least – and he eventually began to grow suspicious.

"He called his daughters into his chambers one by one and asked them directly if he was still in power. Then he did the same with each of his wives. They all lied to appease his pride. So he called them in again in the same fashion and asked them which of his family loved him best. Of course, all claimed to love him more than anyone else, and this he considered proof that his wives and daughters were patronizing him. If they were lying, certainly his servants and courtiers were lying as well. Angered, he considered having them all beheaded, or strung up or racks, on stung to death by jellyfish, but his thoughts of revenge only made him angrier as he realized that he could never be sure that his orders of execution had been carried out. In fact, he couldn't be sure that any of his orders had *ever* been carried out at all! Instead of flying into a rage, as he always had in the past, he took a deep breath and sat down to think. He thought for a long time about his pride and about the way he had treated the people around him. Even the wicked do not wish to be wicked for the most part. Often, the greatest evils are born of innocence. The blind king realized he had been a tyrant and resolved to change his ways.

"But before he called his family in to tell them his epiphany, he thought about all they must have been doing to him. Were they any better for deceiving him? For stealing his power while he signed treaties on napkins? Perhaps nothing they had ever said to him had been true. And so, unfortunately, he became angry again, in spite of himself. That night, he left the castle in secret and journeyed far across his kingdom until he reached the cave of a witch who had been exiled by his father."

"How did he get around if he was blind?" Ruby asked.

"Perhaps he had a stick," Michael grinned.

"No, not a stick," Ruby said. Her face lit up. "Sonar! He is a king of the deep sea. Of course he can navigate with sonar. Like a whale!"

"You should really be telling this story. I must have heard it from you anyway! As I said, you have always been the tale Weaver, Majesty. Not I."

"You're doing fine," Ruby said. She pressed against him and closed her eyes again. There was something familiar about the story. It reminded her of home, wherever that was. A thousand miles away, perhaps. Across the ocean. "He got around by sonar. Go on, now. Then what happened?"

"Well," Michael continued, "he reached the cave of the witch. She was old, of course. All witches are. And she was ugly, too. Just as ugly as he was. And she knew the way he'd been manipulated. He poured everything out to her – his anger and his pain – and she sympathized. She was living in exile, shunned by all. She was not blind, but the kingdom was blind to her, and that was almost as bad. She saw an opportunity to have her revenge.

"The witch told the king about a magic mirror that could restore his sight. It was far away, beyond the surface of the water, on the top of a mountain, in the care of three guardian beasts. The king could not go to get it himself, of course. The witch said that one of his kin must fetch the mirror, and he despaired. They would not do as he asked. They would lie to him or trick him. He was a useless old man! But the witch had a solution. She had a powder that would make whoever touched it incapable of resisting him for a whole night. She said that she would sprinkle it on the sea lilies, and that the king's youngest daughter would get the powder on her hands when she came out to pick the flowers in the morning."

"This is all very convoluted," Ruby complained. "I don't think you're telling it right."

"Perhaps not," Michael replied, scratching his head. "I thought I remembered how this story went!"

"There is no powder," said Ruby. "It's all a trick to get the king to take poison! Isn't it?"

"Why would anyone go to all that trouble just to poison him? He's blind, right? Couldn't they just put it in his food?"

Ruby considered this. "Where's the story going?" she asked at last. "I'm getting sleepy already; and I just wanted to hear you talk anyway."

She was lying on the ground, the Tidestone in her fist and her head in his lap. His dagger was stuck in the dirt near the fire. Now he stood and helped her back to the bedroll. She wondered if she was supposed to be the witch or the king. Or maybe she was the youngest daughter. As Michael tucked the bedroll tight around her, she imagined living at the bottom of the ocean and picking sea lilies.

"His daughter goes to the surface," Michael whispered, gently pulling a leaf from her hair. "She meets a prince who helps her find the mirror. In the end, I think, he looks into the mirror and his sight returns. He sees how ugly he is, but it turns out that he thinks he's beautiful. And the daughter marries the prince and they rule a kingdom on the land, but the king goes on being a tyrant."

"He doesn't learn anything?" Ruby mumbled. "He doesn't change?"

"That's the moral of the story," Michael said. "Sometimes, no matter what he learns, no matter what he gains or loses, a man doesn't change. It takes more than a magic mirror to change a person. We make ourselves, and if we want to be different, it has to come from inside."

Ketha did not come in the morning. Ruby and Michael ate breakfast quickly and then packed up camp. Michael was anxious to move on.

"It's no good to stay anywhere for too long," he explained. "The Nixie patrols expand their range every day, and then there are the dire-dogs to worry about."

"You said they wouldn't come," Ruby said. "You said it would be all right."

"I said they didn't like fire. The fire is out now, and it's best to be going. I don't know what's happened to Ketha, but if we have to find this outpost on our own I would just as soon get an early start."

Ruby moped and dragged her feet, but she was actually feeling more together today. They hadn't been in the aspen forest long before she was humming to herself and clinging playfully to Michael as he picked their way through the forest.

Lockwood was beautiful and open. Ruby was taken with its energy. The canopy was kinetic; the slightest breeze set flame-orange leaves quivering for miles, making a rustling sound that was almost like a song. The trees themselves swayed slightly even when the wind wasn't blowing. Their bark was white with patches of brown trunk showing through beneath. In some places, it hung in shags where some animal had clawed it, and elsewhere it was pearl-perfect and wrapped in wisteria, racemes huge and pendulous. And all about the purple-hung vines, blue butterflies crowded. They followed Ruby and Michael everywhere. Sometimes, they even seemed to lead.

The sun raced up to the apex of noon. It shone down blandly, disinterested, but it could not diminish the splendor of the autumn colors. For the first few miles, the air was sweet and wintry. As they neared Southunder, however, the breeze became hot and smelled more and more like coal and kerosene. Their way soon began to disappear beneath tangles of boxthorn. Dewberries grew in abundance, trailing to snag unwary ankles, but Ruby learned to spot them by the moths that gathered on their leaves. Occasionally she would pick a dewberry or a bright red wolfberry, but something in the soil made most of the fruits growing here taste sour. Michael said it was the chemicals leaking into the groundwater from Southunder.

"It's well known," he told her, "that you shouldn't drink the water there without boiling it."

Dusk fell cold, and with it came the howling of the dire-dogs on the lawn to the north. At this, all other animal noises in the forest ceased. Ruby and Michael came upon a deer that was standing as still as stone, coiled like a spring and ready to bolt. Not even her ears moved. She was an old doe, large and lithe, and she was panting with fear; the panicked hitching of her abdomen was the only sign that she wasn't some hunter's decoy. Ruby went to her side and patted her and she blinked her deep, brown eyes.

"Don't worry," she began, her own voice quavering. She was about to say that the dire-dogs were only hunting the sward tonight, but the deer sprang away before Ruby could open her mouth again.

"Will they come into the forest?" Ruby asked Michael as the doe vanished.

"Those were not hunting calls," Michael replied.

A terrible crashing splintered the hush, and Ruby started. Michael stepped forward to put her at his back. He drew his dagger slowly, and the ringing hiss of the blade as it slipped against the sheath was chilling. And then, in the weird glow of blue aspen leaves, a shadow appeared.

Even hunched, it was huge. The shapes on its back may have been flagpoles. There were gaps in its left arm and in its chest through which a few vine-wrapped tree trunks were visible in the growing dark. Ruby peeked past Michael to watch the thing advance. It clanked, it thudded, and it blew steam from its joints. Its face was a block with a bulb for an eye. Its hydraulics creaked as it approached them slowly, turning its head as if thinking. It was a Nixie.

It clacked at them. Its voice was a sickening grind, a churning and a clicking of ancient motors. Michael began to back away, trying to push Ruby with him. Beneath a wave of annihilating panic, Ruby withered until she was nearly paralyzed.

"Don't move unless you run," Michael whispered to her. "And don't run unless you can get away."

Now the Nixie prepared to charge. Its grating voice poured out of it as it bent one knee. Then, it leapt forward in a burst of steam. It was all fire and fury, thunder and power and motion, a mindless juggernaut with its arms raised to crush them. Michael brandished his blade, and Ruby very nearly broke out laughing. The thought of him trying to fight off rushing death with a long knife was hilarious in that moment. But it was also brave and noble. Her heart broke for Michael, but her mind was stopped, and it would not start again.

There was a crack. The Nixie staggered, tugged backward, and before it could regain its momentum there was a loud bang and its head spun around. Its face sparked. The Nixie swayed, circled, and then fell forward in a swirl of fallen leaves. Michael turned and scooped Ruby up. He carried her into the forest at a run, arms wrapped around her tight. Ruby didn't see the shadows dropping from the trees and crawling from the underbrush. When they swarmed over the Nixie, pulling it apart while it screamed in its awful, grinding voice, she pressed her head against Michael's chest, only looking up when Michael let her go.

There was a fire burning somewhere. She was on her feet, and Michael's arms were up. His dagger shone from the leaf litter.

"Knees," said a young voice. "Now."

Michael complied, and he pushed on Ruby's shoulder until she did the same. She looked around, eyes wide. The firelit form before her was made of shapes that fit together poorly. It didn't look like anything. She breathed hard, trying to gasp the fear from her.

"Where you headed? Who are you?" the young voice asked. It was smooth and certain.

"North," was all Michael said.

"Ain't going north. You was goin south, weasel. Don't you know your directions? And who's this?"

"We got turned around," Michael tried. "You know the way things have been. It's the Forgetting. We have no business here. No quarrel with you."

"Wrong on that," said the young voice. "You've business in Southunder now. And a nice quarrel with me, it looks like. 'Specially if you don't get your paws on your head and stop resisting."

The fire behind them was dying out. Several voices were shouting to one another. The Nixie was dead, pulled apart; it was no longer croaking in anger. Now, Ruby saw a spear tip come out of the darkness, followed by the whiskery, gray face of a bearcat. Its hazel eyes searched Ruby's. Its big, wet nose twitched.

"You first," said the bearcat. But then he stopped, eyes widening, and his mouth opened in abject surprise. He tilted his head back casually, as if he were going to look over his shoulder, and then he dropped his spear and slumped to the ground, bleeding. The jet of blood from his throat went high into the dark. Ruby didn't see it sparkle in the distant firelight.

Michael stood. The hooded stranger had found them at last. Ketha sheathed his scimitar and helped Ruby to her feet, and then he bowed deeply. She saw at last that the hood was not a piece of Ketha's clothing.

"Time is short. I'm sorry, Empress. Take this, and follow." Ketha handed her another cloth-wrapped bundle. It was a dagger in a belted sheath. She hurried along with Michael as they followed Ketha into the dark, and she did not strap the sheath on. She left the dagger in the hide, terrified of it.

The three crouched in a shallow pit beneath a hedge of Juliette thorns. They watched in silence as the fire went out and the seeker from Southunder split into parties to search for the young bearcat. When they found him, they swore amongst themselves, and there was a brief scuffle over who was to blame for the botched arrest. Ruby remembered what Michael had said about wickedness starting with innocence. She couldn't tell which she was seeing now. She pitied the searchers for the upbraiding she was sure they would get when they got home. There would be a funeral; the bearcat's mother would be in ruins. It was a terrible thing to have happened to the ones who had saved her from the Nixie. She wrapped her fist around the Tidestone and wondered what mirror they would have to look into someday.

Five

The Passage West

Ruby's heart was hammering in her chest. She felt that mad pulse behind her eyes and heard it roaring in her ears. It was worse than the howls of the dire-dogs. She shut her eyes and tried to slow her heaving breaths. Adrenaline burned in her veins; she felt sure that it must be lighting her up like neon. The hunters from Southunder would see. She was glowing like those mutant leaves. They would come and pull her out and Michael with her. For a terrible second, she was more certain of this than she had ever been of anything else – at least as far as she could remember. The Forgetting lay upon her like a predatory animal.

"Who are they?" She had to ask.

Michael put his arm around her shoulders. His paw went over her mouth.

"Shh," he mouthed. "Quiet."

The searchers were leaving. They didn't even come close to the hiding place under the brambles. They took the dead bearcat and disappeared among the aspens, still arguing, and they left the Nixie where it lay. Was it dead? They had put out the fires, and now the wind smelled liked burning oil. She squirmed, and Michael must have known she was close to screaming. He pulled away his paw. She wriggled, turning as if to face him, and earned a few new scratches on her arm. A thorn lodged in her shoulder, and she hardly felt it.

"The second one," she said in a hot whisper. It might have been a minute since the men had gone. It might have been an hour. "Where's the second one?"

Michael's eyes widened. He looked at Ketha, who seemed about to say something. But then there was a sound behind them. The bramble disappeared in a rush of air, and there was a Nixie standing over them, limned in the moonlight like a glacier.

"No!" Ruby screamed.

The horror was not gone. It was pounding at her again, invasive, penetrating, hot and huge above her with its hand raised. Michael and Ketha barely had time to gasp in surprise before the Nixie's fist came down.

The impact was enormous. Ruby screamed. She was crushed half into the dirt, but she fought back. She was on one knee, her hands up. Michael and Ketha were looking at her. Ketha's horrible, unblinking eyes were shielded behind a clear membrane. They both gaped, unharmed. The Nixie pushed, but she was holding it.

She looked up at it from within a coruscating bubble of reds and pinks. An iridescent dome stretched from her palm, shielding the three from the Nixie's attack. It sparked as the Nixie tried to push through it, but Ruby gritted her teeth and kept it in place. It was the fire of her outrage, the protrusion of her fury into the physical. It was the soul shield, and the Nixie could not break it. Momentarily confounded, the Nixie took a step back and let its arms drop stupidly. The shield disappeared in a shimmer, and Ruby climbed out of the ditch and stood up. She approached the Nixie with her arm outstretched and her palm open wide. The sad moonlight made her flesh look as pale as chalk.

"No!" She said again. "No."

The Nixie sat silent. It tilted its lump of a head, as if considering the situation. Ruby advanced upon it once more, and it vented steam. There was a whistle from within it, then a clack and a clank, and it remained motionless.

"Stop," Ruby said. She was sure and strong. She was getting through to it. "Back off."

The Nixie rocked in place. It clicked again, and this time it brought both hands down on Ruby. She got her shield up in time, but sustaining it demanded intense focus and effort. She couldn't maintain; with a long cry of despair, she felt herself failing. She pushed back with what remained of her strength, and the dome expanded to tip the Nixie over its copper heel spurs. Its slow, dumb fall made Ruby laugh; she was still laughing as Michael swept her up and followed Ketha into the woods. She couldn't tell which way they were going. She only clung to

Michael and pressed her chin against his shoulder, looking back at the fallen monster, until they slid on flat blades of loose shale into a gully and it ascended beyond her view.

It was a brief slide. At the bottom of the gully, Michael and Ketha resumed their frantic retreat. They tore through the trees, limbs threshing at them, moving with the bottomless power of the young and certain. They finally stopped in a clearing beside a pool that was poured out from above by a chuckling waterfall. Cedars crowded together here, and about their feet were little tufts of stillweed and flowering clover. They were at the source of the river Owof, which flowed southwest toward the Great Confluence at the Pearlshores. They were west of Southunder, then. This memory came dancing up from cold confusion, winking and magnetic, and Ruby clung to it as her strength waned. Just then, it was her only bulwark against the Forgetting.

We are west of Southunder. The mindless repetition reassured her. *This river flows toward Pearlwater.*

She sagged from Michael's chest as he laid her on the grass. Ruby realized she'd left her dagger under the brambles. She was exhausted, waning like a petal in the autumn cold, and when she tried to tell Michael about the dagger, her tongue felt huge and clumsy.

"Just relax, Empress." Michael told her, and she was thrilled to see him smile.

Under the dim spill of early stars, Michael fed Ruby hard bread and gave her water from the pool. Ruby was drained but unhurt, and her strength returned quickly, though she remained misty-headed for some time. She couldn't describe how she had generated the shield of light.

"It came out of me," she tried. "Out of my feelings." She was sitting by the little stream that ran south from the pool to become the river Owof at the edge of Lockwood.

"Your fear?" Ketha asked. "Your anger?" His voice was a sibilant whisper.

Ruby tried to avoid looking at Ketha, but found that she couldn't. He fascinated her. A forked tongue flicked from between his scaled lips. His bright and wary eyes shimmered in the moonlight like variegated pearls. His small head was perched beneath a spreading hood. He was a cobra. When he held Ruby's hand, his skin felt bloodless and alien.

"No," Ruby said. "Deeper than those."

"I've seen it before," Michael said, watching the water falling in the dark. "That deep force. In Dimwood. The creative force."

Ketha stroked Ruby's hair. Then he stood, and from within the folds of his robe he produced the dagger that he had brought for her. He laid it beside her and then dipped his canteen into the pool.

"Strap that on," he said, lingering over the S. "Beautiful as it was, my Empress, I think it would be unwise to rely on that deep force in the future."

Michael helped Ruby fasten the belt around her waist. The knife hung heavy at her hip, too large and too dangerous for her. Her mother wouldn't have let her near such a thing. But she was glad to feel it there, nonetheless. She fondled its hilt and admired the silver etching on the leather scabbard.

"The camp," Michael said. "We waited for you at Hearthmeade. When we didn't find you in the forest, I feared you'd been captured. Those were rangers, weren't they? The South'nders back there?"

"Not among the elite, surely," Ketha chuckled. The sound was like toenails being filed. "Scouts, I imagine. They dealt handily with that Nixian, but I suspect that the one they felled was damaged. They certainly didn't know to look for the second one." He sat down and began thumbing the blade of his scimitar.

"I'm sorry I failed to meet you. The Forgetting…it's too convenient an excuse, but it must suffice. I couldn't remember when I thought you would arrive in Lockwood, how far away you'd been when we met on the Fields of Silver, or even if we had planned to meet in the forest itself. It was only by luck that I found you. And, of course, the loudness and inexperience of those scouts. There will be even more about now. And the Nixie patrols have expanded again. With the rangers in the forest and the Nixian influence expanding, Lockwood just isn't safe anymore – not that it ever really was.

"The outpost is gone. Bernard and Peter are dead or in prison. We were too certain, Michael. It was reckless. We underestimated

Southunder. It's nearly a southern capital now; the Nixians have so much sway there. Empress…"

Ketha bowed awkwardly before Ruby.

"We failed you," he said, sadly. "But I did what I could."

Ruby put her hand on his hood and smiled at him.

"No work done for the greater good can ever fail," Ruby said. She wasn't sure she really believed this. It sounded like something an adult would say – or a child pretending to be one. "You have my pardon."

Ketha's tongue flicked out.

"Wise as always, Your Majesty," he said. "Even after all you've been through." The sinister, ophidian stare. The expressionless face. Ketha was a hard one to be grateful for.

Michael swallowed a cheekful of pemmican.

"So we're to go on foot to Pearlwater, now," he said, deflated. "Our journey grows ever longer. I hope you'll accompany us, Ketha. The more blades the better."

"Unfortunately, I have business in Dof'wom," Ketha said.

"Lampblack?" Michael interrupted. "That far?"

"We have long arms and many fingers," Ketha replied. He might have smiled if he had been capable of such an expression. "There are pockets throughout the south that may help us when the time comes. I am moving back and forth between them. My travel journals barely fit in my pack now! I must go to Lampblack, but you will not be alone when you leave for Pearlwater – nor will you be on foot. Follow me to the spring, and I will show you how you will travel."

There was a path around the pool and through the cedars. They mounted the high bank on rough-hewn basalt steps, clinging to each other in the light spray. At the top of the waterfall, the path continued a little way beneath a blanket of fallen leaves, the brook whispering to itself nearby. It ended at the mouth of a cave which wasn't much more than a dripping depression in a high hump of rock and leafy detritus. Here was the ultimate source of the Owof, the spring that originated deep beneath the Auburn Mountains, in the flooded halls of the gnomes of old. Under the low overhang, pressed against the back of the cave entrance, were two large, woolly rams. Ketha had tied them to a peg, their leads latched to simple collars. They bleated anxiously as he brought them out, and he calmed them with pats on their horned heads.

"These," Michael smiled, "are not horses."

"Indeed! They are *gofan* from Gigdhinug – Northover rams." Ketha lead one of the large animals over to Ruby, who immediately began to stroke its fleecy side. "I know I promised horses, but I'm afraid those were seized. These will have to do. I was lucky enough to be able to get them here just this morning."

"They have no saddles," Ruby said. Her ram nuzzled her. Its face was black, and it wagged its little tail when she petted it. "How will we ride them?"

"They won't wear saddles," Ketha explained. "Too proud, Empress. The breeding lines go back hundreds of years. It's often said that they know their pedigree; they push other sheep around, strutting across the feeding pastures, happy to be so prized. Or so it seems to the breeders! And to me, as well. I had difficulty getting them to stay here in the mud. Anyway, you won't need saddles. They're the softest sheep in all the north. You could sleep on them! And they're fast. They'll get you to Pearlwater, at least. And then, if you haven't fallen in love with them, you can get yourself a nice big horse to get bucked off of."

"Steer with the horns?" Michael asked. "There's no bridle. They don't mind?"

"It's what they're bred for. And you'll find them useful on mountainous terrain as well, of course."

Ketha offered to help Ruby onto her ram. She had already decided to call it Rachel, though she suspected that it was a boy because of its horns. Ruby put her foot into Ketha's hand carefully. She gripped Rachel's near horn in one hand and his wool coat in the other. She expected the animal to bleat or kick and she was preparing to be embarrassed when she fell onto her duff, but Rachel accepted her calmly. His tail beating the air, and when Ruby was positioned comfortably on his back, the ram tilted his horns to allow her to get a solid grip. The animal was powerfully built. Ruby could feel its muscles moving beneath her. It bore her weight without losing its balance.

"He's so strong!" She beamed.

"And fast, too!" Ketha replied. "Treat him well, and he'll carry you west without stopping."

"If only I'd had the foresight to bring such a steed from Dimwood," Michael said. "You've done so much for the Empress."

"Hindsight is failing in these dark times," Ketha replied, "and it is tearing foresight down with it. But there is a light in the sky. I can feel it. The world is changing, Michael. The shadow is pulling away."

Michael approached Ketha and the two shook hands on the bank of the brook. The deepening night had swallowed most of the stars. What lights were left in the black were obscured by trees.

"I'm sorry about Bernard and Peter. I'm sorry that has been your only reward for all your work."

"The work has been its own reward," hissed the snake. "It's said more often than it's truly meant, but I mean it now. I live to serve the Empress." Ketha bowed to Ruby again. "The *true* Empress. Safe travel to Pearlwater, Your Majesty, Lord Underbridge. Go west carefully. These lands are falling one after another. Ride north if you must, and avoid Seer's Knob. I'll see you on the Pearlshores or in Dimwood when the last day comes."

Michael said, "Safe travel, Ketha," and dipped a bow of his own.

Ruby put her hand on Ketha's wrist.

"Thank you," she said, earnestly. "You *will* be rewarded for all your work. Safe travel, master snake."

"Empress." Ketha bowed one last time, and then he was gone into the shadows of Lockwood forest.

Michael and Ruby lead their rams northwest until they came again to the great lawn between Lockwood and the Fields of Silver. The Auburn Mountains dominated the darkling horizon, and Seer's Knob was just visible against a bank of storm clouds coming up from the Pearlshores. There, though Michael was loathe to take the risk, they had to camp. They were both too tired to travel any further, and they would be useless tomorrow without a good night's rest.

"These rams will earn their keep," Michael said as they lay in the grass, watching the rain rolling in. "Tomorrow we'll head toward Seer's Knob. If we're lucky, we'll be able to cross that open country unharassed. But if the way is blocked, our only recourse will be the Valley of Silk."

Ruby lay for a long time in silence, the Tidestone glowing softly in her hand. The Forgetting was receding from her. She felt her selfhood emerging from the mists. It was a transcendent feeling – liberating – like being born. At last, she spoke, not knowing whether or not Michael was still awake.

"I wonder if they've forgotten me at home," she said. "I hope the Forgetting hasn't spread that far."

Gasping in a nightmare. Battered senseless. Wrapped in squeezing weight, crushed in the hot dark, drenched to the bone and choking. And now she was filled up with something, a vileness, a hook that threatened to pull her apart from the inside. Above it all: the howling hounds of Nirfang. Within it: the smell of burning oil and the clacking, rattling speech of the Nixies. She felt the deep force, as Michael had said, but it was destructive instead of creative. It was wasteful. Tossed about on a bitter sea, she gagged in horror as that force moved in her. It would not generate the soul shield. No – you had to have a soul first. Hers was hiding. She woke on the shore, rolling in slime and seaweed. Seabirds pecked at her, beaks pinching her cheeks, wings beating about her shoulders. She rolled over and tried to bat them away. The dream went on, draining into something more abstract. She was grateful for that. The deep force could heal her now.

Ruby woke with her mind still chained in dreaming. The nightmare called her down haunted corridors, a shadow of wounded anger, and for a while she felt the small flame of her consciousness guttering. Control and presence returned at last as light was growing in the east; the Forgetting swallowed all indiscriminately, and the nightmare finally vanished into it.

At dawn, Ruby and Michael headed east down the Hearthmeade. The rams were fast and seemed indefatigable, and they responded immediately to even the smallest touch on their horns. Ruby imagined the horrible training the animals had to endure to build their sensitivity. She didn't like forcing Rachel, grabbing him by the head and pulling, but he didn't even begin to complain, and he certainly seemed proud to be doing the work he was bred to do. Rachel leapt easily over most obstacles. His gait was pompous and precise. Riding on him was comfortable even when he would bounce to gain more distance. Ruby tried to sink into his wool. She put her face in that thick fluff and inhaled, filling her nose with his strong farm smell. She had to remember what it meant to be real.

The Hearthmeade rolled low toward the coast, and the ground became spongy. The sky opened wide before noon, and a strange autumn fire spread across the blue. There were thunderheads piling over Seer's Knob. Gold light poured west, leaving the reaching fingers of black clouds soaked with blood. The crumbling walls and arches of ancient castles loomed high and haunted near the southern end of the Auburn Mountains. There was Mount Bolding, squatting with its crown below the snowline, the hills humped at its feet collapsing beneath the press of time. The gnarled woods below Bolding peak were nameless and unvisited anymore – except, perhaps, by Nixies. When Michael had set out from Dimwood, this great mountain sward had been free and open. Now it was Nixie country; that much was increasingly obvious. Patches appeared on the lawn as they rode further west; large Nixian contingents moving through the area left the grass burned black and drenched with oil in places.

Late that afternoon, Michael and Ruby made camp just inside Lockwood forest. They tied the rams to an aspen; Rachel sat patiently, chewing grass, while Michael's ram fussed at the rope.

They made no fire. Ruby had grown sick of hard bread and forcemeat, but she swallowed her cold and fatty dinner with swigs of spring water, nonetheless. She was tired and sore. Her throat hurt, and her inner thighs were red and sweaty. No saddles needed, she thought, but chaps would have been a blessing. Her hip was lightly bruised where the dagger had bounced against it. Michael was more fit and had fur to help protect his legs from chafing, but he was complaining, too. He drooped with fatigue as he unpacked their light camping kit.

"Here's where we make our big decision," he told her at dusk. "The Empress has a foothold here; I know it. She's been expanding east so quickly. If there isn't a Nixie stronghold at Seer's Knob, I'll be surprised, though I don't think there was when I passed earlier."

Here, he stopped and made some frustrated noises.

"I remember seeing fire," he went on after a moment, "and I remember the fisher cats of Hawkport, but Seer's Knob might as well be on the moon for all I recall. My journey east is slipping away. We can only take Ketha's advice to ride north. If we chance going south past the Knob, we could be seen and swarmed. Travel through the deep forest now presents the risk of being caught by Southn'der rangers. They might be looking for us. They probably are." He put his head in his paws and sighed. "I wish Ketha hadn't said that Lockwood isn't safe. If I were ignorant of the rangers' push deeper into the forest, I might consider passing Seer's Knob through Lockwood."

"And if there's no outpost?" Ruby ventured. "And if the rangers don't catch us? There's bound to be risk no matter which way we take. You mentioned the Valley of Silk?"

"We may be better prepared to deal with the Nixies," Michael joked. "Arane doesn't take sides. But that, at least, is a danger I know. It's less of a risk. Fewer variables, I suppose."

"I'd rather not risk getting caught," Ruby said. "But we don't know that we won't be able to pass Seer's Knob without anything happening. We can move through the forest silently. We're here now, aren't we? There are no rangers."

Michael considered this for a long time, chewing like a ruminant and staring into the middle distance. Finally, he said, "The Empress has been trying to cut off the Eastfair for almost as long as she's been on the throne. Forgive me, Majesty. I can't think straight through this fog! I've tried to resist the Forgetting, but nothing slows it down. Nothing stops it. I'm confused…and this is the worst possible time to be indecisive!"

"It's on me, too, Michael," Ruby said. "I feel it every minute of every day. Some days I'm more myself than others, but most of the time I feel like a puppet being moved by my real self somewhere else."

Michael nodded, suddenly somber.

"Let's not decide tonight," Ruby continued. "We'll scout ahead tomorrow. If the Nixies have Seer's Knob, then, with Southunder all but controlling Lockwood, our decision will be made for us."

"Your wisdom does not fail, Empress."

With this, Michael began a song. Halfway through it, he forgot the lyrics, so he simply hummed the rest. When he was done, he sat silent for a long time, though Ruby could tell there was much he wanted to say. She looked at him in something like wonder. Her memories of him were still winking in and out, but as they slowly developed, she grew fonder of him. He was loyal but sad, direct but mysterious. She wondered how much of him had always been beneath his surface. How much of him had she ever really known?

Michael looked at Ruby, a light in his eyes, as if he had heard her thoughts. He smiled, and she found it strange that he could smile and Ketha could not. Smiles seemed to burst from him, fighting their way through pain and worry to manifest. He smiled as if he couldn't help it, no matter how hard he tried.

"Another story, perhaps, Empress?" Michael asked.

"I'd love it," Ruby replied, and she didn't add, *if you can remember one*.

"After the first war," Michael began, "in the dark years of the rebuilding, the Halcyon came to Melidora in the form of a woman. She was very beautiful, and wherever she went to teach there were men who followed her and fawned over her. They approached her in droves to make advances upon her, and eventually her suitors became more numerous than her students. She tried to minister to them, to teach them patience and self-control, but most of them did not listen. It wasn't her message that mattered to them, you see. She was an alien, a goddess, perfect in every way, and there are people who feel compelled to defile perfection. To debase the holy. They were so broken and so hateful, that they wanted only to pull her down into their mire and make her as corrupt and powerless as themselves. This was the lesson that she left when she went away for the first time.

"After Melidora was remade, when it was even greater and more fully formed, the Halcyon returned in the form of a man. He went from Westfair to East, teaching and healing, and his power and his ministry grew as his word spread. But there were many who rejected his teachings, who persecuted him and cast him out, because he was a man. They imagined that he was base and power hungry, and they decided that the content of his message didn't matter. All that mattered to them was that they reject any powerful man outright, that they establish their independence, even if they had to lay scorn upon the back of mercy and ridicule a teacher of peace. They were so afraid of being dominated and of having their individuality taken away, that they wouldn't hear the Halcyon's message. This was the lesson that he left when he went away for a second time.

"It's believed that the Halcyon will come again, this time as neither a man nor a woman. We wonder if we have it in ourselves to accept the Halcyon's word without regard for how he or she may appear. I don't believe we do, if I may say so, Empress. Perhaps the Halcyon was wrong to think that we did. I know that the Halcyon does not fail…perhaps its goal was to show us something about ourselves. I still don't know what, if that's the case. That we are selfish? That we don't really *want* peace?"

"Perhaps she'll come as an old man the next time," Ruby interrupted. "Or an old woman."

"Or a young one," Michael said. He smiled at her again.

"Not if it wants anyone to listen. Nobody listens to children."

Michael heaved a sigh. "Maybe it's not about listening," he said, and he left it at that.

In the early morning dark, Michael and Ruby heard raised voices in the woods. The shouting was indistinct, distorted by distance. Trackers at the spring, perhaps – more scouts from Southunder. Michael thought they were getting closer. There would be no breakfast.

They trotted west into the cold, down the gentle slopes toward where Seer's Knob sat brooding beneath a black mass of anvil clouds. Gold touched the edges of the storm as the sun came creeping over the Eastfair. The rising light was pulling morning shadows from the Hearthmeade by the time Ruby and Michael rode into the rain. Ruby had hoped for a wild and exciting storm, but she was disappointed; this was only a sick drizzle. The drops were fat and oily. The wind swayed the trees in a noncommittal fury – now beating, now caressing, now confused as it tried to blow from every direction at once. It tossed Ruby's hair into a wild tangle.

The Knob rose from Lockwood to the south. Sparse birch woods ran up its western slopes. A mane of red spruce flowed from its crown, with bands of beech and oak dropping over its shoulders like a stole.

The gray city of Alamandra was built into its north face. Its high spires were hung with tattered flags. Its walls of pearl-studded basalt must have been magnificent long ago, but now they were overgrown with pothos and monkey ladder.

"What became of the Alamandrians is a mystery," Michael explained, "even to the gnomes, who once lived in its ruins. Alamandra: jewel of the east."

For a moment, as they neared the southern horn of Lockwood, a ray of light lit the gray city. It seemed then that the ghost of Alamandra's beauty still existed, superimposed upon its ruins; Ruby thought she could almost see it. Then the clouds closed up again and the vision was gone. Only the miserable shower and the cold bite of the wind remained.

The Hearthmeade ended where Seer's Knob fell into Lockwood forest. Ruby was encouraged when she could see no sign of Nixies there, but, as they stopped to take shelter from the storm at Lockwood's edge, Michael showed with dismay that his fears had been confirmed.

"A wall," he said, pointing across the lawn. "It's there, just at the edge of the birch wood. They're blocking the passage east."

Ruby squinted through the rain. After a moment, she saw what Michael was talking about. The wall was to be fortified, and it looked nearly ninety feet high. It was being built in sections, with Nixies standing guard along the finished portions. They were many yards away, but there was no mistaking the way they moved – that clumsy gait, the jerky movements of their limbs. And now there was a thin curl of smoke rising from Alamandra. Ruby swore under her breath and then bit her lip. Lightning went forking across the massive, windswept complex of clouds, preceding an angry murmur of thunder.

"It must extend into Lockwood on the other side," she said. "Right?"

Michael said nothing at first. Ruby saw him trying to work the question out, measuring distances in his mind. She could almost feel his frustration as the Forgetting toyed with his cognitive processes, and she couldn't help but pity him.

"Yes, that's right," Michael finally replied. "That must be why there've been more rangers in the forest. Southunder's resistance won't last long."

He put his paws on his hips and got that far away look in his eyes again. Such a range of expression from those little tar drops!

"We can't pass," Ruby said, crestfallen. She didn't know what it was that Michael feared in the Auburn Mountains. She didn't remember Arane. Maybe it was just the inconvenience of going out of their way that Michael didn't want to face. Whatever the case, Ruby mimicked his concern.

"No going around Lockwood," Michael thought aloud, "and no passage below Mount Bolding. There's no choice to make. I wish Ketha had said something about this. We'll lose so much time now! But you are worth taking the longer route, Empress. The resistance needs you. Rash decisions could end it before it has a chance to begin. We'll ride north to the Auburns. The Valley of Silk is the only way over them."

With this, he untied his ram. Ruby patted Rachel on the shoulders to get him to dip low for her, and when she had found her place on his back she reached down to feed him some chokeberries.

"You're already carrying a heavy burden," Ruby said as they turned north, "don't pick up any more weight. It's the Empress who's in a hurry – not us. Pearlwater will still be there when we come down from the mountains. Stop torturing yourself. We'll do what we have to do."

"The Forgetting tortures me," Michael said, calmly. "The Empress tortures me. Both have one thing in common: *time*. Pearlwater could be gone, Majesty. It could be burned and broken and occupied by Nixie garrisons by the time we get there. Many others have fallen. I worry that I'm not enough…that I'll harm the resistance more than I can help. This is the most significant period of my life. I want to act. I want to shine. I want to succeed."

"That's why you came all the way from Dimwood," Ruby said.

"I had to. You're the key to all this."

Michael straightened his waistcoat. It was stained, and a button was missing from it. To the north, the Fields of Silver ran up against the ragged line of the Auburn Mountains, where they dwindled into a flowering scrubland. Here was Auburn Moor, deep at the feet of a derelict fort that still flew the silver flags of Alamandra. The Wood of Thorns was visible to the north as a green line – the Moonwood that

Michael had sung about. Ruby imagined Leora descending to bathe there, wearing the skin of a woman.

"What will we find in the Valley of Silk?" Ruby asked after a long silence.

"Arane," Michael said. He sounded surprised that she would ask. "And her children. But no Nixies. Nixies won't go there. If the whole of Melidora is conquered, Arane will remain free. She has always been and she always will be."

At last, the pitiful, spitting rain gave way to a colossal downpour. The Pearlmire would be welling with black bay mud. Awnings and tarps would be going up all over Southunder, protecting cowards and criminals as well as honest men. Ruby and Michael did not make the Auburn Mountains by nightfall; by that time, both were soaked to the skin, cold, and sniffing miserably with runny noses. Michael built them a lean-to in a sycamore glen, and for the first time he shared the bedroll with his Empress. He sang a hymn with her as they watched their little fire flicker in the wind, and then he led her in prayer as the moon rose in all her pregnant melancholy.

Six

Into Darkness

The storm gathered momentum. It made up for its mild start by pitching into a twisting, howling fury, the rain freezing into shards of cutting ice. Michael and Ruby were running low on rations, so they tried to hunt during the day, when the gale was at its most forgiving. They skinned hares and plucked pheasants, and they boiled fat with currants and chokeberries. Their canteens flowed with rainwater. When the sun reappeared and then shied away into the north to die in the cold, Michael's ration pack was full again. But the Forgetting crept upon them in their distraction, and they spent two more days trying to remind themselves where they were going and what was at stake. They talked about things they could remember, hoping to find a route back from the mist, and those two days would have been miserable for Ruby if she hadn't been in Michael's company.

He told her of his brother David, who had died in a mining accident. He described the kinds of fish that were to be found in the Charl, and he sang a little mnemonic song from his youth about which kinds of bait would catch which species. And he preached, remembering sermons a word at a time. His parables awakened many of Ruby's memories about her home, and she spoke of these happily while they sat by the fire. It felt necessary to have something of her past to hold onto as she tried to remember her present.

"I was born by the ocean," she said. "Or in a field not far from it. In a town, rather, surrounded by hills and woods and prairies, and the beach was nearby. I had no brothers or sisters…but there were always cousins at our house. Family members and friends of my parents were in and out all the time. My father must have been in some line of work that required him to open his door to all kinds of people."

"A man of the cloth, perhaps?" Michael interjected.

"Maybe." Ruby squared her jaw and then chewed her bottom lip for a moment. "Or maybe the kind of person who talks to people. A therapist. He might have been both of those at one point. But I remember feeling as though my life was very public. I had only a small space to myself – my room – but I wasn't allowed to lock the door. I don't recall ever being bothered in there…but it didn't matter. It didn't feel private to me. Everywhere I went, I was watched. It was important that I be on my best behavior."

"But everyone has secrets," said Michael.

"Yes," Ruby agreed, "but not everyone has their *own*."

"Whose secrets were you keeping?"

Ruby thought about this for a long time. "My mother's," she finally ventured. And then she added, "I wonder what that means."

"It means you're just like everyone else." Michael offered her a smile that warmed her. "That's what I think, anyway."

On the sixth day, they broke camp and headed east, though they were still unclear as to why they had to go that way. Rachel had nothing to say on the subject, unfortunately; he made it clear that he only went where he was told to go. It seemed that the Forgetting didn't affect lesser animals.

At dusk on the edge of Auburn Moor, they met a band of moonrats and hedgehogs moving three wagons east from Moonwood. They were Cholai, wanderers from the North, and Michael was wary of them at first. He refused to talk with Benjamin, the well-dressed hedgehog that came to invite them to join the caravan.

"We offer food, clothes, and warm beds," said Benjamin, wiggling his snout and hooking his thumbs into his vest. He had come with his wife, Moira, a black moonrat with white markings on her head. "Would you rebuff that offer, master weasel? You two look like you just washed up out of the sea!"

"Perhaps we did," was Michael's only reply.

"You can see we're not Nixies," Moira said calmly. She was small and beautiful, and her voice was as smooth and as clear as water. She wore a beautiful brooch with a purple gem set in silver.

"They don't pester us," Benjamin added. "Walk with us. We'll go as far as the fort with you. My dear!" He gestured to Ruby and then rocked back happily on his heels. "My daughter has just outgrown a dress that I think would look lovely on you! And we have tonic for those colds, too. You won't find much hospitality out here in the Stark Lands, fellow travelers. You know that. Please consider our company."

But Michael would say no more, and Benjamin returned to the wagons with Moira to camp for the night. Michael and Ruby camped not far away, and the smells of the Cholai's cooking made Ruby's stomach clench and grumble. When Benjamin came to them with venison steaks, Michael broke down at last. They joined the Cholai that night

Moira gave Ruby a moon-silver dress and a pair of warm stockings. Michael reluctantly accepted a white linen shirt with a silver collar to wear under his waistcoat. He grumbled at first, but he smiled when Ruby said he looked dashing in it, and from then on, he stopped complaining about the Cholai's generosity. Warm in the shared sleeping wagon, they stretched out on downy mattresses with quilts to cover them. Ruby slept well into the afternoon, pressed and sweating between moonrat kittens, and she woke feeling refreshed for the first time since her night on the beach.

"We travelers have to help each other," Benjamin said that day, walking beside Michael and Ruby in the light of afternoon. "Especially in these trying times. If we can't stick together, master weasel, then all is lost."

Wisents pulled the three Cholai wagons. The two main wagons contained supplies packed into crates and bags and stowed with amazing efficiency. While Michael preferred to walk outside with Benjamin and Moira, Ruby spent most of her time on her mattress in the sleeping wagon. Dreams made her feel real. Every bump of the cart left her aching, and she cherished each bruise. Each cramp was an affirmation. She began to use the pain to enter a kind of trance, and in this way she learned to quiet her mind and persevere when the Forgetting came over her.

The Cholai were prolific inventors. Many of their wagons were fitted with strange devices for measuring the weather, preserving food, or catching and distilling rainwater. The children played with small machines that could fly for short distances on wings of gunny cloth. They used something like electricity to power these toys and to light their lanterns; each wagon carried a generator cobbled together from spare parts. They clanked and buzzed and they leaked oil into sinks. Ruby felt uncomfortable around them. They reminded her of the Nixies.

When she wasn't sleeping or meditating, Ruby frequently enjoyed discussions with Leora, the caravan's mystic and Halcyon priestess. Named for the moon, Leora was an ancient shrew with a third of her tail missing. She could gaze into a crystal or read a deck of cards and see the future, but she had the soul of a philosopher. Her real love, as she explained, was not divination but the politics of faith.

"We believe first," she said, "and we listen last. If I come to you with a problem, an observation, and I put the problem in your hand and I say, 'Work it out', then you will feel like a boat on the sea with no rudder and no paddle. You look around, asking for help. It's how we are – in our hearts anyway. The Cholai hearts and yours. For some, it's not the same. They want to self-direct, not rely on anybody. But for us and for those like you, Ruby, we want to reach out. Don't reach out, take everything into yourself quietly, then you break. So leading is easy. Because most *want* to be led. They don't want to do things alone.

Alone feels wrong. Scary. But the leaders...who leads them? At your core, and at the core of those like you, is a misunderstanding about what leading means. You don't know what leadership is. How could you? No one does. We're followers – all followers. Cholai and you. Even the leaders follow. So no leaders, then. Maybe just question answerers or decisive bodies. I don't know. There's no answer. Perfect is bad. Impossible. Broken...just the way we are. Believe first, and listen last. Listen first, you don't believe. Don't believe, don't trust, you're alone. No oars. Rudderless. What I do: tell them what they already believe. Put the problem in their hands, make them think they took it themselves. Then maybe they can solve it."

"Are you saying that you can't really see the future?" Ruby was stunned. "That you just tell people what they want to hear?"

"No, no!" Leora protested, but Ruby saw her knowing smile. "I don't lie. I reassure. That's all anyone wants. 'You can do this. This is fine. Don't worry.' Maybe I see, but that doesn't matter."

"It's not about listening," Ruby said with a chuckle.

"Not for them," Leora said. "But not for me either. Not really. Everybody wants the same thing. You're not going to find a new kind of desire, a new hope, a new thing for people to want. Talk to one or two, and you've heard everything."

Leora was fascinated by Ruby's Tidestone. She spent as much time staring into it as Ruby would allow; Ruby was reluctant to take it off

"Not a seeing crystal," Leora told her. "But something like. From the Halcyon to you. This gem is a special thing, Ruby. Guard it well."

Ruby had taken to staring into the Tidestone herself. Its light had taken on a weird quality. It no longer shone its guiding ray; now it scintillated in a strange, liquid way, its glow rippling and warped as if diffused through water. It still whispered to her, but it rarely made any sense anymore. The better she felt, the better it made her feel. Michael wasn't surprised to hear about this.

"The Halcyon doesn't give gifts in that way," he said to her one night, while she lay draped across his chest and the sleeping wagon was loud with snoring. "It may not be a gift from any deity, but it's clearly linked to you. Whatever changes you've seen in it are probably reflections of changes within yourself."

After three days, Ruby began to remember why they were going toward the Auburn Mountains. When she told Michael, he was ecstatic. A long talk with him helped to reestablish the memory with certainty. Michael had said nothing to any of the Cholai about who they were, and no one seemed to have recognized Ruby. He remained silent even after their epiphany. Despite all their help, he still did not completely trust them. Ruby was complicit in this conspiracy to remain silent. Though she liked these northern wanderers a good deal more than Michael did and felt that she had no reason to distrust them, she was loyal to Michael before all others. Perhaps she believed before she listened; but when she did listen, she could only hear that Michael's reasons were justified.

Just south of the ruined fort, Ruby and Michael parted ways with the Cholai. They would turn their wagons north and make for the Thornwash. Ruby and Michael would camp on the moor for one more day before continuing on toward the Valley of Silk. They said their goodbyes beneath the gloaming sky with the horned moon rising. Moira gave Ruby a pack of rations and supplies for herself. She had also mended Ruby's moccasins.

"They'll wick away any sort of wetness now," the moonrat beamed. "Like a duck's back. The inner lining, as I'm sure you know, was perfect, but I added some down padding at the big toe. Just a little fluff to help with blisters, dear. If you're headed into the mountains, you'll thank me for that later."

Leora also had a gift for Ruby. It was a sword of gnomish make, simple and sturdy, with a sapphire set in its silver pommel. When tilted at a certain angle, the blade appeared blue. At another angle, it seemed velvet black.

"Blackheart," Leora smiled. "Used in the first war a thousand years ago. Made from metal that fell from the sky, they say. Meteors, you know. Use it. Save your life."

There were Melidoran symbols etched on one side of the blade.

ᚱᛇᚾᛕᚴᚨ ᛒᛕᚾᚴᛃᚨᚴ

And on the opposite side was another inscription.

Ruby strapped Blackheart onto her hip. She was about to put Ketha's dagger aside, having no room for it, but decided to put it into her pack instead. Wearing the sword made her feel like a warrior. It came to her all at once that she was riding into battle – that Michael expected her to lead soldiers into war. Her stomach dropped. She wasn't ready. She took a few deep breaths and gripped the Tidestone for reassurance.

"You see it now, eh?" Leora said. Her tone was almost derisive. "Listen first. Then act. Then believe, child. Save your life." She got close now, her ears swiveling, her lame tail curling up against her bristling back. Ruby could smell her. She realized just how weak age had left Leora.

Last of all, Benjamin presented Ruby and Michael each with walking sticks. They were tipped with brass and beautifully carved, and Michael began to lean on his right away. Ruby thought he looked like a proper Cholai now, though she imagined he would be offended if she said so.

"Travel well, friends," Benjamin said, his impresario's grin firmly in place. His eyes glittered darkly. "May the road rise up to meet you."

"And the wind be always at your back," Michael said, and he earned a smile of pleasant surprise from Ruby as he bowed.

"It shall be, master weasel," Benjamin grinned. "It shall always be."

The tails of dust whirling up from behind the Cholai's wagons were still visible to the north when Ruby and Michael reached the Auburn Mountains. Razor-backed peaks marched black into the northern distance. To the south they rose on a gentle slope from a tide of autumn colors, with high snow tracing a strandline beyond the last of the hardiest trees. The western entrance to the Valley of Silk was a canyon cut into sheer walls of red-orange rock, and the moor before it was stony and withering. Ruby and Michael dismounted to lead the rams in on foot, and at first the animals balked. It didn't take too much coaxing before their pride overcame their fear, and Ruby was glad they wouldn't have to leave the rams behind.

They ascended a narrowing passage, walking side by side when they could. The floor was covered in a skin of yellow shale, and the slightest misstep sent blades of it calving off into a precipitous slide. The walking sticks Benjamin had given them proved invaluable here, saving Ruby many a painful tumble. The sure-footed rams were hindered in their ascent only by their being tied behind Michael and Ruby; Ruby thought it was a shame that there was no room to ride them. After they had been climbing all day and the back of Ruby's neck was dark with dirt and sweat, the passage suddenly opened wide. It dipped precariously down a high ledge toward green-clad hills and finally onto the floor of the valley proper, where it disappeared into a spacious evergreen forest.

Above, the sky was dimming to a pellucid amethyst. The crimson fire of the setting sun spread from behind clouds that bunched up like bed sheets. In that failing light, with her hand on her brow to shade her eyes, Ruby could just see that the valley was hung with great, shimmering strands of silver. They drooped across each other or billowed in the wind, stretched above the trees, anchored to the mountain walls. The forest canopy was adorned with smaller strands; it was as if the valley had been blanketed by a fall of silken threads.

"A paradise," Michael called it. "No place like it anywhere else. Tread carefully."

"The *threads*," Ruby said, staring. Rachel fidgeted, afraid again. Ruby patted his head to calm him down. He fell silent, but he continued to halt and fret. "Where do they come from?"

"The children of Arane," Michael said. "Great eastern Weavers." He began to mount his ram for the descent. "It's about a five mile walk to the other side if we don't stop. Try not to touch their webs. This valley is kept pristine – a secret kingdom. Remember, Empress: we don't belong here."

With this, they mounted their rams. Rachel bounded down the cliff as if he'd been born there and made even shorter work of the rubble field below. He bleated, happy to be of use again and apparently unaffected by the extra weight of Ruby's pack and oblivious to the sword Blackheart bouncing against his flank. He virtually skipped across the hills toward the wood. Ruby assumed that the joy of doing what he was bred to do had banished Rachel's fear. To her dismay, this proved to be temporary. On the valley floor, she and Michael dismounted, and the rams recommenced their worried fidgeting. Ruby got down on one knee and tried to look up into Rachel's eyes.

"Don't be scared," she said. "Everything will be all right."

As she petted Rachel's nose she felt warmth in the pit of her stomach. Darkness was falling, but there was a light for a brief moment, holding the dusk in place against the onset of night. When it faded, heat was spreading through all her extremities, and the Tidestone was pulsing on her chest. When she touched the jewel, it began to glow like a lantern's flame.

Rachel tossed his head. His breathing slowed, and fear left him; Ruby watched it recede from the ram's big, yellow eyes. "Maa," was all he said.

Michael came to Ruby's side. Somewhere nearby, an early nightjar began its watery chirr.

"Ever you amaze, Majesty," he said. "I had worried about navigating this forest in the dark. The children of Arane are active at all hours. But perhaps your gem's light will keep them at bay, should they think to descend on us." He did not seem too sure about that at all. "It will light our way, at least."

Ruby got to her feet and let the Tidestone fall against her. She was still thinking about Rachel's eyes.

"Are you so afraid of them?" She said. "The Weavers? What have you heard?"

"Many things, Empress," Michael said, looking apologetic, "and all of them warnings. This land was given to Arane by the Halcyon herself...or himself. It's not quite forbidden, but it sees few travelers. Those it does see rarely have good things to tell."

Ruby's shoulders dropped. "I'm afraid," she admitted, and Michael embraced her.

"We have your light, and you have your new sword," he told her. "And as long as we're together, there's no need to fear."

The Tidestone's light was clear and soft, its circle wide enough to see for thirty feet in all directions. The trees were evenly spaced, almost as if they'd been planted on a grid; Michael and Ruby led their rams down a natural corridor of hemlock, jack pine, nightcap oak, and silver fir. There was evidence of recent massive fire damage in places. For an hour, they walked in silence, and the air seemed to close in around them. It was hot, and the forest was waiting.

Beneath the persistent drone of insects and the high chirrup of tree frogs, beneath the noisy queries of barred owls and the baleful sough of large animals moving through the brush just beyond the light of the Tidestone, there ran a thread of barely audible sound that came from the forest's canopy. When Ruby first noticed it, she thought it was the wind. But she listened further, or was compelled to listen, and after an hour she slowly realized that it was a voice. It was a murmur that followed them over a rise into cycad groves, where strands of silver hung thick. There were large, structured webs here – complex versicolor orbs that shone in the moonlight. Many were torn, most were unnaturally perfect, and one had snared something as large as a pheasant. Ruby didn't like the way the webs moved; they seemed to sway whether the wind was blowing or not. Here, the canopy was open, and the whispers moving across it were less distinct. This was far from a relief. In the new silence, Ruby felt her pulse pounding in her throat. As they passed through the still grove and back into the living sounds of the forest, Michael finally spoke.

"I saw an eastern Weaver once," he said. "In Hawkport."

Ruby heaved a sigh and wondered how long she had been holding her breath.

"It was in a museum," Michael continued. "Dead, but…quite well-preserved."

"That means someone caught and killed one," Ruby replied.

"Or found one. They come out sometimes. To Duskwood." Michael pushed a hanging web away from his face as gingerly as he could. "You find things cocooned in silver. Badgers. Pigs. Even deer. But that's usually it."

"I remember, I think," Ruby said. It felt good to fight the Forgetting now. "I found a butterfly in a spider's web once. It was thrashing, beating its wings. The spider was sitting in a corner of the web just waiting. Maybe waiting to see if the butterfly got tired. I broke the web and freed it, and even then the spider didn't move."

"What happened to the butterfly?' Michael asked.

Ruby thought for a long time. She didn't look at the spots of light out in the darkness. She didn't see the many sets of eyes. There was only the path ahead and Michael's question to think about.

"I don't know," she said at last. "Whatever usually happens to butterflies, I guess."

She fell silent again. The memory of the butterfly had awakened another one – an older one. It was not a memory of home. Her heart began to race as she turned it over in her mind.

"The Weavers," she began. "They…they're not…"

"Shh!" Michael put a clawed finger to his lips. His ears pricked up. The fur on the back of his neck was ruffling, standing up as if he'd been shocked.

Ruby listened, tense as a bowstring. She could hardly hear anything over her own swallowing. There was a sound from somewhere ahead of them – a crash or a flutter, she couldn't tell which. And then a familiar cry rose from deep in the forest. It rode a hot breeze to ring for minutes in the valley, seeming larger than the mountains themselves. It was the baleful howl of a dire-dog.

"No," Michael whispered.

"It's in front of us." Ruby moved to press herself against Michael, to throw her arms around him, but the cry came again and she was yanked back suddenly. Rachel was pulling at the lead, terrified, trying to bolt. And now he began bleating; the high, hitching sound punched through the tension, exploding it.

Ruby stumbled to her knees and tugged on the lead, her mind racing with fear, her heartbeat hammering in her temples. Michael was struggling to control his ram as well, but it was Ruby's strength that gave out first. Rachel pulled free and went bounding away, the loop at the end of the lead wagging behind him before he and it both vanished into the dark.

"Rachel!" Ruby scrambled to her feet.

"He'll lead it right to us," Michael said. His voice was a hot rasp. He nearly dragged his ram forward. Eventually, weakened by fear, it came up to press itself against Michael's legs. "We have to get to high ground."

From far off, she heard Rachel bleating. Hopefully, he was headed for high ground, too.

How long it was before they heard the dire-dog's call again, Ruby didn't know. They turned north and pushed as hard as they could for the foothills. They slashed silver webbing aside, yanked it from their faces and mouths, and it fell on them to cling horribly as they pounded through the brush. There was sap smeared on Ruby's new dress. There were pine needles in her hair. At least Michael's ram was behaving. He didn't even bolt when that third howl finally came, obviously closer this time. It rose like a shriek of maniac laughter, and it was accompanied by a sound like trees falling in the forest. And then it was gone again, and they were left in a heavy, frantic hush that seemed intent on crushing all the breath from Ruby's lungs.

Blackheart felt huge at her side. She realized she had been squeezing its hilt. Webs hung over her shoulders, fine as shahtoosh, and it was no use trying to pull them away; the silver strands clung even faster to her sweaty hands. At last they broke into a close stand of blue spruce, and beyond was bare grass where the ground hunched up into bald hills against the feet of the mountains. Here they stopped to gasp with their heads between their knees, and Ruby risked a long swig from her canteen.

"Quietly now," Michael said, still catching his breath. "If it goes after Rachel, it might pass us by."

This thought brought precious tears to Ruby's eyes. She swallowed a sob and followed Michael as he crept into the spruce grove with his ram in tow.

It might smell us, Ruby worried. *We're a bigger target than poor Rachel!*

She would give her fears no voice; she was afraid to open her mouth.

Michael's ram flicked its tail and tossed its head. It was panting, its pink tongue hanging out stupidly. It stayed by Michael's side, jumping at phantom sounds and at shadows moving through the Tidestone's light. She tried to put her hand over the jewel, but its glow was not easily stifled. She still felt totally exposed as they squeezed in between the spruce branches.

At last, Ruby's heart stopped hammering, and, without her pulse roaring in her ears, she realized that the whispering in the forest had grown louder. It was right above them; that was what Michael's ram was reacting to. She couldn't ignore that sinister muttering. It absorbed her, dominating her attention. Rapt, she was able to make out individual sounds.

W ég. Goj é. Écu.

She pulled these like threads from the hopeless tangle of whispers. They plucked at something inside her, and she didn't have time to wonder why. They were not words, of course. They were carefully structured nonsense, their meaning disguised as gibberish. She could not see that meaning – that particular peak remained shrouded – but frustration felt like a luxury now. She let it roll over her for the time being, like water. *Like a duck's back, you know*, as Leora had said.

The foothills were bare and rocky on this side. Ruby and Michael slipped up their shoulders, picking their way across a fine layer of gravel and pulverized rock. The night seemed very deep when Ruby looked down over the valley floor from the crags, and a searing shaft of pain was running from the soles of her feet to the small of her back. She was lucky to be wearing such incredibly comfortable shoes. They stopped on a flat outcrop of feldspar, and Michael sat down with his back against the scarp face. His ram milled about, distracted, apparently having forgotten its fear entirely. Ruby wished she could do the same. She paced, kicking pebbles into the valley. Nothing moved in the forest. She couldn't even hear the owls anymore.

"Come away from the edge," Michael said.

Ruby ignored him. She was the Empress.

"We can't go back down there at night," she said. "We'll camp here and continue across the valley in the morning."

"We shall," Michael replied. He gulped water and then continued. "I suppose the lesson we learn from this is that, no matter how bright the light you carry, some darkness is best left unexplored."

This made Ruby smile. Her mind was like a cauldron, its contents stirred vigorously and now left swirling. Ideas fused together, burst apart, and then fused again to form new thoughts. Some of them were terrible – the dire-dog munching quietly on Rachel's bones – but she clung to the ones that provided some measure of comfort.

"It was the Weavers whispering, wasn't it?" She asked.

"That was my thought," Michael replied. "Following us. Watching. They watch us even now; I'm certain of that. As much noise as we made, as many webs as we disturbed, I'm surprised they didn't fall on us and wrap us up."

This thought did not provide Ruby with any measure of comfort.

"What are they?" She was still looking over the edge of the cliff. "I almost remembered."

"Many-legged things," Michael said. He looked like he was having trouble remembering himself. "With pincers and eyes...eyes like lanterns. Or embers of fire. And jaws like this." He put his paws up to his snout and wiggled his fingers, simulating a Weaver's pedipalps.

Ruby laughed and came to sit beside him. She leaned against him, and he put his arm around her. The ram folded its legs up under its body and tilted against the scarp face, exhausted.

"No fire tonight," Ruby said.

"No fire," Michael agreed, "though it would keep the dire-dog away. There are eyes here that are best turned from us, and we've already drawn far too much attention to ourselves. I think we've had enough adventure to keep us warm until dawn."

The sun was rising when Ruby stirred awake. A glow of brilliant gold washed through a slab of cirrostratus lashed with long mare's tail clouds, draining to a desaturated blue as cool and clear as powdered glass.

Smalt, her mother would have called it, and now a memory came swirling up from her misty depths. Her mother had been a potter. Was she still, in the lands beyond that sunrise? Might there be a little white candy dish decorated with cobalt blue sitting on a dresser waiting for her? It would still be filled with caramels. She could taste them on her tongue, rich and sweet.

She closed her eyes, warm and comfortable in the bedroll. It had been pulled quite tight around her. The sweet taste sat at the back of her mouth slowly became tart and coppery. Her throat began to feel sore. She opened her eyes again and her vision was blurry. Her head started to ache as she squinted, trying to regain the clarity of that gorgeous sky. She tried to lift her hand to wipe her eyes, but her arm wouldn't move. It was stuck to her side, and there were sparks running from her fingertips to her shoulders. Tilting her chin toward her chest, she shook her head, trying to bring the world back into focus. She wasn't in the bedroll. She was wrapped to her neck in silver thread.

Ruby screamed and her lungs burned. Her breaths came weak and shallow. She craned her neck and could not see Michael's ram, but she could see Michael. He was lying on his back half-wrapped himself and still sleeping. There were things moving over him, many-legged things with red carapaces and black pedipalps twitching around their mouths. She thought of Michael's fingers wagging. They were not spiders. They spun silk from beneath arching tails tipped with stingers. Their heads were heart-shaped. One sat on Michael's chest, its four clusters of black eyes glittering like chips of obsidian. Another worked methodically to wind him in that silver webbing.

"No!" Ruby thrashed as best she could, but she was slipping back into paralysis. She realized that Michael was paralyzed, too. She could just see the wound on his neck where they had stung him.

"No, no, no!" She screamed again, determined to remain defiant. She could feel Blackheart pinned against her leg. If only she could get her hand to move. If only she could reach that jeweled pommel.

But the venom was pumping through her. She felt it as heat in her veins. She was lightheaded; her body was growing weak again. As her eyelids drooped, one of the terrible Weavers pulled itself onto her chest and looked her in the face. The last thing she saw before she slipped back into unconsciousness was her reflection in every facet of its glittering black eyes.

Seven

Arane

In the beginning, Melidora was black and empty. The Halcyon looked down from the other world, and saw that it could be a good place, and she descended with the Tidestone around her neck to bring light to the void. She saw first a linden glade and a river flowing through it with silver willows growing all along its banks. The light of the Tidestone fell upon it like snow, and while it still lay partly in shadow, she named it the Dimwood.

Living things awoke in Dimwood, and the Halcyon gave to their kings the light of the jewel to spread in all directions. She named them Knowers because they went forth to carry the truth and to awaken other things, and she made a home for them in a great mountain. But the Knowers found Melidora unfinished.

Then the Halcyon made the Weavers, and it was their task to finish shaping Melidora after her design. But there were many things in the primal dark that wanted nothing to do with the Halcyon or with the Tidestone's light. They were sluagh and kobolds and grim wights, and they killed Weavers wherever they found them. Then they rose up to make war on the Knowers, and they killed their kings and drove them from their mountain. With the world newly made and already sick with hate and death, the Halcyon placed the Weavers in a secret kingdom to protect them. Then she came with all her wrath and forced the dark things into hiding. But she could not destroy them, for they had been made before her.

Why the Halcyon left Melidora is a secret lost in time. Her truth lives on in the woods and the rivers, under the ice and the roots of the mountains, in the spring wind and the dawn light, and in the songs of birds. And she continues to work from the other world, her plans unknown anymore, and all of Melidora's stories are her stories to this day.

The Weavers' poison gave Ruby many strange dreams. Some were about the Halcyon, and in these she saw the Knower kings with the light of the Tidestone in their hands. She saw Melidora wrapped in silver thread, and the Halcyon on the face of the deep. In some, she sat in a chair beside a window. It was winter outside, and she was frozen in place. Paralysis followed her into the other world, closing her throat and sitting heavy in her muscles. The Tidestone was gone, and all was dark for a long time. And then she was clawing toward lucidity, fighting as if trapped under ice, the surface just visible. When she opened her eyes at last, the world swirled back vividly. The colors were unreal; the lines were perfect and crisp. She might have been inside a painting.

Slowly, the world spread open around her. Pain descended along its strands, a chaperone for the cold specter of fear. She was in a vast chamber, bound on the wall with silver thread. There were Weavers all around her. The floor seemed to writhe. Two huge pillars stood at the back of the room, and there was a hard, unsettling shape between them. Gems traveled its dark surface like ants upon a carcass, shining in the vertices of its irregular angles. It made Ruby feel sick to look at it, but she was compelled to stare. After a long moment, she realized that it was a throne – though it was nothing anyone of healthy proportions could sit upon correctly.

The chamber was decorated with ancient reliefs. The remnants of the pigments used to color them were still visible in places. The level of sophistication in the carvings was incredible. From all around her came a chorus of insectile whispers; and now, from that muttering chaos, a single voice emerged, and all the others fell silent.

"Are you truly she?" Asked the voice.

A woman rose from the palpitating mass on the floor. Lank, black hair swayed at her jawline. Her eyes were like chips of beryl.

"You will go east," the woman said. Her lips barely moved, but her voice was huge and queenly. Arane, certainly. The Weavers were her children. Ruby remembered. "That is the best I can do. I'm sorry. The nightmare is almost over."

Arane reached up. She might have touched Ruby, but Ruby couldn't feel anything; she was alive and thinking in a body that was dead. She might have been crying.

"Don't worry," Arane continued. "Don't fear. You've come back, but they don't know you. They don't know you, but we do – your servants. We have an operation. I will do what I can for your friend, but they are careful. I cannot promise anything, Empress. I cannot promise anything for him."

The queen of the Weavers looked into Ruby's eyes. It might have been fear on her face, it might have been real and total love, but it was probably only hunger. This cavern was cold with a depthless hunger; Ruby would not have been surprised to see the wall open up and the Abyss gaping behind it. Then Arane stepped away, and it was not the

Abyss she saw next but two colossal golem shadows drawn across the cavern by torchlight. The pulsing sea of Weavers parted, and a pair of Nixies took hold of Ruby and began to peel her from the wall. There was a small, slim figure between them.

Arane doesn't take sides, Michael had said, but he had been wrong.

"Yes, that's the one," the slim figure was saying. "That's the one I paid for. Take her."

Then the world began to swirl away again, the brilliant colors bleeding into darkness, and Ruby lost consciousness once more.

She was sitting motionless in a gray room, and it was winter outside the window. She was sitting on a bench in the back of a charabanc with its top pulled up, and there was a face before her speaking. Its words sank away. It might have been a man, it might have been a cat, it might not have been there at all. She turned her face to the mica window, and watched the world rush by in a meaningless blur of autumn colors. Red became gold, gold became green, and green faded from blue into gray. The Forgetting pressed hard upon her. It took her in its cold fist and squeezed, and her mind filled up with smoke. It was a short step from gray to black again.

The Nixies headed east in a long caravan. Six wagons of ebony and white pine left the Auburn Mountains and the Valley of Silk on a wintry day. At the head of the caravan were two spider phaetons with dark little drivers tugging their gilded reins. Their quirts flew back in graceful arcs, pestering huge black stallions to speed as they crossed into Duskwood. Nixies walked on the outside of the column, two to a side, guarding open wagons crowded with prisoners. These were the large kind, the hulks, shambling along in their haphazard way, and they fouled the air with the smell of oil and coolant steaming from their sagging innards. There were smaller Nixies as well. They stood in the charabancs or atop the two carriages, lean and well-formed and almost humanoid, and they watched all through the scopes of copper-barreled carbines.

Ruby remembered fording the Golrace not far above churning waters that fell madly toward Hawkport in the south. There, Mount Golrace loomed gray and lonely, a lost peak left over from the breaking of the Auburn Mountains in the ancient past. Ruby saw it in the red dawn light, a spire striving for heaven itself, dark and terrible against the cloudless sky. A black fortress sat high on its misty shoulders. Once a gnomish stronghold, it had been empty for centuries.

The Forgetting was a specter in the corner of her mind, waiting in shadow wearing the shape of a man. It would step forward, and it would lock the door behind it. She was alone in her bed, still and silent as a fossil, in a room full of faceless hands.

The webbing had been cut off her. The Tidestone was gone, along with her pack and, of course, her sword. A chain connected shackles on her wrists and ankles, and there was a lead attached to a collar around her neck. A black and white cat held the other end of it – her owner, she presumed. He sat across from her on the charabanc, avoiding eye contact. He was handsome and had an aristocratic air about him. She imagined that only the very rich could afford to buy slaves from the Nixies. And he was in league with them, of course. He turned a blind eye to their cruelty. He profited from it, in fact. Sometimes, the cat would try to speak to her, but she ignored it. She hated it more than she'd ever hated anything, and it didn't seem to care. Ruby remembered that this was the way of cats: they took what they could as long as they could be bothered, apathetic about the difference between self and others. She made up her mind that she would do what her master commanded only insofar as a cat would. What would he think about that?

A wide wagon track cut into Duskwood through a grove of cypress, juniper, and black willow. These gave way to locust and poison sumac, hickory and persimmon trees. This forest was where the Halcyon had departed from Melidora the first time. What remained of her first light was here – or so the story went. Ruby remembered this in a fever dream, from which she was shaken awake by a metal hand.

"You were seizing," said the cat.

A Nixie was looking down at her. Its eyes were like goggles. Ruby only leaned against the backboard and looked out at the forest. The Halcyon's light was dimming from this part of the world. It had been dimming for thousands of years. It was midday, but the canopy was thick, and the trees were old and tall. All the wood was shadowed. The wagon drivers didn't seem to mind; they lashed on whatever the conditions, needing neither rest nor food.

Once, the caravan broke out of the woods to cross a bridge over a deep gorge. This was in the morning and after Ruby had spent many days in the dim and the hush. To see the light of the sun again, to feel the air moving upon her, made her smile for the first time since the Valley of Silk. If anyone saw this, no one said anything. She prayed that a wheel would break and that they would be forced to stay under the sun all day, but the dark little drivers kept up their demons' pace. Ruby sagged as they returned to the dark. A few tears pearled up and tracked a short way through the dirt on her cheeks, and she was happy to be able to feel them.

When they crossed the Charl, Ruby was in a deep sleep. Dimwood lay just to the south, its great capital dreaming beneath towering lindens, larches, and lonely stands of dawn redwood. Silver willows wept low over the river. The wagons crossed the white stone bridge carefully, one by one.

Beyond Duskwood towered the knurled horns of the Nirfang Mountains. Ruby watched them with shadows swirling in her periphery. Her anger roiled with the deep force. It burned like a coal at the top of her throat as the caravan finally broke into the open. There was a Nixie outpost at Owl's Head Peak; the caravan stopped there for a night, and Ruby was allowed to get some exercise. She walked in a pen with other prisoners, Nirfang gigantic above them, stygian black and cold, clawing up at the sky as if in anger.

Most of her fellow captives were moonrats, as the Cholai had been. Some may have been Cholai themselves, but she recognized no one. There was a pair of otters, a badger with a terrible scar across her face, and a large-eyed wolf cub that wouldn't stop crying, no matter how much the Nixies kicked him.

The Nixies left a charabanc full of prisoners behind when they departed, and they cut northeast across the prairie at breakneck speed. Ruby hummed quietly to herself, trying hard to remember Michael's song about the moon. She imagined Leora descending, nude and pale, to bathe in the Wood of Thorns. As the wagon bounced through sedge and spikerushes, Ruby imagined she was sitting at the source of the Gray River, watching the moon-maid rise from the water. Her belly would be round and full. Her hair would be adorned with stars.

When pain would grip the base of her neck or when sadness would bulge up into her mouth, Ruby tried to give in to the Forgetting, which only grew more powerful each time it consumed her. But something in her mind fought back. The Weavers' poison was gone from her body. Now, it was the war of memory that left her sick. When the caravan arrived in Gowspin, the Nixies delivered her cataleptic into the hands of her new owners.

Eight

The Hills of Connemara

She awoke on an alabaster slab in a little garden, sunlight streaming gorgeous from a cloudless sky. A warm breeze mixed the fragrances of freesias, jonquils, and mignonette. Intermittent showers of violet blossoms blew down from a single jacaranda by the wall. She sat up, breathing deeply and feeling rested, all her aches gone. A sliding panel door opened on the garden from a small, red-roofed house.

From beyond the walls, she could hear a constant, pulsing murmur. Ruby rose and padded barefoot to where a flutter of blue butterflies were puddling in a low birdbath. One delicate arch planted on the birdbath's rim, she pulled herself up and peeked out at the ocean. The tide sucked lovingly at the pebbly beach, which curved to the north and south as far as she could see. It was noon, and the water shimmered as if scattered with diamonds. There were large, black sea swans floating well beyond the shore. Now and again, one of them would spread its wings and trumpet, and the sound was like a swift wind lashing the brass curve of a church bell. White birds circled in a cloud, diving. They gathered on the shore to bicker and preen in great flocks. They were kittiwakes, and the sight of them brought a sob up to catch in Ruby's throat.

She went back to the slab and sat, wiping tears from her eyes with the heels of her palms. There were florid bruises on her wrists and ankles. The moonrat's dress had not been as pretty as the flowing, amaranthine gown she now wore, but she lamented its loss all the same. As she pressed her thumbs into the aching ball of her right foot, it occurred to her that her stockings were gone, too. This brought a swell of horror very close to her surface. She remembered that she was now a slave, and she hoped that it had been a nurse who had removed her stockings and not her new master.

"The cat," she said, thinking aloud. "Oh, Michael!"

Those horrible Weavers on him, their silver webs and their stingers bobbing pregnant with paralytic venom – it was all her fault. She was the Empress; she had decided to go north through the Valley of Silk. She reached for the Tidestone and remembered, mid-motion, that it was gone, too.

She was on the verge of a good, hard weep when someone came out into the garden through the sliding door.

"Ruby," he said in a gruff voice. "Empress, you're awake!"

A small creature bowed before her with deep formality, his knee out and his head on his arm.

"Sir Arturus Merswin Periwinkle," he announced, "at your service."

Sir Arturus Periwinkle was a guinea pig. Most of his hair was blond and stuck up in broad curls despite obvious attempts to smooth it back. A white strap across his upper half matched a splotch on his face that ran around one eye and down to his wiggling pink nose. He held his bow until Ruby stood, touched him on the head, and told him to rise. Then he beamed at her and rushed to her side to take her hand.

"Sir Arthur," Ruby said. Her voice felt hollow and robotic. Shock was a difficult feeling to deal with today. "What do you mean?"

Arturus bristled. Ruby guessed that he didn't much care for that name.

"The circumstances of your arrival are strange, I know," he began. "Please sit down, Empress, and we'll explain everything."

"By the bird," said another voice. "I told you the fresh air would do the trick."

The cat came into the garden over the wall, skipping easily along the top on all fours. He dropped onto the grass by the jacaranda, removed his Lincoln green cap, and made a little bow of his own.

"You," Ruby frowned. Her eyes became dark, and Arturus squeaked as she squeezed his paw.

"I," the cat replied, "am William, and I am sorry for the way this all came about." He placed the cap easily between his ears. "We had hoped that you would make it to Pearlwater from the Lockwood outpost, but that plan was scuttled almost the instant it was laid. And we didn't know the path south past Seer's Knob had been blocked until recently. It appears the Nixies have all but claimed the Eastfair for the Empress."

"Even the Gray River has been taken," Arturus added. "Butterbush Barrens is cut off, though Eggplant continues to resist. And ever it shall! Certain parts of it, at least. My kin will not be cowed, especially not by Nixies!"

"Indeed," said William. "Sir Periwinkle's illustrious Eggplant may be the last stronghold of the north, for what that's worth. But this is all too much for now. Sit. Sir Periwinkle will bring you some tea, and *I* will do my best to bring you up to speed."

Arturus made a defiant face, but he complied. As he disappeared into the house, Ruby sat back down and William lowered himself onto the slab beside her. He searched her face with eyes like pools of honey. There was a certain calculating intelligence there, a deep light of age and wisdom that she found fearsome and entrancing.

"Allow me to apologize again, Empress," William began, "and to assure you that this is a safe place. We are emancipators, friends of the resistance working within the Nixian empire to sabotage their slaving." He removed his cap again. His tail was curled around his middle, and as he spoke its tip began to move back and forth. The cold light in his eyes invested his face with a predatory aspect. "The Nixies need workers for their factories. They dig underground, mining ores and gems. They need engineers, metalsmiths – tradespeople of all kinds. Some go north to work the ice. Some go south to Nirfang. The rest are shipped here to work the docks or to the Cradle itself, under certain circumstances. There are always trades going on; slaves may be taken into private households for all kinds of reasons. Periwinkle and I buy slaves and free them when we can, or we take them in from other places. There is a network to help them to safety. We're a small part of it. The resistance is growing every day. There are still safe places left."

"Michael," was all Ruby said in reply.

William frowned. "The Nixies own the Auburn Mountains. Apparently, Arane was put in a desperate situation; now she works with us to move as many slaves to safety as she can without being caught. She got you here with great risk to herself. Your friend, Lord Underbridge, must have gone south, Majesty." William's eyes were wet. His ears were flat against his head. Ruby was moved by the sorrow on his face. "Sometimes, what we do is not enough. But, as long as there is something we can do, there is hope."

Arturus returned with a tray. The teacups were tiny. The clay teapot looked like a toy.

"Oolong," he said, with a dramatic flourish. "Drink and regain your strength. We've been treating you for some time. The Weavers' toxins are powerful; I worried you'd die."

"Not dead," Ruby replied, taking a cup by its miniature handle and sipping. "Just lost." The tea was hot and bitter. She swallowed calm with it. In a single, burning gulp, she swallowed focus.

William patted her calf. She could see that he was disappointed that she had not acknowledged his apologies. Ruby thought there was very little good to be done by apologies now.

"Rest here awhile, Empress," William said. "I must make some appearances today. We cultivate our image as necessary to avoid falling under suspicion. Tonight, we'll talk about the next step." He stopped in the doorway, and turned, looking back at Ruby with a taut, feline smile. "It warms my heart to see you again."

The house was cozy and well furnished. Ruby followed Arturus into a sitting room, trailing her fingers over surfaces of solid oak and cherry. There was a heavy smell of mint in the air; on the kitchen table was a beautiful arrangement of flowering catnip. Paintings on frameless canvasses were hung on the walls. Ruby could follow William's brush strokes through the oil and trace the contours of the colors as they flowed over each other. Here was a seascape, and Lockwood in fall colors, and here was Pinwale Harbor from behind shining rows of fishing line. She recognized some of these scenes from the glass at the Bay of Mirrors. More paintings leaned against each other in the hall and behind the enormous settee. One of these was of a red-headed girl, lanky and beaming, with the sun at her back. Walking through the house was like exploring the body of a lover. She touched the banister affectionately and ran her toes along the pine baseboards. Arturus sat on the loveseat with his pink feet up on an ottoman, letting her roam while he chewed dandelion heads.

"I remember this house," Ruby said, only slightly interested in whether or not Arturus was listening.

"Come and sit," Arturus laughed. "You remember how to do that, don't you?"

A little annoyed, Ruby did as she was told. She fell onto the settee and found it deep as well as sublimely comfortable. Her legs stuck out above the floor as she sank into the cushion. It smelled old and expensive.

"Of course you remember," Arturus continued, picking a yellow petal from his whiskers. "You've been here before. You're the Empress."

"I've been forgetting so many things," Ruby explained. "Everyone has. Right? Michael said the Forgetting had settled on everybody."

"It has," Arturus replied. "But it's slowly losing power since you've come. Everywhere you go, the Forgetting starts to recede. You bring a light, Empress. You always have. It's why we need you."

Ruby looked at Sir Periwinkle. "Tell me about yourself," she said, fist pressed up beneath her chin.

"You don't remember?" Arturus said with a wry smile.

"Knight of Eggplant," Ruby replied, "Butterbush Barrens – yes, yes. But I want to hear it from you."

Arturus crossed his paws behind his head and leaned back. He was quite a bit more flexible than he appeared. His twitched his whiskers and look at the ceiling as if his response might be written there. Ruby followed his gaze and saw only immaculately applied stucco.

"A Butterbush man, that's right," Arturus said. "And knighted for gallantry in service to the crown, yes indeed. And on top of all that, a Periwinkle! A triple threat, as they say where I come from. My father was Feodor Periwinkle, and his father was Arturus Feodor, master of Foxburrow. He fought in the battle of Gowspin, you know. And Feodor died on the Thornwash in the North War, fighting ten kobolds at once.

They were heroes, and their ancestors were heroes, and now is *my* time. Have a look at this."

He hefted himself up and crossed to the mantle. He picked up a hinged box covered in green felt and handed it to Ruby.

"The Periwinkle seal," he said, proudly. "Our family crest. Handed down since the name was Barewingle. We lived in the east then. There's one just like it on an escutcheon in my father's house."

Ruby opened the box gently. It was quite heavy for its size. Inside was a silver medallion engraved with the image of two guinea pigs in suits of armor standing on either side of a flame encircled by an oblong shape that might have been a wall. The corner bore Melidoran letters; each time she looked at those strange symbols, they seemed more familiar to her. Now they settled into her mind and she understood them at last. The feeling was thrilling and deeply satisfying. Her memory was finally knitting properly.

"Constant, Fearless, Righteous and Right," she recited, and Arturus seemed to swell up with pride.

"Our family motto since time immemorial," he said. Then his voice became an awed whisper. "Do you know it's said the Periwinkle line first rose to prominence in Alamandra? Look at that flame there encircled by the wall. The wall of the gray city, if you ask me!" He took the box from Ruby, closed it, and petted it for a moment before putting it back in its place of honor.

"Heroes," he muttered. "And now it's my time."

Ruby sipped her tea and listened long into the evening while Arturus boasted about his heritage and the deeds of his forebears. He appeared to have done very few deeds worth boasting about himself, but that didn't stop him for a second. Every brave moment, every display of his inherited superiority he inflated shamelessly. He told of his knighting ceremony and of the row his uncle had started with a member of the royal family while it was still in progress. He found it offensive that the King of Eggplant was an otter, but he went on at great length about the beauty and virtue of the queen. He was a passionate pig, that much was clear, and obviously quite impressed with himself. Ruby imagined that working in secret chafed him, and he confirmed this as the sun was slipping down behind the garden wall.

"William is a good fighter," Arturus admitted, "but he's intent on creeping about in the shadows. I suppose that's how cats are. I long for the day when Pearlwater and Dimwood march on the Cradle! Living under the Nixies' noses – or whatever they've got for smelling – makes my warrior's heart sick for battle. But we've done a lot of good here, if I can say. William's got a good head. Me, I talk a lot of bluster, and I charge in nose first no matter what fight there is to win. He keeps me from getting myself locked up, or worse, I suppose. For that, I'm thankful."

"The fight is coming to us soon, Arthur," Ruby said. "The work you've done here is almost finished. You'll have your glory in battle."

Hearing *Arthur* again, Arturus made a face, but he didn't protest. She was the Empress, after all.

"I hope so, Majesty," he said, looking into his empty teacup. "I hope we've done enough."

Ruby sat back into the couch, long legs folded under her. Someone had painted her nails while she was unconscious. She could imagine William worrying that she needed some color on her hands and feet as he and Arturus nursed her back to health. She began to pick at the polish and thought about the slaves the Nixies had taken. Was Michael underground, working the bellows? Was he hammering an anvil, making war machines to raze Dimwood to the ground? Was he lying dead on the banks of the Charl?

She voiced her concern to Arturus, who thought for a while and seemed to be unsure what to think about the concept of selfless concern for others. He was not a stupid creature by any stretch, nor was he a narcissist. Ruby thought that "emotionally immature" described Arturus most accurately. But he had done so much for the slaves – risked his life to help them to safety. Ruby could not help but admire him.

Finally, he seemed to see why Ruby might be so concerned about Michael.

"My best guess is that he's at Nirfang," Arturus said. "They keep a small number of slaves at Owl's Head, mostly for mining. But if he knows anything about Pearlwater or Dimwood, they'll be holding him for questioning. I've heard tell of their methods, lass. It's best not to think about what they might be doing to get him to talk."

"But I do mean to think about it," Ruby announced. "In fact, I mean to rescue Michael. He and all the slaves at Owl's Head, if I can." She remembered the little wolf. It was all or none.

"An attack on Owl's Head?" Arturus's eyes widened. "It's a small camp, but still…it'd be suicide. Three could never do it, not even with a year to plan."

"Three?" Ruby smiled. "You would want to join me?"

Arturus looked stymied for an instant, and then he narrowed his eyes at her and grinned wickedly.

"I've been there," he finally said, virtually growling with excitement. "I know how they place the guards – and I know how to get you in."

"There's hope then. It can be done."

"A mad hope. And slim. The slimmest. You're insane to try it – begging your pardon, Empress. It's reckless. But, by damn, I like reckless."

They spent the rest of the night talking and planning. Arturus said Ruby had been asleep for almost a month. In that time, Southunder had finally fallen. The city's lord mayor had been killed when dire-dogs crossed the borders, and the Empress of Nix had supplanted him with a mechanical man – a homunculus. It was now the Nixian capital of the south, and Hawkport was set to fall next. From their stronghold on the Gray River, Nixies were hunting Cholai openly in Moonwood. Every few days, a group of Cholai slaves arrived in Gowspin. But the Cholai were cunning, and Moonwood was dangerous territory. Arturus was certain that hope yet remained for the wanderers.

"We will want the Cholai as allies," Ruby said. She was feeling less like a child by the hour. "We'll need all the friends we can find."

By the time the moon had hauled herself west and was sinking silver into the sea, her stars dimming to honor her descent, Ruby and Arturus had a rough plan for their attack on Owl's Head Peak. They had factored William into it, though Arturus was sure he would disapprove of the whole thing. Stealth would be critical in the first stages.

"We'll let him in on it when he returns," Arturus said. He was eager and agitated, and he paced the floor incessantly as they went over their plan again. "And then we'll have to spend all day talking him into it. But we'll have his bow, I'm sure. Eventually. Besides, he can't refuse an order from you, Empress, if it comes to that."

But William did not return home that night. Ruby and Arturus fell asleep in the sitting room, all the tea in the house gone and the cherry coffee table covered with empty cups of every shape. When the first rays of the noon sun were angling through the front window and William still hadn't appeared, Ruby grew sick with worry.

"I can't do too much obvious looking," Arturus told Ruby as he rushed to assemble his light armor, "but I'll stop by some places and see if anyone's heard anything. I have a vague recollection of where he had to go last night. The fog lifts, yes, but slowly. So damn slowly! I'm sorry, Empress, but if they've found us out, they will come looking. You have to hide."

He pulled on a suit of silver plate. Heavy boots rode up to his knees, and his sword in its scabbard sat upon his back with its hilt over his right shoulder. Ruby couldn't decide if he looked heroic or ridiculous. With all his gear on at last, he led her into the basement, clanking proudly down the stone steps. There were bookshelves on the east and north walls; a door on the west wall was illuminated by a crystal mounted above it. Within that crystal, faeries danced, the blue light of their auras amplified by the crystal's meticulously cut facets. Arturus turned away from the door and, with a grunt, slid the book case on the north wall to the right. It moved with a grinding shriek on a track that was recessed into the slab floor. Beyond it was a small apartment.

"It's got all the necessaries," Arturus said. "But I wish like hell I didn't have to put you in here. We knew it might come to this, though. It's built for several occupants. We've had as many as twelve in here at once."

He rushed through a tour of the apartment, showing her the bed and the bookshelf as well as the vents that ran up through the ground outside. This space was lit with faerie crystals as well. Ruby patted the one in the small kitchen, watching the tiny, winged creatures swirl about inside it. The kitchen had an ice chest, and Arturus showed her that it was stocked with food.

"I don't mean for you to be down here for very long," he assured her. "I'll be back tonight, and I'll open the door. Don't open it yourself! You'll hear me come down the steps singing."

"What song?" Ruby asked.

"Does it matter? 'The Hills of Connemara.' When I unlock the door, there'll be three clicks, and then I'll start to slide it. Any fewer or any more, and it won't unlock and you'll know it isn't me."

He embraced her at the entrance to the secret apartment. Ruby put her chin on his blond head.

"I'm sorry," he said again. "This is no place for an Empress! But I could say the same for Gowspin itself, I suppose. These are trying times."

Now he turned to the bookshelf on the east wall.

"If you hear three clicks and it's neither William nor I that comes through the door," he placed something in her hands, "use this."

It was Blackheart. Ruby held it up and slipped it half out of the scabbard to see the symbols etched on the blade. Before she could thank Arturus, he offered her something else from the top of the bookshelf.

"And this," he said.

Ruby's eyes lit up. She put the Tidestone around her neck and spent a moment gazing into it. It glowed, its voice in her head whispering relief.

"Thank you," she gushed, "I thought they'd taken them!"

"They had," Arturus smiled. "Luckily, 'they' was us." He looked over his shoulder with wide eyes. His ears pricked. "I have to go now, Majesty. Remember: three clicks! Stay safe!"

"Find William," Ruby replied. "And come back for me."

Arturus bowed and seemed about to say something more, but he only slid the bookcase back along its track, looking in on Ruby one last time before he pushed it hard into place. After three clicks, Ruby heard him clanking up the stairs.

First, Ruby went to the kitchen. There was a pantry she hadn't seen earlier. She opened it and took out an apple, and while she chewed she went to look at the faerie crystal. The creatures inside it were little more than balls of light with what looked like butterflies' wings. They moved in random patterns, dimming and brightening. She wondered what they could sense – what they could feel. They seemed to react to the light of the Tidestone; as Ruby leaned close, the faeries swarmed in its direction. She backed away, worried about upsetting them.

Then she went to the bookcase. It shared a room with a number of small cots and a vent that opened as a round hole in the wall. Through the vent Ruby could smell the beach and hear the steady pulse of the tide. Now and again, the cries of the kittiwakes echoed through the tube

Most of the books on the bookshelf were about Melidora: there was *The Lords of Melidora*, *The Singing Statue*, *The King's Eagle*, *Heroes of Butterbush Barrens*, *The Secret of Dimwood*, and a few collections of short stories, as well as a book of maps and names. She chose *The Legend of Dallie Bratcher* and opened it wide as she sat on the bed. She stuck her nose in the binding and inhaled; she had always found the mixed smells of ink and pulp and paste to be intoxicating. After another deep breath, she smiled broadly and placed the book in her lap. She felt a warm wave of relaxation spread across her shoulders. The close quarters and the heavy, musty air made her nervous, but she would lose herself in this story and forget about the fear. She would forget about the pain that was finally returning to her body after the long wagon trip from the Valley of Silk, and the horror that churned her stomach when she thought of how she had failed Michael.

The book's cover was richly illustrated. On it, young Dallie Bratcher was setting out from Southunder with the Auburn Mountains before him. There stood Seer's Knob, and old Mount Bolding was a towering shadow behind it. The author's name was Elizabeth Lynn, and Ruby sat for a long time staring at the florid, golden lettering that spelled it out.

She knew the name. It was huge in her mind, loud and urgent. She searched for the connection, digging through layers of memory like an archaeologist. There were so many old fears, so many memories of betrayal and loss. She cataloged them, filed them away, but she found that she could not interface with them.

They are my thoughts and my feelings. They are part of me, but not all of me. I am a separate thing.

At last, she came upon the sought-for stratum. The truth was buried deep, and she hauled it out fully into the light of recollection only after a herculean effort. She thought sadly, *I must not want to remember.*

But remember she did. At some point, she could not stop the memory from surfacing, and her breath caught in her throat as it came to her. In a long-lost world, where her father had smoked a pipe by the docks and her mother had made her a candy bowl decorated with smalt, Elizabeth Lynn had been her sister's name. Elizabeth Lynn Fisher.

Ruby opened the book at once and started reading.

There was no publishing information and no note about the author. The pages were thick as hide. The book was in hand-printed Melidoran, and Ruby struggled to read the first sentence for more than an hour. Frustrated, she put the book down and took another one off the shelf: *The Secret of Dimwood*. This one was just like the other; she could barely get beyond the first line. She thought of the Periwinkle family crest with its motto.

Constant, fearless, righteous and right.

"Once," she strained, halting after every word, "there was a blind king of the sea."

The symbols sat deep in the skin, pressed like tattoos, shimmering dully with ink that seemed alive. As Ruby watched, the black pools opened, and they were bright at their bottoms with pearls of meaning. The truth came billowing up, stirred from the depths by Ruby's searching hand. Melidoran opened before her at last, and the Tidestone blazed with the revelation.

The apple dried out on the table beside her. She turned the pages faster and faster, her fingers moving beneath each set of symbols. The sea king's son went to search for the magic mirror. He had to complete nine tasks, each more dangerous than the other. He surmounted every obstacle, thwarting gods and devils alike, and proved himself a hero. But when he delivered the mirror, his father saw nothing in it.

"'I'm beautiful,' cried the king." Ruby barely noticed the grumbling of her stomach. She squinted, nose nearly touching the page, and read in a triumphant voice. "'I'm beautiful! I knew it!'"

She had finished the introduction, and now she was hunched like a crone. She was sore from slouching over her knees, but it was the kind of soreness she felt proud of. She dropped the book on the floor and lay back on a nearby cot. The story stayed in her mind like a dream, obscured and distorted by strange mists. Her sister's words played across her lips. How much of Elizabeth was in this book? Was there a little bit of her in each one? If she read every book on this bookshelf, would she be able to rebuild Elizabeth – to piece her together out of memories left pressed in ink? Perhaps the result would be something like a homunculus: assembled piecemeal from scavenged parts, dark and imperfect. Something like a Nixie.

Suddenly tired, Ruby rose and went to put her ear to the vent. She listened to the sounds of the ocean. In the crystal on the table, the faeries pressed against the glass, excited by the dangling Tidestone. Her shadow grew long on the wall. She couldn't tell what time it was from the sounds outside. She had just made up her mind to take *The Legend of Dallie Bratcher* into the kitchen when she heard a commotion begin above.

Ruby took her sword from where it lay on the cot and hurried to the secret entrance. Above her, heavy footsteps rushed across the house. She heard things crashing to the floor, doors banging against walls as they were thrown open, and then a pained creaking as someone descended the stairs. At last, she heard a voice warbling down into the basement, and she gripped Blackheart's hilt high beneath the silver guard.

"Gather up the pots and the old tin cans
The mash, the corn, the barley and the bran
Run like the devil from the excise man
Keep the smoke from rising, Ruby."

She smiled, but it was not Arturus singing, and she didn't trust herself to recognize William's voice just yet. She stood with her feet apart, bracing herself with Blackheart straight out in front of her.

The hidden door clicked once, a hollow sound from deep within it. Two more clicks and the bookcase began to slide. When William's white-whiskered face appeared in the doorway, Ruby breathed a happy sigh. She was relieved that she hadn't uncoiled like a spring when she saw him.

"Those aren't exactly the words," she beamed.

"Those are the only words I remember," William said, sliding the bookcase all the way to the right. "Come, Empress. Our time here is through. We are moving on to greener pastures."

He took her by the hand, but she pulled free.

"Where are we going?"

"It's a sad tale," William said, looking irritated now, "and I shall have to tell it on the road away from this town. Come. 'Tis best we quit this place; to stand our guard would be unwise."

Ruby took *The Legend of Dallie Bratcher* and *The Secret of Dimwood*. It pained her to leave all the others, but the books were so thick that there would only be room in her pack for two of them along with her necessary provisions – if William had kept her pack, that was. Books in hand and sheathed Blackheart pressed into the crook of her arm, Ruby ran up the stairs to find William pulling on a green hood and Arturus wrapping a bedroll.

"They've found us out," Arturus said, woefully, "but we have the jump on them. I've got your pack. Are you taking those books? Give them here and I'll stuff them in. Then we're off."

"To Owl's Head?" Ruby asked.

William looked at her. His amber eyes widened and then narrowed to slits. She couldn't tell if he was expressing surprise or disgust.

"Owl's Head?" he repeated, that cold, feline neutrality returning to his face. "That would be the fire, milady. I plan on leaving this frying pan for a far cooler situation."

"We'll discuss it on the way," Arturus said, interrupting Ruby before she could begin to argue.

Ruby had just enough time to hang the sword at her hip and pull on a new pair of boots William had obtained for her. She was sad to learn that her lovely moccasins were long gone. She hopped out the door on one foot, trying to close the last snap on her left boot as William and Arturus rushed toward the stable.

It was dark out, and there was a chill in the air that left Ruby's throat burning. William mounted a horse that stood waiting on the lawn. Arturus led his steed from the stall: a bird with a large, colorful bill and a fleshy comb to match the purple wattle swinging from its throat. Its upper tail coverts stood tall, fanned out behind it like a hand, and shimmered from green to smalt-blue in the moonlight. He saddled it quickly, fumbling with the buckles in his haste, and it let out a ringing cry that brought a neighbor to her window.

"Climb on with me," William said, offering her a paw. His horse was char black with a white mane and tail. Its eyes looked angry, and it stomped the macadam impatiently. Ruby was a little afraid of it. "Time is never on our side, but this evening it is far less charitable than usual."

Ruby took William's paw and clambered up into the saddle behind him. She put her arms around him and clasped her hands against his chest, squeezing hard and shivering as the horse stomped again. It puffed steam from its huge nostrils, chest heaving powerfully. Ruby wanted to laugh at Arturus on his bird, but she couldn't find it in herself to do so just yet. At last, William cracked the reigns and spurred his horse into a furious gallop.

They pounded down stone-paved streets, past quiet homes and manicured lines of flowering shrubs that squatted in the dark like spectators. Further east, closer to the gates, they transitioned onto tar. Here, black buildings brooded windowless in squares that were dominated by military pavilions. Ruby expected to hear the clatter of riders giving chase. She imagined seeing the faces of their pursuers lined with shadow in torchlight, blocky and featureless with goggles for eyes. She was certain they would be stopped, but they reached the gate unharassed and rode out into the field with no one behind them. Rather than being a relief, this worried her.

"South," Ruby said into William's ear.

"But not to Owl's Head," he replied. "We'll camp on the Barrens. Then we can discuss riding to our deaths, Empress."

"I won't leave Michael."

William sighed.

"Every failure is a step to success," he said.

He let his horse slow to a speed it could maintain without collapsing, but the ride was still hard and fast and cold. Arturus kept up, his bird squawking and fluttering, hopping across the freezing ground with its purple comb bouncing ridiculously. Butterbush Barrens was hosting its first frost of the winter. The wide fields glistened in the moonlight like a sea of glass shards. In the south, dire-dogs were hunting. An icy breeze brought their faint howls to her like whispers of prophecy. Ruby finally stopped looking back and pushed her reddening face against William's shoulder.

They rode until Leora began her slow creep west, and then they stopped in a copse of alders. They made camp, but there was no more talk that night – of Owl's Head or of anything else; William was asleep on the bare ground before the fire was going. Ruby hurt all over. A dry ache seized her body, penetrating to her bones, and squeezed her for all her strength. She and Arturus ate a little in anxious silence and then retired as the sky was brightening and the stars were winking out.

Nine

Rescue

Ruby woke before the others. The morning was still and cold, and the alders whispered in the breeze. They swayed knowingly, tilting in concert. As Ruby lay watching them, she felt a weight in her chest like a hand cupping her heart. *Elizabeth*. The trees knew her name. She was in every leaf and every root tendril. She was in the earth and the wind just as she was in the books on the secret shelves. Her mind. Her life. Her ghost. Ruby listened, rapt, as the chickadees began to pipe in the trees. They praised the dawn, but Ruby never saw them.

Elizabeth died when I was very young. Ruby mouthed the words to herself. She heard her thoughts as if they were coming from the land around her. *And this is her world.* This glowed behind her eyes, a truth, simple and real. Ruby took hold of the Tidestone and felt it pulse in time with her heart.

William was ravenous when he awoke. He had to stop himself from devouring all their rations as they sat around the fire in the morning. In the light of day, Ruby could see that William had a scabbed cut just above his ear. His fur was matted with blood, and his eyelid was a little swollen. After a pan of bacon and some cubed tuna, he sat back against the bole of an alder and licked his paws. The last of the tree's shriveled catkins drooped above his head.

"I had an appointment with a bear last night," he said, "a Nixian commander named Dég. I'd been led to believe that he had come from Northover with four Cholai he wanted me to try to sell. I was to meet him at the harbor. Of course, I did some reconnaissance first. From the roof of the fish market, I saw that Dég was in full police regalia. Three Nixies attended him: magogs all. It was obvious that he was there to arrest me." He paused for a moment to run a finger over his wound. He winced, and his ear flattened reflexively as he traced that angry curve over his eyebrow.

"I underestimated them. It was a well-planned operation; they had shut down an entire pier. There were gogs on the adjacent roof as well as in the crow's nest of a ship docked across from me. I took some fire attempting to escape, and my descent from the roof was not as graceful as I'd hoped it would be. The fall left me bleeding, but I was lucky. This will scar, and I imagine I will look distinguished. Perhaps not so distinguished as I might have looked in a pine box," he crossed his paws over his chest and stuck out his rough, pink tongue, "but I'm willing to sacrifice appearances for my continuity."

"I hit the streets early in the morning," Arturus said, and William looked annoyed at the interruption. "I did a bit of looking, but nothing too conspicuous. A friend had taken him in. It took me forever to get a whisper. I was scared for him." Arturus gave William a pat on the back.

"I fear for *her*," William frowned. "And for the transfers we've moved in the last month. This can only mean the Gowspin network is collapsing. All our work… has it been for nothing?" William shook his head and looked down at his calfskin boots. Again, the trees were swaying. Only Arturus's bird had anything to say.

"Tee-whit," she whistled. "Tee-whit-willow!"

From far off, Ruby thought she heard an answering cry

"Hush, Junie," Arturus said, dismissively.

Finally, William said, "I don't want to think about what the coming days shall bring."

"Hopefully, most of them will get to Dimwood or Pearlwater," Arturus tried.

"Tee-willow! Tee!"

Ruby shifted uncomfortably. The Tidestone was whispering. Its voice was like wind on sand. She listened closely, closing her eyes, but the stone's voice drained away. She thought of all the paintings William had left behind. There had been one of a red-headed girl in the sun. She was a galvanic figure, a hero and a leader. *Constant, fearlesss, righteous, and right.*

"To Pearlwater," Ruby said under her breath. Her voice felt as weak as the Tidestone's. "William, Arthur and I stayed up all night working out a plan. We think we can get into the camp at Owl's Head."

William nodded knowingly. "You and *Arthur*, eh? His plans never leave any room for surprises – or failure. Majesty, we must go to Pearlwater. Once there, we will raise a force and attack Owl's Head on more even footing. I understand that Lord Underbridge is important to the movement, and that's why we can't risk ourselves for him. If we fail and he dies, the resistance will suffer. It may only stumble at first, but if it falters it could collapse. The Nixies are squeezing now. Their grip tightens, and we lose more and more every day. It's too risky."

Ruby nodded. She sat back on her heels, looking straight into William's amber eyes. There was always a judgment brooding there – a criticism. He watched the world in condemnation. It was his nature.

"Thank you, William," Ruby finally said, "your opinion is important. I understand. I want to assure you of that."

"You've already come to your conclusion," William sighed. "My participation is mandatory."

"I didn't say that," Ruby said, smartly. "I won't leave Michael to the Nixies any longer than I already have. I know that you don't agree with this idea, and I appreciate that. I don't know you, but Arthur trusts you with his life. I've seen what you've sacrificed. I won't order you around, threaten you, or force you to comply. I'll tell you what I shall do, and I'll ask for your help. Will you help us, William?"

William sighed again, but then he dipped his chin in a bow.

"I suppose I'm honored to serve. Tell me your plan."

It was a short day, and Ruby and Arturus spent most of it trying to remember what their plan had been. The Forgetting was weaker, it was true, but it still sent threads into every mind.

"Until the Empress is unseated," William was certain, "it will continue polluting us."

It had been a sketch to begin with but now it was less than that. It was a skeleton without the means to move or hold together. The finer points hung forgotten, like the remnants of flesh and muscle. All that remained was the goal: to support the rescue effort. Ruby was frustrated. Just when she was beginning to feel like a leader, her power withered like the alder catkins. She was grateful for William, who worked with them to develop a new plan based on what she and Arturus could remember despite being pessimistic about their chances.

"Owl's Head is no more than a waypoint between the Cradle and Lampblack," William explained. "There was talk of a larger fortress under construction in the Nirfang Mountains, but I have never seen any proof of such a thing. It's unnecessary; Nixieland is almost finished expanding. So the camp is small, but it will be guarded by magogs."

"Big nasties," Arturus explained, and he puffed out his cheeks and spread his arms wide, making Ruby giggle.

"'Big nasties', yes," William rolled his eyes. "The magogs will be our secondary concern. Our primary concern will be gogs."

"Little nasties," Ruby interjected, beaming mischievously, a snicker hitching in her throat.

"Snipers," William said. His tone was curt, but he was smiling. It never ceased to amaze Ruby the way cats could display two contradictory emotions at once and be genuinely honest about both of them. "The Nixies with the carbines. The guns. I can't remember whether or not any are stationed at Owl's Head, but it's a good bet that they are.

"Even if we lose the bet," Arturus said, "we win."

William nodded. "We'll have to approach from the east, which will leave us at quite a disadvantage. The camp is mostly on the west side of the mountain. But there will be good cover in the woods."

"Bill can handle the gogs," Arturus said. "He has a *way* with his arrows. It's like nothing I've ever seen. The big ones will be for me, at least until you can sneak in." He addressed Ruby, who nodded. It seemed simple enough.

"Man yet mistakes his way," William said. "We have the misfortune of being thoughtful, while meaner things, led by instinct, go astray so rarely. In all likelihood, this plan will collapse. We must not be surprised, and we must not lose our wits. Empress, you have a sword. Have you ever used it?"

Ruby shrank a bit.

"No," she admitted, and Arturus patted her on the hip.

"It's easy, Majesty," he said. "Hold it up and block, and swing when you can." He drew his beautiful, pearl-handled blade and mimed a duel. His exaggerated expressions, the little grunts he made as he rolled about, and the size of the sword in the three-foot Sir Periwinkle's paw left Ruby clutching her stomach laughing.

"Let's hope it'll be that easy," William mewed. "The Halcyon delivered us from our pursuers in Gowspin. We should pray he will not abandon us now. Owl's Head is two days' ride from here, Empress. I suggest we away at dawn."

Dallie Bratcher was born at the bottom of Southunder's Patamore district. He grew up poor and wild in scrapyards and quarries, a child of the dirt and the slag with few friends and nowhere to go but up. That was the story they told anyway, because they needed a meteoric rise. He was brilliant and misunderstood; he stood out, but he was passed over. Lost in the crowd, he resolved to become a shadow. Because he felt meaningless, he would be meaningless, and the people who pushed him away would regret their callousness and superficiality when he vanished forever. If it ever occurred to him that no one cries when shadows fade, he never admitted it. Gnomes came to Southunder, and Dallie saw the factories and foundries he loved destroyed or seized. He went alone to Nidavir to kill the gnome king, and he was a hero when he returned. They say he rode the winds of a storm, called lightning from the ground, and held fire in his hands. He pulled a thorn from the paw of a dire-dog and earned its eternal gratitude, and it came without complaint when he summoned it to desolate the castle of Sinigroth.

A person may be a hero, but a hero is not a person. Dallie was reduced to an ideal, to a story; the man disappeared beneath the myth.

Old age found him bitter and wilting in Dimwood's holes, caged behind linden roots on the banks of the Charl. He had no loves to mourn, and he had no fame anymore when he met Luna. She was on her own journey, and it may have been that he saw something of himself in her. Dallie whispered advice to her as she passed out of his chapter in *The Secret of Dimwood*, and what he said is unrecorded. But Ruby thought she knew what Dallie told Luna. The words were as clear in her mind as the rest of the words on the page, now that she was reading Melidoran at a brisk pace:

No one can tell you who you are.

Dallie's appearance in *The Secret of Dimwood* was Ruby's favorite part of that story. She felt that it put *The Legend of Dallie Bratcher* into perspective. Lying propped against a quaking alder with the Tidestone shining at her breast, Ruby read one book after the other in a strange euphoria. Elizabeth's words rose like peaks from the mist; they were hidden in another tongue, but Ruby drew them out. She closed her book in the early morning dark, and then she listened to the wind in the trees until the sun came up. It no longer seemed that Elizabeth was speaking to her from the other world. Now, Ruby felt that the words were an extension of herself. She spread out over Butterbush Barrens and then south to Lampblack. She was blowing east with the breeze, stretching across the Cradle and the Golrace and the Auburn Mountains. Her heart swelled with the feeling of being part of everything, her blood cooled into moonlight, her skin softened into tide-washed sand, and she was left astonished by the grandeur of her smallness. She remembered her first morning on the Fields of Silver, when she had watched Michael with Ketha and had felt her energy standing apart from her. She was Elizabeth's shadow, and Elizabeth was the shadow of Dallie Bratcher. Ruby saw herself in Luna, too. This reminded her that there was much more to be discovered. How had she come here? As for who she was, she had decided that no one could tell her that.

William, Arturus, and Ruby set out across the meadows when the sun was but a burning crown upon the Auburn Mountains. They rode over pathless fields of scrub dotted with tanoak copses. The axe-head peaks of Nirfang leaned into the south, black as char below the snowline. Clouds piled high above the Veldt of Skies, gold-edged with wet violet blooming in their hearts, and pierced by the aureate lances of dawn. Beyond, the smoke of Lampblack was just beginning to rise;

Ruby thought that little blue-white coil looked like a dragon's tail. She thought of Ketha, who'd had business there so long ago, and she wished she hadn't lost his moccasins. William rode his steed hard across the flatland, trailing an aubergine sail. Ruby's gown wasn't the most practical attire for adventuring, but it flowed over her skin like a spring breeze. Its caress was intimate, almost knowing. Ruby wondered where William had found it. Was the girl this had belonged to still alive?

She thought of Michael. She thought of the wolf cub and his hurt sobbing. She had not seen his parents on her charabanc. Owl's Head Peak was hot; fire burned within it, smoke sometimes rose from its top, and no snow would last upon it. Ruby stared at it and thought of Gowspin burning, Dimwood razed, blood in the tidewaters of the Pearlshores. Then she turned her gaze east toward Duskwood and the Cradle. The Cradle Spire was a black wedge emerging from a sea of murky green. Luna had ascended it in search of the Halcyon's ring, but she had found nothing on that rocky top. If, as it was rumored, the Halcyon had departed Melidora from the peak of that spire, she had left nothing behind but the ever-fading light and the pall of sorrow that poisoned Duskwood.

At noon, they came to a creek in a little pine wood. They filled their canteens and ate hard bread smeared with some tasteless paste, and then they went over their plan again. There was a new light in William's eyes and a surprising enthusiasm in his voice when he spoke of the attack on Owl's Head. Arturus picked up on this, and it came out of him amplified. He showed Ruby a few basic parries with her sword, and she had to stop him when he became so forceful in his feigned advances that he frightened her. He was positively bloodthirsty now, and William let him roar and rage without interjecting. She could not imagine what they had lost in Gowspin. They were grieving in anger now, and she shrank from them.

"I hope you can pour all this out at Owl's Head tonight," she said to them, arms crossed on the bank of the stream.

"No catharsis will ever be sufficient, Empress," William said. It was almost a boast.

"We'll have to wait on that," Arturus laughed. "I can't say for sure until I've tried."

It took a good amount of time to get Arturus's bird over the creek. Junie balked, complaining, and she was strong enough to resist all three of them when they resorted to tugging on her reins. It was only after Arturus had fallen into the creek that Junie decided the water would not sweep her away. She stepped over Arturus as he sat fuming in the mud, and William laughed. Ruby thought it was a manic, desperate sound.

As they were leaving, Ruby almost brought up the books she had found in the secret apartment. She had been considering it for a long time, but the idea felt unfinished. It still seemed private, and now Ruby was worried that reminding William and Arturus of the home they had lost would be a bad idea. The issue remained private, then, and she mulled it over with her chin on William's shoulder.

The day was long and comfortably warm, but the temperature dropped suddenly in the evening. Time stretched out huge behind them. Ruby looked back on the way they had come, and the Barrens seemed to go on forever. She couldn't see anything she recognized. On the other hand, the road before them contracted. She drifted into a light sleep with her arms around William's waist, and she started awake with Owl's Head Peak dominating the distance. In a moonlit grove that sloped over the Nirfang foothills, they tied their steeds to the remains of an iron fence.

"There was a gnome city here," Arturus whispered. "It was called Nidavir. It was here for a hundred years or so, and then it was empty. The forest grew over it, but you can still find walls standing up here and there. Doorframes and staircases and such – all short, you know. For the gnomes." They squatted in the bush while William looked through a spyglass. "But the rumor is that Nidavir was built on top of another city, and that Alamandrians used to live here."

"Nidavir was in the Auburn Mountains," Ruby whispered. "I read about it in my book."

"The city here was called Cutting Deep," William hissed, "and it was built around a gnomish cobalt mine, so watch your step! Any sinkhole could drop you five-hundred feet into the ground." He lowered his spyglass and looked over his shoulder at Arturus. "And *every* legend says the Alamandrians had a secret city somewhere. Now please keep your voice down!"

Ruby patted Sir Periwinkle on the back, and he smiled. Paws on his hips, he turned up his nose and wiggled his head. Then he reached out to pull on William's tail, which was puffed up like a bottle brush. William looked back, eyes blazing, and coiled his tail up underneath him. Ruby put her hand over her mouth to stifle a giggle.

"Always so serious," Arturus whispered.

They were a little less than a mile from the Owl's Head camp. William complained that he couldn't see much through the trees, but said that what he had managed to see was promising.

"I think there are only two magogs at the gate," he said. "Big Nasties. I didn't see any gun barrels in the hills ahead of us. It's a good bet that they're in the woods to the east, looking at the camp from the front."

Arturus drew his blade. It hissed into song as it left its sheath, and the blade glittered in the moonlight. It was only the size of a long dagger, but it looked fierce in his paw – as if his anger was radiating through the hilt.

"We don't have a plan to get out, do we?" he asked.

"No," was William's matter-of-fact answer. He then added, "We might be able to steal a wagon."

"I'll have to leave Junie." Arturus was crestfallen. "She's been a good bird. I hate to set her free in dog country."

"Let's not get ahead of ourselves," William replied. Now he looked at Arturus with compassion. Ruby was glad to see his eyes soften. "We don't know how this is going to play out."

They crept forward, crouching, freezing at every rustle in the forest. Ruby's heart raced, pumping acid into her extremities. She looked up at the rocking canopy. Cedars interspersed with cottonwood and cockspur thorn dominated the forest. Sequoias towered far to the south, their tapering tops forming a line to mark the northernmost bounds of Lampblack. The wind breathed through the trees like a warning. They were blind, but their arms were long, and they spoke of everything their fingers touched in their ancient murmuring language. A bird began to shriek nearby, sending a shock of cold up Ruby's spine to the base of her neck, where her hair stood on end. Her arms broke out in gooseflesh. She scanned the trees and was able to pick out the black-eyed mask of an owl's face glowering down at her from the high branches of a beech. As she watched, it spread snow-white wings and glided silently toward the deeper reaches of the woods, disappearing into the dark.

Agents of the trees, Ruby thought. *Spies.*

The approach to the camp seemed interminable. The morning's euphoria dissolved. When they finally lay on their bellies on the shoulders of a beaten-down hill, Ruby felt as if the full weight of the night was on top of her. She was the dirt, and the trees were digging into her, crushing her lungs so that her breaths were ragged and shallow. The mountains themselves were collapsing onto her back. Arturus complained of pains in his knees and his neck, but William seemed unfazed. He was lean and strong and flexible. Ruby found it strange that she envied his youth and vigor; he must have been older than she was. He produced his spyglass and sprawled motionless for a long time, looking through it.

"There they are," he said. "I see the copper barrels." He pointed over the hill toward the woods beyond the camp. "Let me get set up."

The Nixie camp was pressed up against the lee side of Owl's Head Peak. A broad dirt yard flanked by small bonfires ran up to a knot of black buildings that reminded Ruby of the windowless structures in Gowspin. Nixie buildings. Ruby saw several clockwork behemoths milling about, patrolling in small circles. William had been wrong; there were four of them. Two Nixies stood guard beside the row of pens to the south. These were set back into the rock face, and Ruby couldn't see into them from where she was. She remembered walking the dirt yard, but she didn't remember Michael being there. She had been so far away then, so removed from the horror; she thought it was a wonder that she could remember anything at all about that camp.

"They don't have many weak spots," William said, "but there is a place just at the base of the neck. It's a control cluster of some kind. An actuator. If I can hit them just right, I think it will scramble them. I don't know how long it will take them to recover." He was up on one knee now, his yew bow in his paw. He let his arrow hang for a moment before nocking it. "Just give me a moment."

The owl shrieked again. This time, the call set another owl screaming as if to wake the dead.

"Don't miss," Ruby said.

Arturus put his paw on her arm and said, "He never does."

"You exaggerate," William purred.

Now, William drew his bow. The arrow was very long, deep brown, and fletched with blood-red feathers. The point sparkled gem-blue. He put his head low and narrowed his eyes, his ears flattening back, his whiskers fanning out. Until now, Ruby hadn't realized how many whiskers William had. Stiff and white, they sprouted in great profusion from around his nose, from his round cheeks, and even from his forehead.

"Fly straight," he whispered, his lips inches from the shaft. "And kill."

The bowstring snapped with a thrumming twang. The arrow disappeared into the distance, and William remained motionless. Seconds later, there was a loud report, a clear and ringing clang to which the owls replied with a chorus of shrill screeches. Arturus winced. It was a lot of commotion. Ruby thought she saw the shadowy mass of woods beyond the trees shudder where the gog fell, but she couldn't be sure.

"Louder than I'd hoped," William muttered, and he drew another arrow from his fantastically embroidered quiver. "Let's see what the magogs do."

They waited in taut and freezing silence. The magogs in the dirt yard continued their aimless shuffling. They were featureless hulks in the dark; it was only when they were near the fires or after the hissing issue of steam from their thick bodies that Ruby could be certain where they were. She had moved down the hill a bit, and she could no longer see the Nixies by the pens.

"There he goes," Arturus said. "Wait it out."

One of the Nixies had finally decided to amble toward the source of the sound. Ruby's shoulders ached. She slowed her breathing in an effort to relax, but this made her chest feel heavy. She had tucked the Tidestone into the front of her gown, and now she felt it digging into her skin. She shifted in the leaf litter, glad that the stone wasn't glowing for once. Maybe it knew the stakes. It whispered to her, as always, and she thought it was telling her to slow down, slow down – to breathe and wait and let herself go slack. That was easier said than done. The pain in her shoulders expanded to her back, just below the base of her neck. It grew sharp and terrible, like a knife carving into her.

"What's happening?" she whispered.

"It's turned around," William, replied. His voice was so low she can hardly hear him. "I'm going to take another shot. There's one to the south. It's a good distance, but I think I can make it."

"Not yet," Arturus said through clenched teeth. "It's too soon. Let them wander a bit, or they'll get suspicious."

"It doesn't look like they care one way or the other," William replied, nocking his second arrow. "I think they're too stupid to figure it out." His head dropped. This time, he kissed the shaft of the arrow.

"Fly straight," he crooned. "Fly far. And kill."

The bowstring snapped. The arrow vanished as if into thin air. Ruby hauled herself up on her elbows and looked over the hill, but the woods beyond the Nixies' fires were just a wall of shadow. There was a muffled noise in the distance, and William smiled, showing star-white canines.

He turned and looked at Ruby. His mouth moved, and Ruby thought he was about to say *I never miss*, but then he was rising from the hillside with his eyes as wide as saucers. William was being hefted off the ground by the scruff of his neck. Before Ruby had time to do anything more than gape, her gown went tight around her throat. She kicked the air uselessly as she was lifted, and a huge hand that smelled of oil clamped over her mouth. Arturus leaped to his feet, his sword ready, and he had some luck in fending off the Nixies as they tried to surround him. He beat them back for a second, but they regrouped and overwhelmed him, knocking the glittering sword from his paw. A magog wrapped its colossal arms around the guinea pig, and Arturus screamed and bit.

"Unhand me! No! Lumbering curs!" He shouted and beat at the Nixie. Small as he was, he was usually loud enough to puff himself up. In the Nixie's arms he was like a pet, tiny and defenseless.

"Unauthorized," ground a straining voice. "Illegal access to private premises."

Then the Nixies turned in unison as a great baying started up in the east. It was an old and empty sound, and it rolled over the Barrens like a flame. The fires went out at the camp below the hill, and the canopy was suddenly filled with fleeing birds. They rushed to the air with a roaring of wings, their voices raised in a cacophony of fear. Ruby felt the howl in every muscle. It crawled from her pores and swelled behind her eyes. It was like a burning hand in her body, intruding, seizing her spine, and she felt the deep force moving over her mind. The Tidestone sparked awake, now glowing nearly as bright as the moon. She screamed, and the Nixie that was holding her staggered.

Her soul shield blazed to life, trapping the Nixie's hands and arms as Ruby writhed to free herself. The Nixie pulled backward, stupid and oblivious. It could neither break the shield nor move it. Its arms separated, hyperextending, and then they pulled free from its torso and it fell over on its back. Ruby dropped into the leaf litter gracelessly, and crouched between the two masses of metal she had rendered useless.

The Nixie that had picked up William was still holding him by the scruff of his neck. It turned toward the howl, tilting its head quizzically. It clicked and buzzed from somewhere within its thick torso, but William put a quick end to that. It had been a mistake on the machine's part to leave his limbs free. He drew his knife from his hip and drove it hard into the control cluster at the base of the Nixie's wire-wrapped neck. For a brief moment, a dazzling cataract of blue-white sparks lighted the woods, and then the Nixie went as stiff as a pillar. It crashed to the ground in a dumb heap, and then William was on his feet. The baying became a low, haunted whistle. It was drawing nearer to them, and now it was accompanied by a violent ruckus in the brush and a blast of searing air – like a whirlwind of flame raging from the east.

William dashed for his yew bow. Ruby turned, blind with emotion, and saw Arturus still struggling in the grip of the remaining Nixie. The thing was standing and clicking, struck by the clamor at the bottom of the hill. Arturus beat on its arms and kicked against its chest. He screamed his little wheezing scream and leaned back, bracing his paws on the Nixie's wrist. Pushing with his feet high near the joint of its shoulder to its arm, Arturus let his strength explode from him. The Nixie's arm began to creak and break. Thick, black ichor seeped out of it – oily blood that stank terribly as it smoked on the ground. Arturus was pressed to his limit, groaning from exertion; he was incredibly strong, but it was not enough. Ruby stood sweating and grinding her teeth. She held out her open hand, cords standing out on her neck, and the wind tossed her gown back to spread it behind her like red-violet wings. With a barn-owl shriek, she pushed the deep force upward and knocked the Nixie off its feet. Its arm tore in half, and Arturus squeaked in pain as he hit the ground.

A whisper emerged from beneath the howling and the crashing tumult in the forest.

"Fly straight, my sweet."

The Nixie was clacking in something like panic. With its companions out of commission, and massive structural damage severely impeding its efforts to regain its vertical base, its stupidity burned away. With an angry hiss of steam, it heaved its uneven bulk from the forest floor.

"Assault," it quacked. "Response!"

The bow string snapped. William's blue-tipped arrow struck the Nixie in the neck as it teetered. There was another brilliant shower of sparks, and then a pop came from within the machine. It tumbled backward smoking, as lifeless as it had been before its activation – a pile of parts excavated from gnomish ruins at the roots of mountains.

Ruby was drooping like a half-cut sapling. The enervating rush of her emotional outburst had left her all but useless. Her legs felt like lead. Her arms hung from shoulders that blazed with pain. But there was no time to rest; William and Arturus collected themselves and hurried over the hill toward the terrible howls, and Ruby forced herself to follow. She didn't have the energy for fear anymore. Her feelings were locked in torpor, inaccessible. She trudged up the hill and practically fell down the embankment toward the darkened camp. As she regained her balance, she saw the forest explode, and from the blast of splintered wood and charring leaves there came a pack of dire-dogs running as if the whips of Hell were behind them. They barked and whined, tails between their legs, their yellow eyes wide as they turned south and bolted for the walls of Nirfang. For a moment, the forest seemed to swell with darkness and heat, and then a slavering horror emerged onto the field, its head held low and its mouth filled with glittering scythes, and let loose a howl to shake the foundations of the earth.

At first, the sound was all there was. It crashed against the mountains like a sea; it shook the sequoias like a mighty wind. Leora dimmed, and moon shadows grew long as the enormous dire-dog approached. William and Arturus were left frozen, dwarfed in fear before it.

"The Lord of the Dogs," Arturus whispered, awed.

William's voice was a gasping croak. "Vanreah."

The enormous dire-dog stood at the edge of the forest just within the circle of light spilling from Ruby's Tidestone. The Nixies began to crowd about it; they were nine feet high hunched, but it dwarfed them even at the shoulder. A shock of fire-gold fur poured from the crown of its head to bristle thick across its back, which bunched into an arch above its massive forelegs. It crept forward, tensed to pounce, its paws spreading huge with black claws like daggers. Red eyes burned in its skull, shining in the dark like perfect rubies.

And then it was in motion, lashing out at the Nixies with terrifying power. They struck at it and it battered them to pieces. They ran from the woods, the muzzles of their carbines flashing, and it gnashed them apart in the hell of its mouth. When the field was strewn with smoking, sparking wreckage, Vanreah turned its wrath on the camp itself. It tore through the dirt yard, ripping up fence posts and scattering kindling and ashes. When it fell upon the pens and began crushing the iron bars in its teeth, William and Arturus finally found the will to move again. Vanreah tossed prisoners aside, mangled and screaming or dead and gutted, as it rooted under the rock.

"Here!" William shouted as he ran towards the beast with his bow drawn. "Dog!"

He put an arrow deep into Vanreah's right flank and was rewarded with a high cry and nothing more. Arturus took a single throwing axe from his hip and hurled it, but he failed to hit the dire-dog at all.

Constant, fearless, righteous and right.

Arturus ran headlong toward the massive Vanreah, two paws grasping the hilt of his sword, and all weakness left Ruby. It seeped from her heat in a single, sick pulse and seemed to drain through her feet. She stepped forward, determined, her face hard as stone. Her hair whipped about her cheeks and neck. In the Tidestone's light, her features were cast in shadow. Blackheart slipped from its sheath before she was even aware of what she was doing, and it sang ruefully as she lifted its tip toward the beast.

"Vanreah," she said. Her voice scraped from her throat, deep and terrible.

The dog turned with a moonrat hanging from its mouth.

"Stop," said that deep voice. Ruby could scarcely believe it was her own.

This is her world, she thought, and it was the only thing that kept her back from the brink of collapse. She held out her hand. William stood back, clutching Arturus by the arm. Vanreah seemed to consider Ruby. It spat out blood and flesh; the body it had been chewing fell in pieces. There was a silence that might have gone on for an age, and it was even worse than the Doglord's howling had been. It was terrifying in its spaciousness, pregnant with malice and charged so that the very air seemed to spark with it. And then Ruby took another step forward, and Vanreah leapt upon her.

For a long moment, Ruby wondered whether or not she might fall backward forever. She imagined falling through the ground as if through water, the woods and the mountains disappearing above her in a splash of dark colors, and then dropping into an abyss of air never to come to rest. Perhaps that was all the other world was. Or perhaps she would shatter, and her mirrored fragments would be scattered to the four winds. Did the north wind blow toward the north or out of the north? She would finally get to see.

She closed her eyes as Vanreah crushed her into the grass. It leered over her, pushing its muzzle into her cheek. Its mouth was too wide, its teeth crowded together on multiple rows. She sucked its searing, rancid breath and her stomach contents swirled into her throat. A hard swallow left the back of her tongue burning. A growl pulsed from deep within the dog's huge chest as it dug into the ground with its rear paws. Ruby beat the heel of her left hand against Vanreah's muzzle and lower jaw, trying to shove the heavy head back, but the dog's strength was boundless. She saw its whole body quivering just before it lunged downward to snap at her neck. Wrenching her torso up and twisting away from the bite sent pain ripping through her body, and she cried out. Her deep force had abandoned her. She had poured herself out, and now she was left with only her body's meager strength. She balled her fist and bashed at the dog's crimson eye. It snapped again, and this time its jaws closed on her hand.

At first, her hand went numb. She tugged hard in an attempt to free it, sobbing now, gritting her teeth and yanking with no thought of the consequences. It could shred her hand apart, remove it completely, or she might pull it away flayed; when the pain gripped her, none of those fears mattered. There was only the pressure and the heat and the bursts of lightning shooting down her arm. Vanreah would not let go. It tried to twist its head, to lift itself up on its forelegs, but it couldn't. It was caught on something; and now it let out a whine as it was wracked by another spasm. With each paroxysm, Vanreah's tremendous strength was ebbing away. It still held Ruby's left hand in its mouth, pierced by crystalline fangs, but Ruby's right hand was closed fast around Blackheart. The sword was in the beast's chest, lodged between its ribs.

Vanreah shook again and tried to howl in pain as the blade finished cutting through its heart. It could only produce coughs and a piteous whimper. Ruby was warm with blood. The dog was dying on top of her, its fearsome eyes searching her own. The dog would find no fear there. With great effort, Ruby twisted the hilt of the sword in her hand. The tang broke with a dull pop, the blade came away from the hilt, and Vanreah breathed its last breath of hot and horrible stink into Ruby's face before it collapsed.

Now, Arturus and William were pushing at the dire-dog, stabbing it, kicking it, and slashing at its sinewy neck. How long they had been there trying to help her, she did not know. They called to Ruby, and their voices were like the whispering of the Tidestone; they drained away into a windy oblivion. That abyss was opening beneath her at last. She closed her eyes, drenched in sweat and rank with blood and spittle. The pain in her hand was going away. The huge weight upon her, the hairy mass of dead muscle, useless teeth, and blind garnet eyes was like the sweet breath of spring sighing into her hair. William rammed with his shoulder, Arturus put his back against the beast and heaved with all his improbable might, and Vanreah's horrid carcass finally rolled aside.

"Empress!" Arturus was heartbroken. "Oh, Majesty!"

He blubbered, dropping to his knees to touch her as if she were the broken shards of a priceless mirror.

"It would have flattened a horse!" William was trying to find the best way to help Ruby up. He looked lean and wild in the gem-light – like some dangerous jungle thing. "Can you move? The prisoners!"

Ruby rolled over onto her right side. She felt used-up and wasted. She was sure that her spine was twisted and that her legs had been crushed to powder inside, but she was able to get to her knees. She put her bleeding left hand on the dead dog's face and brushed its gimlet eyes closed under her palm. Then, with William and Arturus helping her, she was able to stand.

"Rest now," she whispered, standing askew with her left arm sagging and her legs uncertain about bearing her weight. "Be at peace, Vanreah, Lord of the Dogs."

There was howling in Lampblack. William and Arturus all but begged Ruby to sit and rest, but she refused. The brittle feeling in her bones was an affirmation. She walked the dirt yard in the pain trance she had learned in the Cholai's sleeping wagon, seeing all both vividly and darkly. The dead lay on the field in tatters. Vanreah's blind fury had left none injured. In the mouth of the rock, huddled in the ruins of the pens, Ruby was elated to find living souls. She called them, and some flocked to her. Some stayed cowering, and William had to coax them out. The wolf cub was terrified but unharmed, as were a dozen or so Cholai and a handful of warriors from Pearlwater. There was a badger poet from Dimwater; Ruby remembered her from the scar across her eye. The wolf cub clung to her, and she guarded him like a mother. Even while she petted him and assured him that the Empress had come to rescue them, he wouldn't stop crying.

Michael of Underbridge was in the last pen, balled up in a wet little pocket in the rock wall. He was scarred, his right eye closed by a bruise, and his left ear torn. He limped to greet Ruby, and she fell to sobbing when he embraced her. He was weak and hurt, and it had been her fault.

"Blame is an indulgence," he said, with a deep cough. "I knew you would come, Empress. I never doubted. Never."

She pressed her battered face into his chest. Her cheeks were red-black with grime. She felt as if she might blow away.

"The dogs are coming," Arturus urged. "It's best we hurry on."

"There's a ferry in Dimwood," croaked a green-eyed otter.

"Is there a wagon?" William asked. "A carriage, even?"

But Vanreah had smashed every stick of timber in the camp. If there had been a wagon, it was now indistinguishable from the rest of the debris.

"I'll give up my horse," William said. "And we have a rilla bird, too."

"Junie can carry a little one," Arturus added. "I'll gladly walk to help support any who need it."

"If you're strong enough to lend a paw, help out," Ruby said. At least she had found her Empress voice again. "We'll make camp in Dimwood if we can. It's going to be a long walk."

Ten

Robinegg

A low plain dropped south to separate the talus slopes of Nirfang's foothills from the shadowed forest of Duskwood. It tapered to sandy benchlands near the shore, but it opened wide on pine moors at its north end, unfurling toward Butterbush Barrens. This was called Wolf's Way, and Ruby set out across the plain along with the Owl's Head refugees as the morning darkness was purpling in the east.

They walked in the light of the Tidestone, bedraggled and sore, supporting each other. Some were recovering quickly; they had only been in the pens for a few days. But most were sick and injured, their skin like paper, their eyes sunken and downcast as they struggled to hold up their heads. Ruby thought they were like walking saplings. The refugees talked quietly amongst each other. Most were grateful to be free, but some walked in a waking nightmare, and could only babble about the coming of the great dog and the visage of death that persisted before them even when they closed their eyes.

The rose-pink jewel's glow washed through Ruby, trying to heal her, but its voice in her head was the shriek of the owl saying, "Not safe yet. Not safe yet."

Michael was one of the weakest. He leaned on Ruby, and they lagged behind the others across the Way. The tracks of Nixie wagons carved across the corridor, deep in places where the ground was red clay, and filled with blood-dark rainwater. Ruby put her foot in one such furrow and caught herself in a fall as she felt her ankle turning. After that, Michael helped her watch for wagon ruts; it was almost as if he was the one supporting her.

Arturus walked with the wolf cub who was riding Junie the rilla bird. The badger poet fawned over him, and he held her hand instead of the reigns. Forced to plod, Junie fretted, and Arturus calmed her down by singing. His voice was low and very clear. His song was the anthem of the knights of Eggplant, which told quite a grim story of war and loss. The wolf cub enjoyed it though, and the badger poet seemed to know quite a lot about its author. She talked to Arturus about him at length in admiring, if hushed, tones.

William led his great black steed with a mother fox in the saddle, her broad-eared kit bouncing in front of her against the saddle horn. Despite being dangerously gaunt and having one arm in a sling, the kit was bubbling with energy. He pointed at everything, and his mother named things for him patiently.

"A butterfly, Peter. Yes. It's blue! Look how pretty. It's late for them, isn't it?"

Peter giggled and pointed.

"Those are two halves of a chestnut bur. You don't want to step on that with your bare feet!"

"Ouch." Peter grinned.

"That's right."

Peter laughed, and others laughed with him. He began to draw a crowd of the most frightened survivors, his light the brightest in the dark and his impeccant warmth their only comfort in the chill of fear.

As the sun rose, the little group's mood tipped toward hopeful. There was not much food to go around, but Ruby, William, and Arturus shared until they had next to nothing left for themselves. Word of

Ruby's ordeal started to circulate, and when the group began to ask her about it, Ruby found herself reluctant to tell the story. If anyone recognized her as their Empress, no one said as much, and for this she was grateful. She felt frail and scared and ineffective. The dog hadn't been quite the size of a house, no. And it hadn't breathed fire. It had fallen on her blade, and that was all. She was no more a hero than the rock that breaks a Nixie wagon's wheel. Despite all her deflections and her attempts to minimize her achievement, the rumor grew legs, as all rumors do. She shuddered to think what it would become once they reached Pearlwater.

"Vanreah," Michael said as they dropped back to the rear of the procession. "You can see that everyone has heard the stories. Quite a few of us here were told by our mothers that he would come to eat us if we didn't go to sleep. I always thought the Lord of the Dogs was a myth."

Ruby looked up at him and smiled sadly.

"He will be now," she said.

The day crept along, the sun hanging lazily above them. As they day was dimming, they came at last to Duskwood's eastern edge, where Wolf's Way dwindled, denuded of much of its verdure. Two statues guarded the head of the path that would lead them to the Charl; one in the shape of a woman's face and the other too worn to resemble anything. Here, the group stopped to rest just inside the forest. Ruby sat with Michael near the statues, their backs against cherry trunks, and she listened as the worn statue thrummed. It was shaded beneath the boughs of a big cypress. When the wintry wind would toss the branches, the statue was left in open sunlight. Then the stone would sing, scattering strange, high notes that seemed to drop in time with the wind.

"I'm sorry, Michael," Ruby said while the statue wept its rolling song. "I came back as soon as I could. The Valley of Silk was my idea, and it was a trap. I should have seen."

Michael said nothing for a long time. He stared out across Wolf's Way and absently rubbed the bruise over his eye. A murmuration of Duskwood starlings lifted light as air from the grass where they were feeding, startled by something Ruby couldn't see.

"You've grown so much," Michael said at last. "Your hair. Your face. I thought you were getting more beautiful every day. Now it's been many days, and you're gorgeous. Regal – as you should be. As I remember you."

Ruby took a few strands of her hair between her fingers and looked at them. They were wren-brown now. There was even some white showing through. Her fingers were longer; her soft white hands were tanned and creased.

"What did I say about blame?" Michael continued. "I don't blame you. This is the road we are on, and I will walk it wherever it leads. There's no use for blame among friends, Empress. I firmly believe that's what love is: the end of the War of Blame. And don't blame yourself, either."

"We could have died," Ruby said.

"We could die now." Michael was beaming out across the field. "You bring a light, Majesty. Don't you know that? Don't apologize for the shadows. I didn't tell the Nixies anything they wanted to hear. I stayed alive and waited for you, and you didn't abandon me, Empress. I trusted you, and you came for us. That's the way you are. It's the way you were made. If you find fault in yourself, find good, too."

"You see the good in everything," Ruby replied, and she put her hand on Michael's paw.

"That," Michael smiled, "is the way *I* was made."

The Gray River flowed from a lake high in the Mountains of Halcya and cut across sandy fields to enter Moonwood. There, it filled perfect chalk basins that dropped together in terraced clusters. These were the Moon Pools, and it was believed that the body of Martan Thorn Bratcher was preserved beneath them. As the Gray left Moonwood, it met the river Thorn, whose bad, black waters also bled up into Cutcheon Mud. Between the two was the haunted Thornwash, where stump trolls bred and warred for a thousand years. Finally, the Gray fell deep beneath the Cradle Spire to rise in the lowlands, and there it was called the Charl. In Dimwood, it split to form the wild Dimwale, and it emptied at last into the sea over Dreaming Cape.

In the early days, when much of Melidora still lay in darkness, the Halcyon had a house on the banks of the Gray River. The Gray loved her, so it gave her a son from its waters. The child was wild and beautiful, and the Halcyon adored him. He called her his mother, and she called him Robwillow. Filled with the good waters of the Gray River, Robwillow was a bright and happy child. But he also had the Thorn running within him, and his heart turned black as he grew old. He awoke giants in Duskwood, filling them with angry spirits from the roots of the world, and he sent them to break the wall of the Auburn Mountains in the south. Her generosity betrayed, the Halcyon met Robwillow in battle, and she struck him down on the Fields of Silver. But she remembered that Robwillow had called her his mother, and she could not kill him. She raised a mountainous spire in the heart of Duskwood to cradle him until the fading of the world.

The Halcyon left sadness in the land she had hoped to shape as a refuge.

Ruby's heart sank as they crossed into the gloom. Everdim took the afternoon sun for all its power, and the party fell quiet again. The light faded constantly, but it never died. Not even the light of the Tidestone could light that half-shadow. It seemed a heavy thing, tangible as mist, and it swirled with strange eddies left in the wakes of faeries. Orbs moved in the Everdim, gem-blue on fluttering moth's wings, following the refugees and remaining just out of sight. They began to bunch around her Tidestone, to land upon it and to bounce against it, undeterred by Ruby's efforts to shoo them away.

"I never liked these woods," said one of the otters. He squeezed his wife's paw. "There are things in it watching us. I can always feel them."

"They have no minds," the badger explained, "but they are drawn to sorrow and injury. They swarm, but the fae are harmless."

"Catch a few if you can," Michael joked, trying to cut the tension. "Three in a bottle make a good lamp for a few nights."

This idea was not explored. The hush that fell on the group was oppressive, and none who spoke felt like saying much. Ruby's enthusiasm waned, but, like the Everdim light, it never vanished completely. Duskwood was a place of decline toward no end. Hope shrank there to dwindle forever, neither real nor false. The weary band pushed on into a mild rain that had turned to snow by the time they could hear the Charl chuckling nearby.

The path ended in a wide glade that lay snow-brushed in beautiful, open daylight. The sun was obscured, but the clouds were bright with its diffuse rays, and even that scattered light was welcome after the gloaming dark. The group lingered here for as long as they could stand the cold, and Michael sang to them of his home in Dimwood, where they were headed. The badger poet performed a rousing recitation of an original work in Melidoran, and Arturus, not one to be left out of the spotlight, sang another song of death and battle before they decided to move on. The badger poet began to lead them east out of the clearing, when William stopped her.

"Where are the otters?"

"Mara and Sres," said the Vixen. Peter was asleep in her lap, Duskwood having taken its toll on even his energetic spirit.

"Yes," Arturus looked around. "I saw them while Michael was singing."

But the otters weren't in the clearing, and they didn't answer any calls. The refugees dispersed through the woods, though William urged them to stay together, and they went about searching for signs of the couple. The sun was on its descent now, and it seemed to have picked up speed. Michael and Ruby tried to bring the group back together, but they were slow and tired. Gloaming violet was spreading across the clouds when the band finally returned to the clearing. By then, a moonrat had gone missing as well.

Fear settled upon them. They moved on in terrible silence, the badger wiping tears from her face. The river murmured to itself in the gray darkness. Closer to the banks, the air smelled of honeysuckle and lilacs. The clouds broke as the sun set, and the snow began to melt, turning the gentle slope toward the Charl into a muddy slide. They passed under a stone archway carved with images of butterflies and onto a basalt slab that served as a berth, where the ferry was tied.

The river Charl was as clear and pale as heliodor beneath the canopy. Trees reached for each other across its swift shimmer. Looking downstream from the berth, the Charl hooked east toward Dimwood, which was just visible beyond the bend. The ferry bobbed on pontoons, a flat raft of planks sealed with tar and fixed with outriggers. It had apparently been intended for the transport of goods into Dimwood, and it looked large enough to accommodate two magog Nixies standing side by side. Ruby and Michael stepped on first, and then they helped the others board. The refugees slouched, exhausted, and sat down in a loose circle in the center of the raft. Junie flapped her wings and dropped into the water to float with her neck curled back like a swan's. Peter laughed at this, and a smile or two appeared in the grim crowd.

"She's not so good a swimmer," Arturus said, "but she can float all day."

William's horse balked at the water and would not be soothed, so he removed its tack and left it on the bank standing proud and stubborn.

"He was a Nixian steed, anyway," William sighed. "Perhaps the last slave I liberated. May he live through the winter and join the wild herds of the north in the spring."

Arturus put his paw on William's back, and the two shared a look before William freed the ferry.

Michael stretched out as best he could, extending his injured leg and holding his right arm to his bruised chest. Ruby sat with him and tried to help bandage a gash above his knee, but the pain in her left hand rendered it mostly useless. She had no doubt that it was broken; the fingers were mashed together over a penetrating hole in her palm, left ragged by the dire-dog's tooth.

"You'll need to bandage yourself first." A moonrat came to sit beside Ruby. She was a wisp of a thing, shrunken and bowed, and her eyes were the color of turmeric behind the lank, white curtain of her hair. "Let me help. It's the least I can do."

Her dress was cut in the Cholai fashion. Ruby remembered Leora had worn a similar garment during a card reading. A red sash was knotted at her hip and cuffed with a folded square of dark silk. She wore no undershirt, and her robe was stretched out and deformed with tears at the sleeves. With one pale claw, she cut a strip of cloth from her hem.

"I'm Filwa," she said. She wrapped Ruby's hand gently, binding her fingers straight out. "If only I had some salve for that wound. I remember you, dear. From the Grayplains – the Fields of Silver."

"Moira's mother," Michael said.

"Her grandmother's sister," Filwa corrected. "Hold still, master weasel."

Ruby cut cloth from Michael's sleeves and collar and helped Filwa wrap his knee. The shadows of trees passed over them, and a chuck-will's-widow began calling far off in the forest. Long fish glided under the raft, nipping at the surface with round mouths full of needle teeth. Their scales glowed green and silver. When Filwa brushed the hair from her face, Ruby could see that the whites of her eyes were pricked with red specks.

"I remember," Ruby said, and it felt wonderful. "Benjamin and the others?"

"Safe," Filwa said with a smile. "At least for now. I told the machines I was the queen of the Cholai. They took me and left the others alone."

"A wise lie," Michael said. "But dangerous."

"Is it a lie, now, master weasel?" Filwa patted the makeshift bandage on Michael's knee carefully. Then she turned back to Ruby. "It was a young one that went off into the woods. A southerner. He was the son of a very important Cholai. Led off into the murk by those will-o'-the wisps, I imagine. Up north to old Robwillow's grave. Like the otter pair, those sweet things. That's what happens. The faerie lure is strong."

"You knew him," Michael said.

Ruby looked at Filwa sadly. "I'm sorry."

"The others felt things were watching. Taking them," Filwa explained. "Wanted to go, and it was best to go. A sad thing, yes, but I am safe. I am free. Because of you and who you are." She gave Ruby a conspiratorial wink. "They don't know. The Nixies don't know, either. I'm seeing it more and more – you're so much more yourself now. I wanted to thank you. You did a good thing. A brave thing. And you put my grandniece's sword to good use. The Cholai owe you a debt now."

Ruby looked past Filwa toward the lights of Dimwood. The raft rocked in the water, with Junie paddling hard beside it. Arturus held her reins as the current swept her on toward the bend that would take them at last into Michael's city. Ruby could smell the cooking fires burning.

"Will they fight for us?" Ruby asked.

"They will fight, yes," Filwa replied. "Will fight for *you*."

Ruby nodded. She suddenly felt very old.

"Good," she said, and then she turned to Filwa with a smile. "Then that's all I ask."

They passed from the dark into the moonglow of Dimwood. At Northgate, the Charl narrowed and the trees grew higher, arching over the water to form an arbor tunnel. Faerie lamps hung in the drooping boughs of silver willows, which lined the banks between great lindens and larches draped with banners. Ruby could see flecks of sliver drifting in the lamplight. The hedges were meticulously maintained; here grew laburnum still in spring gold, and here a damask rose bush bloomed despite the chill in the air. There were bright shapes in the trees, moving glimmers in the cruxes of boughs or sitting against garlanded trunks. A sound came from them that was at once like a song and like a gentle heat pulsing into the air. The Tidestone responded with whispers of peace and with pulses of its own, and Ruby felt a lightness in her chest. She inhaled deeply, warmth spreading across her face. She felt a deep calm come over her and tried to sink into it, to prolong it as much as she could.

Four marten bowmen greeted the company on the raft from a white bridge hung with wisteria. Their captain stood in a crested helmet and cape with a patch over his eye.

"Where are you going?" He called.

Michael stood, a little stronger. Ruby helped prop him up as the raft moved under the bridge.

"Robinegg," Michael answered, "to see Tia. And to Elmway after that."

"I'll send word," cried the captain, now with his paw to his mouth, and one of his bowmen headed east to disappear beyond a hedge of hazel. "Welcome back, Lord Underbridge!"

Night had fallen, but Northgate quay was awake and bustling. Soldiers stood beneath lit inn windows, smoking and laughing or staring down the stone streets in grieving silence. Vendors wheeled their carts out of the district down lanes that curved around towering oaks. Two large groups of freed slaves stood at one pier, hugging joyously, drinking, and singing their salvation to the delight of a crowd of onlookers.

A tall stoat in a green jacket met the arriving refugees on a marbled slipway. His attendants pulled the raft over the stones with barge poles and helped the refugees up to where a low charabanc waited.

"From Owl's Head, then?" the stoat asked, extending a paw to Michael.

"There are others worse off than me," Michael said. "See to them first, and I'll find my way to the healer." He nodded toward Ruby. "She'll need a private room, if you can spare one, and lots of rest and treatment for her hand."

The stoat now helped Ruby from the raft. He looked at her quizzically, as if he wasn't entirely sure whether he should send her to the healer or kick her into the water.

"The dog-slayer?"

Ruby nodded, blushing.

"Ruby." She introduced herself.

"Ruby, indeed!" Now the Marten dropped to a knee. "Empress! You shall have your own carriage, of course. After so long, you're back. It's a good day in Dimwood."

"I want to ride with the others," said Ruby. "If that's all right."

"Certainly, milady. And I shall follow behind." He tipped a bow to Michael. "Lord Underbridge. Let the birds see to you."

A team of canaries laid the weakest of the group onto gurneys. They were lean and bright-eyed and nearly as tall as Michael, with clawed hands and feet. Their wings spread over their shoulders like cloaks, stuck through sleeves on the backs of their nurses' robes. Ruby was fascinated with them. She whistled, trying to imitate their tittering language, and they gave little chirps of laughter as she boarded the wagon. Arturus stretched out eagerly upon a gurney, crossing his short legs and enjoying the attentions of the canary nurses. William pushed them away.

"I'm perfectly well," he insisted. "But the guinea pig needs all the help he can get."

"And I aim to get as much as I can," Arturus laughed. A few of the shier birds tittered and put their hands over their beaks. "I'm a hero, you know!"

Ruby knelt beside the badger poet, who clutched the wolf cub on her gurney, and Filwa sat on the bench to pet the cub between his ears. Michael sat up with his leg stretched out, and winced as one of the nurses spread salve on his cuts.

"Tia is waiting," said the stoat as he mounted a chestnut horse. "It warms my old heart to see all of you. We'd heard the stories and feared the worst."

"The story isn't over," Ruby said, forcing a smile.

The stoat gave her an awkward salute. "Ah, yes, of course. Perhaps not, milady. Who better than you to say?"

As she lay in her hospital bed, it occurred to Ruby that, before she had arrived in Robinegg to be ushered into care and comfort, she had been functioning by sheer dint of will. She'd had no fire left in her furnaces; she'd been dry as ash and pouring smoke, forcing her gears to crank despite their creaking and complaining. Fear, pain, and hope had been luxuries for which she simply hadn't had the energy, so she'd been operating at the level of a machine. Even the Forgetting had been unable to find a hold in her. But now she was in her own room with a soft mattress and a view of the river. She could see the birds on the pier, moving among Dimwood's musteline populace. Her energy was returning, and she was bolstering it by feeding on the life of this place. Her personhood was accessible again.

One by one, the Owl's Head refugees came to visit her. It was always Tia who admitted him, strutting with her long legs and rounded wings, her quill-like crest up and bright eyes glaring. She had the beak of a snake-eater.

"Take your time," she would say whenever she had a visitor, and her hunter's frown masked a warmth that was appropriate for her position as matron of the healing birds.

Some of the refugees took more time than others. All were recovering well, and all those still able-bodied promised to fight for her when the day came. Her identity didn't stay a secret long, so Ruby had to endure their genuflections. Filwa stayed longest with her, talking of Benjamin and the effort to unite the Cholai in Pearlwater.

"It is a difficult thing, you know," she said, "to get all together. But word is out. Wagons are moving. Nixies are squeezing tight, making travel difficult, but wanderers know of passes that no one else knows. Could've told you of them if we had known where you were going before, yes? Saved you the Valley of Silk!"

"It is as it should have been," Ruby replied. She had come to believe that in the last few days. "If we hadn't gone there, we never would have gone to Owl's Head."

"That is the Empress," Filwa told her. "That good way of thinking – that's Ruby."

Distrusting the canary nurses, Filwa inspected Ruby's wound. It was clean and healing well, though it would never be whole again. Her fingers weren't broken, but Vanreah's tooth had taken some of the movement from her hand.

"All will be whole," Filwa thought. "Rest and take these. All will heal." She pressed four pills into Ruby's palm. "One at night for four nights. Cholai medicine always works."

And then Filwa had gone into the west, and Ruby had taken a pill after dinner for four nights. Now her hand was healing so quickly that Tia and the canaries worried. They were birds of science, but there were rumors. Ruby had reason to believe that they watched her room one night when the moon was full.

William and Arturus ran errands in the south, scouting and tracking Nixie movements along Dreaming Cape and in the vicinity of Donchapel Hill. For two nights, they watched the Great Road that led up to the Cradle Spire, and they brought back reports of a colossal machine moving through Duskwood. This and more they eagerly reported to Ruby when they returned.

On the morning before her release, Ruby called William, Arturus, and Michael into her room. It was cold, but she was wrapped in downy blankets and a satin gown over blue long johns. She had another matter to discuss, but she listened patiently while Arturus told spy stories, gushing as if expecting commendation. William interjected when he could, adding relevant details whenever the guinea pig's bluster buried them. They had come to think of her as their general, and Ruby found this change disturbing. She was aware of drawing near to a verge. Every night, the Tidestone whispered to her, telling her that she would soon have to be so much more than she was. As the deep force returned to reside within her once more as it always had, coiled like a serpent under a bushel basket, Ruby witnessed the rebirth of fear. It passed through her on windy days, when the eaves howled in the gale, and she watched it, cataloged it, and was forced to confront it every night in her dreams. Arturus spoke of her fear lustily. Even William's eyes shone with eager anticipation: war was upon them.

Michael listened, nodding with his chin in his paw. His leg was healed, but the scars of the lash on his back were likely to remain. His body was still dangerously depleted, and he ate six times a day. On the whole, his physical fitness had saved him. He was the real general, Ruby thought. It was *his* war.

"Hawkport has fallen," he muttered after William and Arturus had finished their report. "That will make things difficult when we set out for Pearlwater."

"There is a plan in place," William assured him. "My network remains in place in the south. I have a contact who will provide us with a boat and passage to the Pearlshores if we can get to Thimblewand."

Michael hummed to himself. "And the big machine?" he asked

"What we've told you is all we know," Arturus said. "It only moves at night, and it never leaves Duskwood. At least not that we've seen."

"There are eyes on the forest as we speak," William added. "Information is always coming in."

"You've earned your reputations. I cannot thank you enough." Now Michael turned to Ruby. "Empress?" He searched her face. It was her time to weigh in. She pursed her lips and wrinkled her nose. This was a bitter serum to swallow.

"Besides my own thanks, I have nothing to add," she said at last, embarrassed at her own bluntness. "The resistance could not be in more capable paws, I'm sure of that. When will we leave for Thimblewand?"

"On your order, ma'am," Arturus replied. He was wearing a feathered cap like the one William had worn when she first saw him. "We're ready when you are."

"He speaks too soon," William corrected. "There is, perhaps, a week's more work to do in securing passage to Pearlwater."

Ruby wanted to look thoughtful. She nodded, mimicking Michael. It was not her war. She didn't want it. The hope on her friends' faces made her heart sink; she was putting a toe over the edge. She held their hearts in her hands whether she wanted to or not.

"There's something else," she began, her throat suddenly dry. She took a sip of water from the glass beside her bed. "The real reason I called you all here. These." She put the glass down and took two books from the same nightstand. She had read them both again; it had been almost all she could do at first. "I brought these from Gowspin. There was a whole bookshelf of them."

William, Arturus, and Michael stood looking at each other for a moment. Arturus made a soft little *wheek*, and Michael crossed his arms. She could not read their faces.

"Yes," William finally said. "They were a gift from a friend – one of the first slaves I helped free. She got passage to her home in Heddlegard, and when it was safe, she sent me the whole collection. I thought it was fitting to store it in the secret apartment." He looked at the books, picked one up and thumbed through it. "I'm glad you saved these. They must be worth a fortune now. I believe they're quite rare."

"You're in one of them," Ruby replied. Then she pointed to Arturus. "And there's a song in the other that mentions you."

"Of course," Arturus said, scratching his blond chin.

"You'd probably have found me if you'd picked up two different books," Michael added.

"The author," Ruby said. She found herself getting frustrated. Mists parted. Peaks rose dark. "Who was she?"

William turned the book over and looked at the name for a long time.

"Elizabeth Lynn," William said, and an even longer silence followed.

Ruby tried to guess what the glimmer in Michael's eyes meant. Was Arturus smiling expectantly, or was he being condescending toward her, amused as he might be by a child? The verge opened beneath her. She looked into the abyss, and the abyss looked back at her.

"My sister," Ruby said.

Now the three looked at each other again, and Ruby could tell that they were puzzled.

"No, Empress," Michael began delicately. He sat down on the bed beside her. "Your sister died when you were eight. She was ten."

The abyss looked back, and Ruby recognized its face. She knew its voice, the cold caress of its breath. She was the abyss, and she was looking down at herself.

"I wrote them," Ruby her herself said. In the pit of her gut, she felt the deep force pulling. "I wrote them in my sister's name."

"In her *honor*," Arturus corrected her.

"Elizabeth," Ruby said, softly. She looked down at the floor and then over at Michael. His eyes were like ink. She thought, *It's her world*, and then she stopped herself. *No. It's my world.* She said this out loud. There was no other way to see it for what it was. "This is my world."

William handed the book back to her, and she set it in her lap without thinking. Arturus knelt before her and put his strong paw on her hand. Michael's paw was light and careful on her shoulder. Lord Underbridge: bard, scholar, priest.

"Your world," Michael repeated. "You're the Empress."

Eleven

Mirrors

Michael fell ill, and Ruby spent days at his side. She read to him when he lay awake, panting and shivering, and she pretended to chastise him when he apologized in the morning. William contracted the same mysterious sickness, and in a few days the whole of Robinegg was writhing with it. Ruby rushed through the wards, helping the canaries as best she could. She applied creams and ice packs, dispensed pills and emptied bedpans. Arturus rejected all her aid at first, but when he could not get out of bed without having a seizure, he quickly rescinded his refusal. Robinegg became a quarantine hospital, and Ruby was eventually confined to her room, despite not having developed symptoms of any disease. As the sickness worsened, it brought pain, leaving patients moaning horribly long into the night. What sleep Ruby could get was populated with horrors. Her nightmares were vague and strange, and she often woke from them paralyzed while the dark sat on her chest, crushing her. Eventually, sleep abandoned Ruby altogether.

"It's the Forgetting," Tia told her. "There's no physical cause for this fever. It's in their minds, squeezing, destroying them. I fear many will go mad."

Ruby took to staring into her gem at night. The Tidestone pulsed and whispered nonsense, and she began to see faces moving within its fire. She prayed quietly, eyes closed, sitting with her back against the wall and her knees drawn up to her chest. She wasn't sure she believed in the Halcyon, but maybe that didn't matter. Belief was a strange thing. Her prayers were earnest, and when she was finally allowed to see her friends in their rooms Michael prayed with her as well. None went mad. After a week of panic and horror, a simple cure was found in the milk of a rare orchid.

"The Halcyon provides," Michael told her as he buttoned his new waistcoat. The front panels were gold, and the back was embroidered with stars. He was in her room, still a little weak but fighting it admirably.

"But only if she's asked?" Ruby said.

"I won't claim to comprehend the politics of faith," he smiled. "And in your case, Empress, I wonder if there are any rules at all."

Winter was deepening when Robinegg opened its doors again. The Charl was laced with ice, but, through subtle magic, the gardens of Dimwood remained in wondrous bloom. Crowds gathered, demanding to see the Empress. She had cured the fever, they said. She had killed the wolfgod. She was a bulwark against the Forgetting, the light that Melidora had waited for so long under Nixian rule. Ruby had no more excuse to hide in her hospital bed. She went with Michael to his home beneath a beech tree in Elmway, and he helped to stem the madding tide when she met her admirers. Instead of the queenly gowns she was given, she wore light armor. She refused a crown, and would not bear the title "Dog Slayer." She was praised for being common, which made being common all the more difficult. The adulation quickly lost what little novelty it had had. Ruby felt the hands of the people on her, prying into her – their eyes searched her for weaknesses as if assessing an enemy.

No one can tell you who you are. She could almost hear Dallie Bratcher's voice in her head. The crowd could not tell her who she was, but that didn't stop them from trying. The love of the people felt hostile and selfish, and she was glad when William came to her to report that all was ready for the journey east.

"I'll be glad to be among equals again," she said. They were on the bank, wagons gathered. She was in silver armor, and the sword on her back was a relic that had been on the wall in the Great Hall for years – in Michael's hall, the House of Underbridge.

"The basest of all things is to be afraid," William said. "Fear makes equals of everyone."

"And hope is born of fear," Michael added. "The people are desperate. They've been afraid for a long time."

"The armies of Eggplant are on the march," Arturus said. "With our strength, the union of Pearlwater and Dimwood cannot fail. Fear has heard its death knell."

William looked doubtful. That disparaging gleam was in his eye again. "We shall wait until we reach Pearlwater to decide that."

The morning's snow turned to rain. The trees were hung with colored lamps and signs declaring victory. Behind them, the crowd was swelling in the street, moving like a single organism aflame with fervor and certainty. No barrier could hold them; they were spilling toward the wagons, throwing roses and coins.

"Let's away," Michael said. It was his war after all. "They'll soon be mobbing us."

Ruby climbed onto her roan stallion. It was a war horse, sturdy and sure and frighteningly powerful. Its breastcollar was studded with jade and hematite, its long saddlepad emblazoned with the kingfisher sigil.

She led the procession behind a standard-bearer, who was really leading her. He rode with his back as straight as a beam, his lance bouncing against his shoulder. They followed Water Street toward the east gate with the crowd shadowing them at a crawl, pushing through alleyways and around the boles of massive trees to get a glimpse of the heroes before they disappeared onto the plains of Donchapel.

The forest opened, they turned south, and Ruby could see Donchapel Hill through the trees. It was a black knob on the horizon, misshapen and worn down, its top collapsing. There had been arthewags there, but that was a long time ago. They had fled north onto the ice and grown long coats. The Nixies had forced them out. Her horse's gait was rhythmic and strong. There was no room for fear or doubt in its mind. It would charge into walls of spears for her. It would leap through fire. She wasn't fit for such a steed. Her confidence was ephemeral, and it was weak when it did manifest. The thought of leading terrified her, and Michael knew it. They all knew how frail she was, how little she understood about her own capabilities. The Forgetting seemed to feed on her deep force. Its claws were in her, but it was different now: it sapped her of her faith instead of her memory.

My world, she thought, and tears came to her eyes. *But I'm not strong enough to be its savior.*

The east gate was crowded with guards keeping the masses at bay. Some admirers broke through the barricades to run alongside the wagons. Badger sows gave trinkets to boars in armor, their faces streaked with tears. Marten mothers lifted their cubs into the wagons to be hugged and kissed one last time. Guards stopped the rest from trying to overtake Ruby's horse.

"I'm not ready," Ruby said to Michael. Her horse wanted to run. She tugged on the reins, barely keeping it in check.

"Perhaps not," he replied. "But you're not alone, either."

Oaks and silver birches gave way to osiers and clumps of withering heather at Dimwood's eastern edge. The fields of Donchapel unfurled before them, wet and hilly. Further south, they narrowed into a glen lined with red alder and hornbeam shaws, bare branches stark against the cloud-choked sky. Behind the mound of Donchapel Hill, the Golrace River cut deep into the southern slopes to drain into the sea from myriad mouths. This was Thimblewand, and a few miles to the north sat Hawkport, its spires like dark brushstrokes on the horizon.

It started to snow as the procession passed Donchapel Hill. Michael moved up to ride beside Ruby, and William was behind him on a brindle mare. He had refused the livery of the Dimwood knights, and was wearing his old Lincoln green cloak and hood. Behind William, an ermine captain led two covered wagons; one carried supplies and the other carried soldiers in Dimwood gray and their stout mastiffs. Arturus rode beside the lead wagon, dressed in full armor. He had been offered a pony, but Junie would not let him leave without her. Now she was complaining about the cold, and Ruby saw that he had tied a soldier's scarf loosely around her neck.

They descended into a valley of white, kicking up whirls of powder. Heavy flakes landed to stick in Ruby's hair, building her a rough crown of frost. She was wrapped in a hooded coat lined with lynx fur, and her hands were warm in elbow-length white gloves. Her breath steamed from her lips, which were chilled crimson despite the coating of bee's wax Filwa had applied to them. At last, she put her hood up, and then she felt even more as though she were swimming in her coat.

The fields pitched up hard to the west, and the valley dropped into boggy terrain as they pressed on. The ruins of a keep stared down at them, dark atop Dreaming Cape: the husk of gnomish Argomanse. Its roofs sagged, its walls crumbled, but it still glowered with a strange kind of life. Beyond it, the Charl flowed high-banked in its tilted bed to drop over the Dreaming Cape in a roaring cascade. Ruby listened, but all she could hear was the rush of the wind through the hornbeams.

Morning warmed into afternoon, but the sun remained behind its shroud. A hush fell over the field, undisturbed even by the rumbling of the wagons' wheels. It was a heavy thing, almost tangible, and it made the horses nervous. They pushed deeper toward the morass, and the ground froze. The Golrace was an angry river; it pounded its imprisoning banks with famous speed and fury. Where some of those mad waters leached into the hill country to bubble up into muddy sinks, the ground was spotted with caps of fragile ice. Ruby led the procession up the slope to the trees, and their progress slowed considerably. The standard-bearer began a chilly, wandering tune on his tin whistle as they picked their way through the fens and into the shallow basin through which the Golrace coursed toward the sea. Ruby recognized it as the song of Leora in the Moon Pools.

The fields flattened out and became pebbly. The soil grew firm again, and as dusk was coming on Ruby began to smell the sea. Here, Michael called a halt, and William, Arturus, and the ermine captain rode up to the front of the column. Ruby joined them as they pulled their horses into a circle. A fleeting image made her smile: her sister Elizabeth teaching her to ride in the field behind their house.

"We're crossing into Nixieland," William said, shifting in his saddle as his mare tossed her head. She didn't like being around the other horses.

"They watch from the south tower," said the ermine, pointing toward Hawkport. "There's no way down without being seen. We should wait here until dark."

"I'd like to, Timothy," Michael addressed the ermine, "but I'm concerned about this quiet. It's not natural. I fear Nixie spies may be a lot closer than Hawkport."

"Or worse," Arturus chimed in, and Junie let out a hitching wheeze. "I've felt eyes on me, too. Everyone has. All the soldiers are talking about it. It's the starlings, I think. The Duskwood birds. I say we move south as fast as we can, Hawkport be damned. It'd take an hour to get from the south gate to Thimblewand, and this cold's too much for Junie."

"We've been riding so long," Ruby said, a little embarrassed. She felt as though she was interrupting. "I think a rest might be better than an all-out dash for the coast."

Timothy made a face, and Ruby blushed. She'd said something stupid, just as she knew she would.

"It's a long ride," Timothy said, "and the terrain is bad. We either risk the wagons across the rocks, or we risk the woods."

"It'll take more than rocky sand to break up a Dimwood wagon," Arturus replied.

"I think the choice is fairly obvious, if I may say so, Empress." William dipped his chin in a bow, but his eyes were wide with fear. "I can wait to get some food in my stomach. We'll soon be on the water."

The others seemed to agree. Ruby sat up straight, trying to be regal. Empresses didn't say stupid things or make bad decisions. She tried to think of a way to agree while making it sound like continuing on had been her idea all along, but as she opened her mouth to speak there was a great rush of wings above them. The horses fretted, whinnying their anxiety, their eyes wide and ears pivoting. A flock of Duskwood starlings curled into the air like smoke, startled from the treetops. Suddenly, then there was a horrible smell, and Ruby nearly gagged. The stench burned her nostrils and stuck in the back of her throat. She spit, but it was still there, stinging like needle pricks.

"Bugganes," Timothy whispered, and he spat as well. Apparently, nothing else needed to be said. He pulled his horse hard away from the circle, and Ruby followed. The smell grew worse as the caravan got moving again. They hurried down the embankment and onto the rocky plain, and Ruby thought she saw a vast, tawny shape moving in the woods they left behind them.

After the breaking of the Auburn Mountains, the Weavers fled the Valley of Silk and lived in the Wood of Thorns until the end of the Halcyon's first days in Melidora. The Halcyon scattered the giants that Robwillow had awakened, and some of them went into the north and became trolls. Some fled east into the sea and were never heard from again. Giants were afraid of their reflections, so the Halcyon placed mirrors in the eastern bay as a ward against them. The remaining giants went underground, looking for their father's prison, and in aphotic pits at the hearts of ancient caves they became twisted and wild, and they were called Bugganes.

Many things were held asleep in the Everdim. In those primeval days after the Halcyon's ascent, as the fading fell upon Duskwood Forest, old horrors slowly vanished from the world. How long had the Nixies been working in Duskwood? How deep had they dared to go in search of oil and metal? While Ruby was convalescing, William and Arturus had corroborated stories of fell things moving in the forest, of a horrible smell that came and went, and of the recent butchering of a horse on Wolf's Way.

"It's some mechanical thing," William had been sure. "Another clockwork killing machine."

But what came out of the forest that day was not mechanical.

Ruby spurred her horse into a trot to keep up with Michael, who was circling around to get the wagons moving. William dropped back, and Timothy the ermine captain turned his horse in the opposite direction, riding alongside the wagons toward the tail end of the procession. As they headed down the slope and began to pick up speed, the horses still nickering nervously, a strip of red alder copses parted to make way for a walking hill. Ruby watched the hill grow long arms, and it broke into an awkward lope. It opened a mouth, and its lower jaw was a like a long spade of yellowed tusks. Its back bristled with dull yellow hair, while its chest and arms were covered in bone-studded scales. Ruby's blood went cold, her heart impaled on piercing fear. Down onto the plains of Donchapel came a son of old Robwillow, a grandchild of the Gray River.

The Buggane charged the wagons and the horses reared in terror. Michael and Timothy did all they could do to help the drivers keep them from bolting. The standard-bearer dropped away, and Ruby was left riding alone at the head of the column. Arturus came up beside her, Junie trotting hard and flapping her wings as if in a vain attempt to fly.

"Circle, round!" he cried. "Lead us east!" With this, he drew his sword and, with a lusty cry, pointed Junie's beak toward the beast.

Ruby tried to turn her horse, but it seemed to have its own plans. It didn't appear to be afraid of the Buggane. It tugged away from her and continued pounding south.

The Buggane was drawing nearer. Its huge claws dug trenches in the sandy soil. Snow flew about its legs, billowing behind it crazily, and it lunged at the rear wagon to ram it with its shoulder. Timothy turned his horse in time to avoid being crushed. The driver hauled on the reins, and the wagon tilted frighteningly. Arturus rode toward the beast as it stumbled in the snow, his sword glinting in the failing light, and Ruby tried in vain to call him back. She jerked her horse's reins, now on the verge of panic, and it finally yielded. She made a wide circle back toward the wagons, where Dimwood archers were kneeling and trying to prepare arrows. William was riding toward her now, following Arturus a little way, and then turning abreast of Ruby. He unshouldered his bow and drew an arrow from his quiver just as easily as if he were sitting still. She saw him look down the shaft and knew he was whispering. Then his arrow was speeding away, cutting a whistle through the air. It narrowly missed Arturus on its way to the Buggane's head, where it appeared to shatter. Arturus tipped to the side instinctively, pulling Junies reins, and Junie fell over, flapping and squawking pitifully. Ruby saw William frown as she spurred her steed past him, toward where Arturus lay pinned beneath Junie.

The Buggane clambered to its feet and stood, dwarfing the wagons, its shadow spilling huge across the snow before it. It let out a high, choking scream, and Ruby drew her sword. It was an antique – a ceremonial blade. She wondered if it even had an edge. But Arturus was struggling to get up, and he may as well have been bound and prepared like an offering for sacrifice. The monster's shadow fell over him. Junie rolled off of him and bobbed around, disoriented. The Buggane looked first to the fallen Aturus and then to Ruby, who was holding her sword high.

"Here!" she cried. Two arrows flew by her. One fell in the snow, and the other went wide of the Buggane. The Dimwood archers were not as skilled as William, but Ruby doubted that it mattered. The beast's skin was as hard as stone.

Arturus was shouting something now. He was on his feet, his cape blowing, but the Buggane was ignoring him. It looked past Ruby at the archers, and its eyes lit up with amber fire. It ducked its head for another charge, and Ruby leaned off her horse to try to scoop Arturus up before the beast could step on him. She fell hard into the snow, her breath whooshed from her lungs, and she cried out in pain as something popped in her shoulder. She gritted her teeth and swore; there was no time to be hurt. She forced herself to her feet and leapt, tackling Arturus, and the Buggane roared by in pursuit of the last wagon. Ruby wrapped her arms around Arturus while he struggled. Tears formed in the corners of her eyes; her shoulder felt separated. She was sweating and gasping for breath, and she could not hold him. He fought free and stood in the snow, staring with his paws balled into fists as the Buggane prepared to demolish the wagon.

Ruby watched, astonished. Michael was circling after her horse. Timothy had drawn his sword and was putting himself between the shrieking horror and the charabanc. William rode hard alongside the wagon, trying desperately to help its driver turn it before the Buggane could bash it to pieces in the snow. But there was another rider on the field. A horse had come down from the north, where Hawkport was beginning to glow in the gloaming dark. Its rider was robed in black, his face hidden beneath a hood. He seemed to be swinging *bolas*; the weights made a sinister whirring sound as he spun them over his head by the nexus of the three cords.

The dark rider circled in close, ducking low in his saddle. He veered toward the buggane, leaning dangerously into a hairpin turn, and then he hurled his weapon. The Buggane fell gracelessly, crying out as the cords twisted its legs together. It was down again, thrashing in the snow, and now Ruby saw more black riders on the field.

"Empress!" Michael was approaching from the east. He pulled her horse by its reins. "Sir Periwinkle!"

He didn't need to tell her to mount up. Ruby took up her sword and, biting her lip as her arm filled with heat and stabbing pains, she hauled herself up on the far side of her steed. It twitched away from her, and for a terrible moment she was sure it was going to buck her off. It was afraid after all. It was only an animal. But it calmed for her, and she settled into the saddle as Arturus gathered himself. Junie whistled to him as he wriggled up her smalt-blue flank and patted her neck.

"Go, June!" he told her. "Hup! Here they come!"

The Buggane was hobbled. It beat the ground in a rage, shrieking malice and ancient, horrible hunger. In spite of herself, Ruby almost felt sorry for it. William and Timothy had succeeded in helping the wagons back into formation, and the drivers were beating hard now. The charabancs bounced over the rocks, their frames creaking and flexing precariously. The dark riders split up to cut off the passage south. Michael rode hard along the outside of the column with Ruby and Atruturus close behind. He pulled a flashing saber from his hip and stood up high in the saddle, the blade out to slit the breeze.

The dark riders' horses were small and low to the ground. They blew steam from their nostrils. Their legs swung in perfect rhythm, pushed by pistons and cranking gears, their knees fixed with hydraulic struts. As they ran, their joints whined. The riders were gogs in black, capes snapping behind them, and they brandished short swords or whirled *bolas* as they bobbed in their iron saddles. Ruby's decorative blade came out again, ringing dully, its ridiculous, gemmed hilt glittering in the burgeoning moonlight.

The Nixies were close and closing in; and now they were slashing at her. *Bolas* flew, and Ruby ducked, her eyes squeezed shut. She squealed as a Nixie's blade passed over her head and cut her hood open. Michael met the charge without fear. He cut through a charging Nixie, sending it crashing to the ground to burst and scatter. Arturus let out his warbling war cry as he cut at the legs of the mechanical horses. Ruby had banked hard away from the fray, but now she collected herself. She had faced Vanreah and won. She had drawn her sword against the Buggane. She was the Dog Slayer, and this was her world. She spurred her obstinate steed into a spine-jarring charge.

The third Nixie rider was coming around, spinning its weapon over its head. She met it at full force, driving her sword into its chest. The wave of force that ran up her arms was exhilaratingly painful. There was a deeply satisfying crunch, and she saw the Nixie flying apart in slow motion. Its head rocked off its neck, and its arms shattered. It hit the ground disintegrating, and its horse slowed to a stop and stood like a statue, unsure of what to do without its rider.

Arturus cheered, but Ruby couldn't hear him over the thunder in her ears. Three Nixies were down, but more were approaching from across the field. And now the Buggane was ripping at the catgut around its legs, rending it apart like paper. Ankles free, it lashed out from its knees and ripped one Nixie rider's horse out from under it. A second Nixie fell skewered on a huge claw, pinned to the ground and gushing blue-white sparks. Standing, the Buggane put its back foot on the Nixie's chest and tugged it in half.

Michael came up beside Ruby and shouted to her over the bawling of the beast.

"That's the Empress I remember," he said. His fur flew back wildly from his face, revealing his reckless smile. "Lead us south! And don't look back!"

Ruby regained the head of the column. She ached all over, but she rose in her saddle and lead the flight from the plains of Donchapel with her heart soaring. The Nixies followed them for a few minutes, but they were outnumbered. They turned away toward the screaming Buggane, *bolas* humming. The plains opened into true wetlands, where the Golrace poured through mangrove rushes into the sea. Ruby could hear the southern ocean pawing the marsh, nursing at sinks and hollows of bay mud. At last they came within sight of the coast, and here Ruby brought the caravan to a halt just within the marsh of Thimblewand.

They brought the wagons well-nigh against each other and waited, watching the plains for their pursuers. Night fell, and all was quiet in the north. Snow lay thick on the hills; all trace of their passage disappeared. They kept a watch, and Ruby was not allowed to participate. She slept in the charabanc with the soldiers, curled in her cloak and armor, and woke up cramped as the rising sun stretched the shadows of the sentinel trees. There had been no alarms.

The wagonmaster insisted upon a full inspection, and it was found that the charabanc's frame was cracking in several places. White gum was smeared into the largest fissures, and when it was packed over with snow it turned golden brown. This was an old Dimwood trick, the wagonmaster explained; the sap used to make the gum was found in no other region. With skillets in the fire and coffee percolating, Ruby called a circle together. William roused Arturus, and Michael brought Timothy; they sat on stumps, the smells of bacon and onions steaming around them, and a crowd of warriors gathered to listen as they talked.

"There is no ship," William said first. "The *Melusine* is not in Thimble Harbor. I think it's clear that my contact betrayed us to the Nixies."

"We were lucky," Arturus replied. "We had no inkling. That patrol would have taken us completely by surprise if it hadn't been for that big tusker."

"A fool sees not the same tree that a wise man sees," William sulked. "We'll have to cross the marshes now." "It's the only option," Timothy said. Ruby saw a nervous desperation in his eyes that worried her. "And it's only three days' walk across the Pearlmire."

"Fewer than that, I imagine, with horses and wagons." Michael sipped coffee. His words puffed out in curls of white. "But shall there be Nixies waiting for us? Further ambushers?"

"I wouldn't be surprised to see them swimming up out of the bog." Arturus laughed. "They've been steps ahead of us for so long."

"I wonder if you would go into the bog to see just how far ahead they might be." Ruby addressed both Arturus and William. "I know of no better scouts than you."

"A good scout would have seen this coming," William said. Was he still moaning? Ruby frowned at him. "Twelve years we worked. Now they've got their hands on our networks. All our passages are cut off. They're in the marsh, don't bet against it. Down from Hawkport, no doubt. Sucking it for minerals – Nixie dust. Crushing it dry like a sponge."

"The east has gone silent," Timothy added. "They could be in Pearlwater for all we know."

This brought a concerned murmur from the soldiers. Ruby was disheartened to see how many of them had considered this a possibility.

"Southunder has fallen," said one of the men. "It was the gateway to Pearlwater and the Pearlshores. Even if there had been a boat, the Nixies might have met us on the docks."

"Through the mire then," Ruby said, trying to stem this tide before it drowned their hope. "We'll start today across Thimblewand. We'll cross Heddle Bridge."

"Right above the delta mouth? That's very close to Hawkport," Michael said, not quite chiding. He didn't have William's condescending glower, but sometimes his cool smile could be worse. He showed her his small, sharp teeth, his eyes soft and dark, like the petal where love waits. "There's a lower pass. It shouldn't be too wet at this time of year."

Ruby felt stares upon her – fingers pulling at her attention, searching her heart for tumors of fear. The fear was there, but she realized that she couldn't let it come to light. She stepped past Michael's advice, and she could see it for the intrusion that it was. And she could see where she had to grip the issue, own it, and become involved at last. She sat back, face blank, and sipped her coffee.

"I'll tell you now what I've decided to do," she said. "I need you at my back. Will you come with me?" She was near the verge looking down into the dark. She knew the face was her own. A calm settled upon her – a clarity left behind by the retreat of the Forgetting from her mind.

"The bridge at the Heddle," Michael said. Now his eyes brightened. His smile tilted subtly to become almost laudatory. "Indeed, Majesty. We shall all go."

William and Arturus took two Dimwood soldiers with them on a scouting excursion. One was a robin, and the other was the only mouse in Dimwood's army. She gushed, thrilled to be chosen and excited to be of some use, but when it came time to leave the camp she tried to seem very grim and tenacious. They were in the swamp for many hours, but the morning sun loitered like a coward. When they returned with news of no Nixie activity to the north, it had barely crept out from behind Lockwood Forest.

"There are signs of Nixie movement in the area," the mouse was eager to report, "but we saw neither bolt nor screw of them wherever we went."

"If any foes of ours are there, we saw not one," William added. "But I'd advise caution, nonetheless. If they have been here, there must be something of interest in these swamps, and I'd expect them to be back."

The day grew warm, and the snow began to melt. It ran with shining beads of moisture, like flecks of glass. Ruby led the procession north, the standard-bearer now beside her. There was a newness to the light, a sweetness in the air, and she drank it in as they crossed into the delta marsh. As grim as it all seemed, as great as the weight of fear upon their confidence, she thought she could see a way through. The drowning nightmares seemed far away. They traced the Golrace's rambling track upstream from where it flooded the estuary. Where the river's fury finally abated, it sank into obstructing mud and acres of switchgrass. Above Thimblewand, the swamp was drier; patches of woody vegetation bustled with the calls of long tailed cormorants. Cattails shriveled in the cold, and the ground was pasted with horsetail and desiccated sweet flag. Gases bubbled up from deep pits, where the water roiled and blackened under ragged curtains of duckweed. Ruby looked out over the marsh and could just see the harbors as the Pearlshores glittered blue through the tangle of trees.

The Heddle was a raised bank with a level top standing not far from where the river Hawk split from the Golrace. It had been a high hill once, and there had been a lighthouse upon it, but time had worn it flat. Now it was an island of short grass in a sea of reedy mud. All that remained of the lighthouse was part of a staircase and a broken wall that had blackened with age. Somewhere to the north was Heddlegard, a camp walled in by deep swamp thickets and hidden by faerie magic – at least according to stories. Just east of the Heddle, there was a chasm in the swamp so deep that its bottom was lost in misty darkness. This was the Heddle Hole, and it had been a troll delving or a gnomish diamond mine. Or it might have been a scar left on the land by Vanreah in a rage. It was nearly one-hundred feet wide, tapering near the sea, and a bridge of stone arches spanned the abyss.

The Heddle crouched snow-topped in the morning fog. The wagons crossed the bridge empty, and the others followed it on foot. Though the horses were hesitant and the soldiers were disturbed by sounds from the pit, they crossed without incident. Ruby and Arturus spent a moment staring into the Heddle Hole and listening. She had suspected that it opened into a cove, but the peculiar exhalations emanating from it sounded more like the wind than the waves.

"There can't be anything that far down," Arturus said. "Not anything that wouldn't be flooded."

"Who knows what might have been here before this marsh?" Ruby replied, staring into the pit with her horse fidgeting beneath her. "Maybe a whole continent. Anything is possible."

"With its own wars, no doubt," Arturus chuckled. "We've got enough to worry about on this continent."

Beyond the Heddle Bridge, they passed along what appeared to be the remnants of a marsh hedge dyke. A few hawthorns persisted among decaying beech trunks, interwoven with dense clumps of coarse hay and sawgrass. It ran itself low after a good mile, descending back into the same bog mud that had swallowed up the rest of the land. Ruby tried to imagine a time before the Golrace had begun to flow, or when it had flowed in another direction, and she found herself lost in a memory of darkness and fiery upheaval. Her world had endured much over the years to be called hers. She knew that now. She was aware of riding over bones and blood and graves. Nothing is won which has not been lost; this thought rang in her head, the clarion call of a voice unremembered. She was wandering with this thought when her horse stumbled and reared, throwing her from the saddle.

She tried to turn and catch her fall somehow, but she landed on her right side and her breath rushed out of her. William and Timothy came to try to calm the horse, which bucked and dashed suddenly to the side of the charabanc. Ruby was startled but unhurt. She started to stand, a smile on her face, but before she had the chance to laugh the ground shifted sickeningly beneath her.

Timothy was shouting, "It's not stable," when the sinkhole beneath Ruby gave way.

The plug of leaves and muddy detritus had held a great amount of weight over the years, but the jostling of the wagons over it must have broken it loose somehow. Ruby dropped into the ground in a great shower of wet soil and feculent plant matter, and she landed on her back in a cavernous chamber. She groaned, eyes squeezed shut, her tailbone thrumming with pain. Her left hand ached to the bone.

"It's all right." She tried to shout, but she gagged on her tongue. Her throat felt as if it was squeezing shut. For one panicked moment, she flailed desperately in the leaf pile, and then she started to breathe again in huge gasps. The air was fetid, and she coughed as the powerful stench of mold filled her sinuses. She turned onto her hands and knees, and suddenly she wasn't so far from the Bay of Mirrors after all.

"Empress!" William called to her from above. She heard the wagons moving away and hoped they would find more stable ground. "Can you hear me?"

"It's all right," she tried again, and this time her voice carried. She caught her breath and cried, "I'm all right, William! I had the wind knocked out of me."

"Where are you?" It was Michael's voice. "Can you climb out?"

Ruby slowly regained her feet. Nothing seemed to be broken. The Tidestone began to beam, its pure white light growing subtly from a glimmer to a full blaze in which Ruby could see that the walls of the cavern were smooth and rounded. She ran her hand over them, walking a little further down the throat of this chamber, and found carvings on the walls she could not comprehend.

"I think it's hand-made," she said to the little circle of daylight above her. And of course it was. The floor was level, and she could see the marks of chisels when she looked closely at the walls. "It's incredible."

There was a commotion above. Ruby returned to the circle of light. "William?"

"Stay there, Empress," said William, and his voice sounded very far away. "Just a moment. There's something coming."

Noises from above carried through the stone walls and dissipated into muffled echoes. Ruby stepped away from the hole she'd fallen through, still catching her breath, and advanced down the corridor with the Tidestone in her hand. A gust of air like a cold breath flowed over her, tugging at her hair and her hooded cloak. She swallowed a knot and drew her sword. The corridor ended in a bell-shaped chamber. Near the back of the room, sounds bled together into a single amplified hum that made Ruby's head ache. Her eyes were throbbing, her stomach was stirring uncomfortably, but she pushed on through the reeking dark until the floor sank into a bowl that was partially filled with gelid water. Beyond the far edge, a staircase spiraled up around a stone column and vanished into blackness. Breathing white puffs, she stepped into the pool.

The water was crystal-clear. She entertained the possibility that it wasn't water at all; in the light of the gem, it seemed to move like quicksilver. Sprawling over the edge of the pool, back broken, its long arms and horned skull shining like nacre, lay an enormous skeleton. Those of its prodigious phalanges that were not shattered were gracile and beautifully formed. Its teeth had been smashed out, and they were spread along the bottom of the pool like stars across the dome of night. The single ocular cavity seemed to stare at Ruby, to castigate, and she thought she could almost hear a voice coming from the vicinity of the gaping mouth.

You drowned, it seemed to say. *You're dead.*

She approached the skeleton, her heart pumping ice. It couldn't be speaking. There were voices coming from above her, blending into a ringing whisper. Certainly, that's all she was hearing.

Just like Elizabeth. The beast gaped. *Welcome back, Elizabeth.*

The skull was cut nearly in half. Ruby realized there was a hilt jutting from it and that a blade was wedged at the bottom of the split. The dark was moving around her. She could feel the air stirring over her left shoulder, pressing steadily against her. She stared at the skeleton for a long time, defying it, trying to remember why it looked familiar.

It remembers me, she said, and her voice was like the dead voice of the beast. *Of course it does. It's mine.*

Her mouth went dry and she licked her lips. This was her world. Ruby sheathed her ornamental sword and put her hand in the watching eye socket. Her foot on the skeleton's toothless lower mandible, she hoisted herself toward the crown of its cracked head and reached. The hilt was high above the surface of the pool. She gritted her teeth, unable to stifle a stiff groan of exertion, and then her fingers were curling around it. She swung herself out over the water and planted her boots on the curve of the skull's forehead. Both hands on the hilt now, cranking down and back, extending until her legs were straight and straining rods, Ruby let a low, roaring cry rumble up from her gut to power her pull. She felt the blade slip, and then the bone gave. The skeleton groaned forward, its lower jaw and empty eye socket dipping toward the deep rib cage, and the sword slipped free. Ruby dropped into the pool with her cloak swirling around her, and for a terrible moment she felt trapped. The surface of the pool was ice, frosted white and thick, and she beat against it with her eyes wide and her lungs burning. She heard the voice of the beast again – cool and sure and cruel – but she let it drain away. She thrashed, scraping at the sides of the pool with her heels, and finally she was on the dry floor of the chamber again with the sword heavy in her hand.

She heard the wagons moving. There were voices trying to reach her through the stone, colliding hopelessly with each other to knot into a susurrus curtain of sound. She stood, soaking, and her hood fell over her face. Dazed and in pain, she made her way back toward the circle of sunlight. The corridor narrowed, and she felt herself doing the same. She shrank into a dot, the shadow of a cloud on the mountainside, the first snowflake of a long winter melting on macadam.

"Empress! Can you hear me!?" Michael's voice was clear. She was near the hole she had fallen through. "Take the thread!"

Ruby saw a silver cord hanging into the hole, brushing the floor of the cavern. It swayed strangely, descending straight down without touching the walls. She wrapped it around her fist and arm, but before she could begin to climb she was ascending into the sunlight. The cord was moving on its own, pulled up as if by a million hands. She blinked as she rose onto the snow, blinded by the intense glare. The group around her sighed and laughed relief for a moment, but then they fell into awed silence.

"Memnyr," someone said. Ruby thought it was Arturus.

Ruby squeezed her eyes shut and pressed her palms over them. When she could bear to open them again, the whole company had surrounded her. There was a woman looking down at her with eyes like beryl, her gaunt face framed by lank black hair.

"We have come to pledge our aid," said the woman, her mouth barely moving, "to the true Empress."

But it was not a woman before her. It was a disguise of sorts, attached to the black-striped body of great Arane. Her legs splayed out huge and bristling with cilia. Her body bulged above the snow-piled mud, turnip-shaped, its every undulation vulgar. Arane's horrible human puppet wore a glittering crown of spider's eyes. There were Weavers in the grass. She could feel them around her and hear their dreadful whispering. They writhed in the scant trees, swaying with the uppermost branches.

"Accept us," Arane continued. "Deliver us."

Ruby realized that she was holding her breath. She closed her eyes and steadied herself, and the silence around her persisted. There was something new and bright within her. She felt it surging in the heat of the Tidestone. She heard it pumping in her ears. It was a sweet taste on her tongue, old and familiar. It was a new strength. The deep force, perhaps, matured and integrated into her expanding consciousness. How long ago had she fallen into that cavern?

"Queen of the Weavers," Ruby said. From a great distance, she saw herself smiling. "Fight for me, and I will pledge this sword to you."

"On the sword then," Arane replied. "The Weavers swear."

She bowed, the human puppet's limbs swinging vacantly, and the Weavers nearby whispered their fealty with their pedipalps opening like slender fingers.

Midmorning was burning into noon. The swamp swayed around them, caressed by a chill wind from the sea that left the rushes murmuring. The wagons were stopped not far away, and beyond them stretched the Mire of Pearls. Pearlwater was just beyond, close enough that she could see the gleam of shields upon its walls. Distance had collapsed again, but time was stretching out across great reaches. She felt it extending, and it pulled her heart along with it, making her sick with the pain of the world. This suffering was perverse. Now Ruby looked down at the blade in her hand, and Michael put his paw on her shoulder as she did. She had the answer at last, and she fell into it without a second thought, letting it wrap around her like a new skin.

"The sword," Michael said. "Empress…"

"My old sword," she said, staring into its silvered blade. It was like glass, and she could see herself perfectly in it. Her hair was white. Her face was strong and regal with high cheekbones. Her mouth was thin and drawn tight between webs of laugh lines at its corners. "It was in the skull of a giant. Memnyr – the Mirrorblade. I remember, Michael."

Now they were crowding around her, mouse and cat, Weaver and weasel, a great circle of wondering eyes and gaping mouths, to gaze into the face of the blade. It showed all, the sky and the snow. Arane loomed in the reflection, large and terrible.

"Today," Arturus said from beside her, "the resistance is truly born."

"It was born with the Empress," William said, and the crowd muttered its agreement.

"It was born with the sword," Arane replied. "And with the sword it will end."

The Weavers had come from the north, winding through the trees, shrouded in unnatural shadow. At first, Timothy had ordered his men to arms. The host of Dimwood's warriors had drawn up before the Weavers, but there had been no violence. Arane appeared to present her proposal, and William and Arturus had argued that she had been working against the Nixies in secret for many months. No ally could be refused; that had been Michael's assertion, and all had agreed after some deliberation.

"We bind ourselves with silver thread," Arane had said. Ruby was amused by the incredible formality. "We will honor our pledge."

When Arane had crouched above the sinkhole to send a cord of silk to Ruby, the union of the two armies had become official.

"We thought they were Nixies at first," Michael explained, "or we would have pulled you up immediately. But I'm glad we didn't. What made you explore that chamber? Arturus pointed out that it might have been a kobold lair."

"The sword became available to me when I was ready for it," Ruby answered. "Ready for its truth. And its power."

The caravan continued into the Pearlmire, and now the supply wagon carried Weavers' egg sacs suspended from beneath the canopy. Arane wrapped all in her darkness, and twice the procession moved past Nixie patrols unseen. Beyond the delta at Thimblewand, the earth was dark and wet but firm. Snow lay in patches, running with meltwater that would freeze by moonrise, and coarse grasses strove up from beneath it. Here and there, a strange flower blossomed: a lucent bloom bobbing bright on a rigid stem with spiky leaves, its petals whirling around one another to cup a heart of fathomless purple. Great pearls rose from the shallow marsh, the light upon their surfaces making them seem to live and move. Some were cracked, and from these seeped a white fluid with which the riders watered their horses when they could. This pearl milk seemed to soothe the animals' fear of the Weavers, and it renewed their strength to push east through the sandy muck. Ruby spent nights gazing into Memnyr's blade, and as she studied her reflection and the subtle light that beamed from beneath its surface, the mists upon her mind blew mostly clear, and the landscape of her memory was revealed at last in visions.

Elizabeth's death loomed large. She had drowned, and there had been a collapse. A divide. Ruby had passed into a great darkness then, and through it fell a slant of pale light. The Tidestone burned between lusty lips and then was swallowed, and smoke choked her lungs in the dark. Then a great and wolfish weight had fallen upon her and penetrated her heart with awful force. The black sword had pierced her, opened her, drunk her blood. Wounded, she had fallen into the dark to escape, and she had found Melidora still unborn at the bottom. It would be Elizabeth's child as well as her own, a shared thought to comfort them, and she brought it life to stand against the dark that would have poisoned her.

The sword showed her all this in the light of the fading fire, and the Tidestone pulsed with the power of the vision.

The dark blade had broken and the wolf-weight lifted away, and Melidora had thrived as Ruby worked in the other world. The light of that red gem twinned in Memnyr's limpid silver, she remembered her home by the sea and the other sun rising as she walked in cedar woods.

Lothian, the Tidestone whispered, and she thought it was the most beautiful name she had ever heard.

She was the Halcyon, descending from outside, and she had lit the Everdim and cut the course of the Golrace. She had breathed life into the land and made it real. She saw reflected ages of rule, her ivory throne in the Cradle Spire, and she saw Michael and the host of Dimwood kneel before her. She had poured her passion onto the page, and she had felt Elizabeth's hand writing with her.

It was true, and it was terrifying, and the Mirrorblade denied her mercy.

Finally, it showed her a vision of sickness. The other world infected her, pushing a poison into her muscles to stop her movement. How old she had become! She saw her face sag when she frowned and felt the twist of age in her fingers. But her eyes twinkled still beneath the slightly drooping folds of her eyelids. She saw the return of the darkness, and she felt a grim hand moving within her mind. The dark blade was reforged, but it was a dream that pierced her this time. All monsters return. All dead horrors rise. Light can banish darkness, but it can never destroy it. She saw the wolf reborn – new flesh, but the same hunger. Her life shrank into the hands of machines, cold and blind. She fell again, seeking succor in the crush of the sea – the gray waters off the Bay of Mirrors. Melidora would heal her.

She realized that Melidora had become as real as the other world. There was no line between the two anymore. Worlds were in her mind, truth was broken, and now she had come to reclaim her erstwhile throne. She would rule again, the blade was sure of this. The Tidestone beat in agreement, her heart on a cord.

And then the blade showed her the image of a blue butterfly sunning atop a bobbing flower. All at once, there was a whole flutter of them, and when the last vision dimmed, they remained on the blade, a phantom that no one else could see.

Ruby told no one of her visions at first. She found that they hurt her deeply, and even thinking about them brought tears to her eyes and her heart into her throat. But she confided in Michael after the last, and he comforted her with his easy smile.

"No one can tell you who you are," he said to her, as if he'd read her mind, "not even Memnyr. Look at the way you have brought us together."

"Nothing is real," Ruby said, distant and disconsolate.

"But what *is* real?" Michael asked her, and she had to admit, at the last, that she did not know.

Twelve

Torrilelei

Pearlwater loomed ever closer. As the sun set on the fifth day since the caravan departed Dimwood, they arrived upon the Pearlshores at last. The great wharfs stretched east with tall-sailed ships standing out at anchor or docked while their crews roomed in the nearby apartments. The ships had come from older lands, bringing goods. There were sloops from Northover crewed by bears and foxes. Some had brought obsidian from beneath the ice while others had long-furred arthewags to sell. Farmland rolled northwest and into the Pearlmire, spread across manicured terraces. In the spring and summer, these would be green and flooded for deepwater rice.

At the east gate, the guards stopped Ruby's company and searched their wagons. Ruby found the presence of the deadly Weavers difficult to explain. Though the captain of the guard gushed praise for the Empress and bowed many times before her sword, there was an investigation into their arrival that took nearly a week. Pearlwater had been inundated with freed slaves as the Nixies dismantled the networks of safehouses and closed the secret routes they had taken out of bondage. The Empress of Nix had never been more powerful, and the city was pressed beneath a great weight of desperation. When Ruby's caravan was finally allowed to enter Pearlwater proper, there were given a royal welcome and led directly to the mayor's manor to be received.

The mayor of Pearlwater was named Warren. He was a rabbit with one lop ear and a star-shaped patch of black fur over his right eye. He insisted on meeting Ruby's whole company in person, with the exception of the Weavers.

"It is for the best," Arane said when Ruby expressed indignation. "We do not trust easily, and shall dislike moving about the city during the day."

In his spacious office, the mayor beamed from behind an enormous oak desk and ordered his assistant to serve coffee as the weary company entered. On the desk were a mortar and pestle and several tiny models of flying machines. In the corner of the room, a grandfather clock stood quiet, its face having been replaced with a chart showing phases of the moon. The mayor introduced himself to every soldier, one at a time, stopping to speak with the mouse for a particularly long moment.

"All are called," he said, kneeling to look the mouse in the eye, "and all must answer. Your bravery should serve as an example."

"Only doing my duty," the mouse replied, quivering with pride in spite of herself. "Ain't no job too big for a mouse."

Coffee arrived in prodigious quantities, presented on tin trays with an array of hot muffins and cakes. The mayor was generous, and this made Ruby nervous. At one point in time, she might not have been able to see the fear twisting beneath his openhandedness, but now it was as clear as her reflection in the silver blade of Memnyr.

"Your Majesty," he said, drumming his toes on the hardwood floor. "With introductions out of the way, I want to apologize for the excessive caution. You are welcome here, of course! And Lord Underbridge with you. All of you! A sight for me, indeed. We've been waiting for a long time to hear something from Dimwood."

"No apology needed, mayor," Ruby replied, in her new voice. It was deep, careworn, and husky, and it embarrassed her. "We've seen just how great the Nixie threat is. I'd have expected nothing less."

"Call me Warren, please," said the mayor. "And I thank you for your patience. We're under duress, pressed from all sides with Southunder now breathing in our ears." He stroked his one lop ear absently. "We've been waiting for the hammer to fall, but on the upside, we've been ready. Your arrival lifts such a weight from Pearlwater's heart. Now we can move. We can act! And I have a plan I think your Majesty shall approve of, if you'll hear it."

"Of course, Warren," Ruby said.

Michael added, "It's why we're here."

Warren's face lit up. His eyes were like pools of tree sap.

"Very good!" He went to the wall, where a map of Melidora hung with pins marking specific places. Ruby thought it looked as if a child had drawn it. She supposed she should not be surprised. "As I said, we've had South'nders here throwing their weight around, wearing Nixian sigils, and offering us protection. *Integration.* We know what that means, of course, and we've been keeping them waiting. We've been trying to prevent all-out conflict with Southunder, you see. If they move, then Hawkport will move. Each time they come, they are less civil. They're done with our hemming and hawing. I think the next visit will see them knocking down the gates and forcing their 'protection' on us regardless of what we have to say about it."

"You've done well stalling them," Ruby assured Warren, and he turned to smile at her as he pulled a pin from the corner of the map and stuck it into Lockwood Forest.

"Five times we tried to send word to Dimwood," Warren said, "but the Nixies hold the Mire of Pearls. They use the pearl milk to power themselves; I'm sure of it. It's almost as if they're taunting us –dancing near our borders, snatching up our messengers! When we sent riders north, they disappeared. How did you come to cross the Mire? Did you meet no resistance? Are Donchapel and Thimblewand yet free, for that matter?"

"An uncommon ally," Michael replied. "They can move in secret ways, going unseen even on open ground."

"The Weavers," Ruby said. "You shall have to trust them in this. They are our friends, Warren. Send your messengers to Dimwood under Arane's shadow."

"Arane," Warren said, and he shivered and tapped his foot twice. His ear went flat. "Desperate measures in desperate times! But we're glad for any help we can get." Now he touched the pin he'd placed.

"We will send word to Southunder that we're willing to start talks for integration, as they call it. It will take a few days to draw up our papers and then a few days more to meet with them and go over theirs. Such things take time, you know – hostile takeovers. Meanwhile, Dimwood can move on Hawkport." He put another pin where the Hawk River split from the Golrace. "The danger is getting pinned between them."

"And when Southunder discovers that Hawkport has been attacked?" Ruby asked.

Warren gave her a buck-toothed smile. "We'll have to work out some signal. Or perhaps we'll move on the same night. Southunder has been stockpiling flying machines. We've seen them testing them on clear mornings. While our delegates are meeting with Southunder's, a force will enter the hangars and liberate those flying machines. We'll turn them against their creators, and then Dimwood can move on Southunder. There'll be no time to coordinate their forces, see? And even if Southunder marches on us, which I expect, we'll be ready."

Ruby went to the map and looked at it with her chin in her hand, as if there might be some secret there that would advise her.

"Dimwood troops to shore up your own forces here," she said, thoughtfully, putting her finger on the map. "A larger force for Hawkport, and then someone to slip past Southunder's guards and steal flying machines. Perhaps a distraction could be set up for that night – something that will draw guards from the hangars."

"That could make the task a bit easier," Warren said.

"A fire," Arturus interjected, and the mayor gave him a complex look that appeared to mix excitement and annoyance. Sir Periwinkle stepped to the map, all the room behind him. The floor creaked. The air was thick with sweat and loud with the clanking of armor. "We set a fire in whatever place Southunder chooses to lodge your delegates. Light a fire, get the delegates out, and then perhaps more fires in strategic places. And that would also work as a signal, provided the Dimwood troops at Hawkport have a sharp-eyed lookout." He sent a hopeful glance to William.

"I'm capable of volunteering myself," William chided, "But this plan takes risks that I'm not sure I'm comfortable with, Empress. We can't know how Southunder will proceed with any talks or where they might house any delegates – if they were to at all. It's clear that cooperation is an amenity they are willing to do without if it comes to it."

"There's not much love lost between us, that's certain," Warren agreed, "but I do still have friends in power in Southunder. My father was a South'nder, and what's left of his good standing is likely all that's kept our walls intact through this. A fire is a good idea. I think it's the missing piece. I'll send word to Dimwood today, if your Majesty approves."

Ruby put her hand on Warren's shoulder. He was twitching in his clothes. His shoulder spasmed beneath her hand. She wondered how long he had been staring death in the face.

"I approve," she said. "But man yet mistakes his way. We have to prepare for the plan to collapse completely."

From the corner of her eye, she saw William cross his arms over his chest. She thought he was smiling.

"Of course," Warren said. "Wise words." With this, he cleared his throat and leaned in close. He smelled of lavender, honey, and cedar. "Are you absolutely sure that our messengers will be safe?"

"I'm sure." Ruby patted Warren's quivering shoulder. "Hope is a risk that must be run."

There ensued a discussion that consumed the rest of the day, in which Timothy showed himself to have a remarkable talent for planning. The company worked with the mayor and his anteater captains, marking the map with pins and, eventually, moving small tokens upon it to represent the forces that would participate in the battle. The mayor was so impressed with Timothy's knowledge and intuition that, by the time the newcomers were ready to be shown their quarters, Timothy had been named the leader of the assault upon the hangar. Who should join him remained undecided; the hangar was apparently well-guarded, and the mayor had little faith in the stealth of regular soldiers. Time and again, he asserted that Timothy's team should be specially trained.

"They shall need to sneak well, of course. Like thieves!" He insisted. "And they shall also need to know how to fly."

Ruby put in as much as she could, and she felt more confident than she had on the plains of Dunchapel, but hers was, by no means, a great military mind. She watched often from the wall, where she leaned with her arms crossed, marveling at the enthusiasm of the generals. William would serve as lookout for the large force they hoped Dimwood would send to Hawkport, and Arturus would help to coordinate that effort when the fires went up in Southunder. Warren and his selectmen would manage the diversion, while Michael would be among the captains of the force that would march on Southunder when the main battle began. Despite the fact that she carried Memnyr, none wanted to allow Ruby onto the battlefield, not even Michael. But she insisted, and they were forced to relent. She would liaise with the Weavers, as she and William alone remained unafraid of them.

"They will win Southunder for us," Ruby insisted. "See how you fear them? Imagine putting your terror into the hearts of your enemies."

"That we can imagine, Majesty," Warren said, chewing his lip with his large front teeth. "It's all the other things I can imagine about those spiders that give me pause."

They doubted and they were afraid, and all were anxious for the battle to begin, but they trusted their Empress in the end. She was not a strategist, but she inspired them. She was not how they would fight but why. They did not doubt *her*, they asserted, but their own ability to keep her safe.

"I would lose all of Pearlwater and the Cradle itself before you," Warren proclaimed, and Arturus was stirred to applaud. "You who are the heart of this world and the embodiment of the Halcyon's will."

With the initial plans made and William riding toward Dimwood with Arane, Ruby was taken to the Tower Imperial. On a hill near the quay stood the military complex of Bratcher Hall. The tower emerged from its center, bone-white and skirted with gold. Her apartments were on the top two floors, and they commanded a gorgeous panoramic view. Pearlwater stretched out below her in the late daylight, vast and crowded, with cramped houses lining marble-tiled streets. It was clear that the city had gained much through extensive trade with Southunder in the years before the Nixies. Electric streetlights lit manicured lawns and open markets extending into the lower east end's livestock district. Near the gate were towers clad in bronze and topped with crystal orbs. Factories sprawled across the west end, their high, flanged stacks trailing curls of steam, and beyond them were the great fisheries on the Hawk River.

Ruby leaned against the gilt railing, her Dimwood gown blowing behind her in a winter wind that brought the smells of baking from the shops below. She looked toward Lockwood with sadness cold upon her face. The aspens were bare now, and the Hearthmeade was browning under light snows. The gate at Seer's Knob was complete, a monstrous wall of black topped with iron spikes and horns. Further north, the Auburn Mountains vanished like a dream in the mist of distance. And to the south lay the sea, blue and endless, its deeps unsounded, glistening beneath a twist of gossamer clouds shaded with lavender. She could hear it creaming against the shore, the ceaseless murmur of its breath in the harbors. It was fished by kittiwakes even this late in the year. As evening darkened and the breeze grew cold, Ruby came in from the balcony and drew the shades over the glass doors. A shadow was on her heart, and she was just sitting down on her huge canopy bed to leaf through *The Secret of Dimwood* when there was a knock on the door.

Ruby rose and pulled on a jacket. When bidden, a guard opened her chamber door and announced Sir Arturus Merswin Periwinkle, after which Arturus entered with his nose down. He was wearing a long shirt that nearly touched the floor.

"Empress," Arturus began as Ruby poured him a drink. She'd developed quite a taste for Pearlwater's honeydew wine. "Pardon the intrusion."

"I'll find a way to endure," she joked, lamely. "How are you getting along? Where did they put you up?"

"Bratcher Hall," Arturus replied, "just below. They've gotten to thinking that I'm someone important. I have two rooms to myself."

"But you are," Ruby said. She offered him a smile. "Sir Arturus Merswin Periwinkle, yes? And a captain in my army."

He couldn't help but grin at this, though his eyes were dark. "I won't kid myself; that means nothing here. Not until my knights arrive, of course. I've heard no word…and I don't suppose I shall."

"It means a great deal to me," Ruby replied, "and, putting aside the chilly reception we got when we arrived, Pearlwater's bowing to me has hardly let up." She rolled her eyes. "Your knights have a ways to go, but you shouldn't give up hope for them. I haven't! It hadn't even occurred to me to. I know they will come, though I do understand your concern." She sipped her wine. It was sweet, and the spices burned pleasantly in her throat. The shadow on her heart lifted; she almost thought she could see it swirl out of her mouth when she exhaled. "I worry for Filwa and the Cholai."

"We shall have some unpopular allies," Arturus mused.

Ruby barely stifled a frown. "The Cholai are unfairly disliked. I know what is said of them; I'm remembering more and more every day. I feel that I have finally found all the pieces of myself, and now I know how to put them back together. This brings bad memories as well as good. They love this land, and they'll fight for it – as the Weavers will – and we will have enough swords when the day comes at last. We can't afford to be waspish now."

"Waspish," Arturus laughed. "No indeed. Nor fractious, nor insular. I'll be the first to accept any allies, whether be they spiders or Cholai. Even the swords of gnomes would be more swords than we have now."

Now Arturus took a sip of wine. His smile faded; he fell quiet, and he seemed to be woolgathering. Ruby watched the light from the electric lamps twinkling in the wells of his eyes.

"Forgive me, Empress. I have this dream," he said, suddenly distant. He was sitting in a stiff chair. He placed his wine glass on the pedestal beside it and sat back, crossing his legs. "I'm sitting in a room. There's nothing on the wall, and there are no windows. It's gray, and I'm on a gray bed, and the door opens. I can't tell who's there, but I know it's a man. And just his shape is terrible. The door opens on this square of light, and he's silhouetted against it. That's all that happens, but I always wake up thrashing in my bed. It's not the man or the door or the room; it's something bigger. It's what the man means. It's the waiting, you know? For the door to open."

Ruby mulled this over. She squared her jaw as if she was chewing Arturus's dream. It was familiar; the sword had shown it to her. It was a nightmare from beyond mere memory. She had lived it, and it had followed her here from the other world.

"For how long?" She finally asked.

"Ever since I was young. Longer than I can remember. And I found out that my father used to have a similar dream. I'm not given to nerves, you know. I'd never have become a knight if I were a coward! But perhaps the dream in combination with the excitement of the upcoming battle has left me more disturbed than usual. More anxious. That's why I came to you. Look how you healed Michael! And the fever at Robinegg. Not one of the refugees died on the way to Dimwood either, and some could barely walk out of their cages."

Ruby softened. "You want me to take the fear away?"

"Fear is such a horrible word." Arturus managed a chuckle. "I came to look upon you. To see your face and renew my faith, if you will. Because you are great, I know that the dream is just that. And because you are beautiful, I know that all who swear themselves to you will fight to their last breaths. And you *are* beautiful. You know I'm proud of you, Ruby." Now his voice became different. His Butterbush accent changed subtly. "I always was." He blinked at the floor, and then took up his glass to drain it. "Proud to serve you. Proud of how you've grown since they brought you to us, fair and small." His voice hadn't changed after all, of course. It was high and reedy, just as it had always been.

"Your loss," Ruby said, standing and crossing to him to put her bandaged hand on his shoulder. "Your loss at Gowspin was terrible. Maybe you haven't really grieved for that."

"You get the idea that I'm not really the grieving type," Arturus laughed.

"I do get that idea, yes," Ruby replied. "But you should acknowledge that. Honor it. For what it's worth, I'm sorry I couldn't stop it. Your house and your books. All William's paintings."

"The slaves and the prisoners. All our work." Arturus defied Ruby's expectations by remaining dry-eyed. "It ended badly, but it wasn't for nothing."

"Of course not."

Arturus sighed. She saw in him a heaviness she had not thought him capable of. He was disappointed in himself for being rattled by grief.

"Arthur," Ruby said, and now Arturus smiled at the Empress's name for him, "you are one of the strongest individuals I know. It's all right to be sad or to be afraid, because I know that nothing will take away your incredible strength." She knelt and took his paw. "If you've never been afraid, you don't know how strong you can be."

Arturus squeezed her hand. His little fingers were rough with calluses. His nails pressed dimples into her palm. Ruby was happy to see his old light return as he smiled.

"The ultimate enemy is fear," he said.

"And our enemies fear us," Ruby added.

"As well they should!" He leaped from his chair then and wrapped Ruby in as great an embrace as he could manage.

She felt his terrible strength as he squeezed and heard his small heart racing. When he stepped away, Ruby stood and ruffled the wild mass of fur on his head. Then, taking Memnyr from the stand beside her bed, she addressed him with playful formality.

"Kneel," she said, and he bowed to a knee. "You are to be my first captain." She touched him on the right shoulder with the flat of the Mirrorblade, and touched his left shoulder as she bade him rise. "This shall be official, though I know it's not a formal ceremony. Stand, Sir Arthur of Melidora."

Arturus stood and then bowed again with a comical flourish.

"I'm honored, Empress," Arturus said. Now his eyes were as bright as candles. It was a lark, of course, but it meant a lot to him. Ruby had hoped that it would. "A knight of Melidora! I can't wait to tell the guards in Bratcher Hall. Perhaps I'll be moved up into the tower!"

Ruby bent and kissed him lightly top of his head. "Perhaps you shall," she grinned. "Go with my confidence, Arthur. Take these words and hear them when the fear is greatest: your Empress believes in you."

Arthur bowed again, kissed her hand, and was gone with a word of praise and thanks.

"You do not fail, Empress."

Alone again, with Arturus's footsteps clicking away down the hall and his unfinished glass of honeydew wine warming on the pedestal, Ruby stood for a moment looking into the dark fireplace. She realized with a chuckle that the andirons were cast in a fanciful likeness of

Vanreah. It was chilly, and she considered trying to get a fire going. There was probably someone waiting downstairs whose job was to light her fires for her, but the bedroom began to feel small and the bitter howl of the wind outside stirred troubling memories. Wrapping her coat tight around her shoulders and buttoning it to her throat, she stepped into her slippers and placed Memnyr back on its stand. The crow carved on its golden cross guard seemed to watch her. The blade shimmered as if to entice her to stare into it. Her head spun, and a pain started in her stomach. She had spent too long before the sword. Its revelations were addictive, and even the thought of consulting it again made her feel sick. Still she longed to give in; it was only with great effort that she resisted that urge. Instead, she headed down three flights of stairs and stepped past the guards to knock on Michael's door.

Michael's single apartment was on the south side of the tower. Ruby stood at the oak doors, running her fingers over the gold plate on the key hole. There was music coming from inside. She could hear it very faintly: a gentle pluck of strings over a deep sounding board. She pressed her ear above the space between the door, trying to hear the song. An otter guard stood nearby, spine straight and fat tail curled around his left leg, stealing glances at Ruby when he thought she wasn't looking. She could smell the fire burning in Michael's fireplace and the perfume with which every room was regularly sprayed. Cupping her hand over her other ear, Ruby was just able to make out Michael's careful whisper.

Agmi dhu albūm ufdagofu ix aldūha

Dhu fīg egfadaowath inugséwa

Dhu olmgod dofhan ag gék'an wūha

Ix lahofu. dhu llasilman ix dallasma dim wéwa

Gulm héfulo dhagaollas dodfam dobga

Wagéf solwa baowan, xog-is axgēgwan,

Ogwa dahan mi hadofu waog gad ehig

Lug waog sodfwig aldefdug ugwan

For a moment, Ruby thought she understood the strange Melidoran words. They stood on the brink of her recollection, taunting her – a mirror in the sand, beckoning as she rowed for shore, her reflection in it distorted.

Ruby knocked again and Michael stopped abruptly. He came to the door with a small guitar in his paw, its neck flashing with mother-of-pearl.

"Empress!" Michael smiled. He stepped aside and let her in with a sweep of his arm. "The guard has been handling the door; I've had a number of visitors tonight. The mayor's aides, captains of the army. Consultations until well after bedtime. I imagine you've seen them as well!"

"They must not have considered my opinion worth seeking," Ruby replied. "Arthur came to see me, but no one else."

Michael nodded knowingly. "The air is stifling. Fear is on every face. As stubborn as he is, and as much as he'd like us to think he's impenetrable, he's not immune if he's got a heart."

"A warrior's heart," Ruby said. "Moreso than I! I walked my apartments for a while, trying out different chairs. Sleep may as well be in Northover now; I can't even see it from where I am."

"I've been trying to teach myself to play this." Michael held up the guitar and strummed a weak chord. "I'm all thumbs, but it helps to remember the old songs. My memory is coming back. I can feel it like a light spreading in my mind. It's no wonder Arturus came to you for an ear. You downplay your courage, but there are many who will rely on you when their warriors' hearts quail."

He placed the guitar on the large, velvet couch and pulled a chair close to the fire for Ruby. She sat, folding her gown neatly beneath her, her mouth dipping into a frown between her ruddy cheeks. There was sage burning in the fire. In the white heart of the flames, where the wood spit and whined upon the firedogs, a smudge stick put up rich, fragrant smoke. Ruby inhaled until the smell of cilantro and mugwort burned her nostrils. She sighed and closed her eyes, and after a few seconds of deep breathing, she began to relax. She was tired of being praised.

"Arthur complained of bad dreams," she said. "Have you had any?"

Now Michael pushed the logs with a poker, and orange embers whirled up into the dark, where the chimney opened on the tower's side.

"I rarely remember my dreams," he replied. "This was so even before the Forgetting. Even the ones I had in Robinegg – the fever dreams – are lost to me now, which is probably for the best." He looked at her with his brow raised. "Have you?"

"Sometimes I wonder whether or not the whole world is a dream," Ruby said, her tone wistful. "My life has been like a fantasy – a nightmare where faces keep changing. But then it can feel so real. The Forgetting is lifting away from me, and I'm looking on my past like a newborn, but none of it is real anymore. It's there. I feel it. I see it. But it's ephemeral. A shape in a cloud."

"Pareidolia," Michael smiled, and he crossed his legs and put his paws in his lap. "Seeing faces in clouds and such. It's all memory is, I suppose. The past is gone. Imaginary."

"I've been thinking about Elizabeth Lynn," Ruby hesitated to admit, "and how you asked me, 'what is real?' When you found me, I could hardly remember my name. We camped on the Fields of Silver, and my mind was wrapped in mist. You described memory as a land of many rivers crossed by bridges. I wondered what was real then, in that long confusion, and I still do even with my awareness returning. The sea was real, and the mirrors were real. The beach and the birds diving into the bay, the crush of waves on my back – it was real before I remembered anything. Wasn't it? Now here, in this place, with battle ahead of us, I feel like I should finally have an answer for you. But I don't. I can't trust what I see." She chuckled. "You've put quite a question to me, Lord Underbridge."

Michael held up his paws, guilty.

"You should expect as much when you ask advice of a priest." He laughed. "Questions are all we have. We aren't trained in answers. But I know what you mean. It's a deep matter that troubles you. I can tell you what I think if you're willing to listen to another of my stories."

"Always," Ruby said, feeling very grown up. "Please – preach to me."

Michael tilted his chin toward his chest, and now he was the one staring into the fire. He seemed to see something there that Ruby could not. She wondered then what else Michael might be burning in his smudge stick.

"This is a story about Torrilelei," Michael said. Then he sucked a deep breath and blew it out slowly, and he put his paws flat upon his thighs. When he continued, his voice was low and careful.

"Once there was a boy. He was wild and brave, and he dreamed and he loved and he trusted simply. He ran through the fields, and he walked in the forests, and he was known in the hills and the mountains. The wind carried his name to the sea, where the gulls still sing it. Even when he stood looking down into the utter deeps of the ocean or up at the calving shoulders of creeping glaciers, he found nothing in the world to fear.

"The boy met a wolf in the woods. Its pelt was as pale as moonlight, and its eyes were like embers of coal. It brought him to its den in a dark place, where creeks ran black and haunted and the cattails swayed like beckoning hands. Wolf-shapes followed them through the brambles, crouching in the shade of sagging sycamores. At the mouth of his cave, the wolf announced that he was the king of the woods and that his packmates were obliged to serve him.

"'I can give you any wish,' the wolf king said. He saw that the boy had a pure and valorous heart, and those, Empress, are hard to come by. 'Ask me now for whatever you want, and I and my pack will bring it to you.' The pack began to howl, saying 'Ask for the moon!' or 'Ask for the blood of the greatest elk in the woods!'

"But the boy said that such things were for wolves and that he would have no use for them. He asked for the one thing every boy his age wants, and that is never to have to grow up and abandon the freedom of his youth. Whether the wolf was who he claimed to be – whether his pack could even have brought the moon or killed the greatest elk – it is not said. But they were able to grant the boy's wish easily enough. They fell on him; he would not grow old, he would not forget his youth. They ate his pure and valorous heart, for that is the way of wolves.

"But the boy rose from the shade of the sycamores. He left the rushes beckoning and the dark water running into the heart of the earth. He left the living world and came before Torrilelei, the great ash, moon-white and beautiful in its garden. And there was the serpent gnawing at its bronze roots, and there was the stream of dew flowing from it, with which it watered the world. He ascended its mighty trunk, and in its branches he saw worlds and worlds within worlds. He saw the wolves in his own world, and he saw the heaven of his hopes connected to it as if by a spider's thread. And he saw in each world the seed of another, and it seemed to him that all the worlds were dreams that came from the same mind. He was not destroyed; he was only leaving one dream for the next. It is because of him that we know of the tree at all; he retained a strong bond with the world he had left even as he roamed the fields of eternal youth, and his descriptions of the tree have reached the ears of scholars and priests, who wrote them down."

Here Michael stopped and poured himself some water from an amethyst decanter beside him. He took a sip, cleared his throat, and then looked at Ruby with a smile that comforted her.

"Many branches," he said, "one tree. Separate but together, each nourished by the other – dreams and other worlds. All accessible to some extent – made and then not made by a single mind.

"I've been thinking about that boy a lot since my memory began to return. He went on to weave new worlds as a dream collector. He is a symbol of the well of souls, and sometimes I can feel him in my dreams." He smiled a tight smile and then added with a wink, "When I remember them, of course."

The fire was going out. Michael left the poker where it was and let the scraps of the logs collapse into white ash. Embers glared from beneath the remains of the smudge stick, sullen and hostile. Somewhere, the dawn was growing. Light was cascading down mountainsides and up into the sky to tint the horizon with gold-flecked blood. Across green fields, the shadows were shrinking. Ruby wondered where. In what world was the sun rising? It was dark in Melidora.

"I think it *is* about listening after all," she said.

"What's that?" Michael was picking up the small guitar and plucking the strings gently, tuning it.

"Everything," Ruby replied. "Who I am. What's real."

Michael only nodded and picked a somber arpeggio. She sat with Michael while he played, and he sang her the song he had been practicing before. He had to stop often to check his fingering, form

Melidoran was difficult and somewhat monotonous to listen to after even two verses, but Ruby understood it, and that was what mattered. She had always understood it. Melidoran was her language. It always had been.

It was not yet light when Arturus returned to Ruby's apartments. He found her propped against a settee in the small living room, her gown askew and her hands caressing Memnyr's silk-wrapped handle. She had not slept. He called her name, but it was only when he put his paw on her arm that she took any notice of him. She started and pulled the sword against her chest covetously. Her wild expression faded first into a smile and then into a look of concern when she realized what was going on.

"Begging your pardon, Empress," Arturus said, his eyes wide with embarrassment. "I didn't mean to startle you. Word's in the barracks that the Cholai arrived last night. Came over the Black Mountains, I heard!"

With Arturus's help, Ruby got to her feet. The sword sagged in her arms like a murder victim.

"Excellent news! I'll get my coat," she said, shaking her head clear of visions. "Will you show me the way?"

"I don't know that I'm any less likely to go wrong than you," Arturus said. "I'm a norther! I'm just as new here. I've brought a guard who knows where they're being held."

"Held?" Ruby paused with one foot in a slipper.

"It seems there are some concerns about safety with them, Empress," Arturus explained. He ducked his head, trying to hide his outrage with sudden, cloying correctness. Ruby decided that euphemisms were not Arturus's strong suit. "From what I heard, they're being housed near the gate in dugouts with light guard presence. And they've been asking after you."

"I shall clash with the mayor," Ruby said, sadly.

"Unpopular allies," Arturus said. He made a show of shaking his head.

Ruby stormed for the door. "We'll see about that."

Thirteen

Warren

Ruby left the Tower Imperial in full armor. She considered stopping to wake Michael, but he had been through so much. She couldn't bear to disturb him.

There was mist on Pearlwater. Beneath it, the streets were wet and the lamp standards burned fraying halos. A jackal led her down the hill in funereal silence. Arturus trailed them at a jog. Houses huddled close along the streets, shrouded in the stillness. They followed the main road north and then turned onto a broader lane where trees looked down over the cobblestones. They were bare and black in their winter sleep, and the light pouring through the mist behind them split into fantastic rays between their branches. A frigid drizzle began, and Ruby shivered as ice crystals bit the back of her neck.

They passed through a park. Pearlwater opened in the east to let Lockwood Forest spill in, virtually uncontained. Watchtowers stood like hierophants in the open space, draped in fog. Beyond the park, the street collapsed into a narrow choke just wide enough for a single individual to pass through on foot. Guards stood all about, armed and armored, and the jackal nodded to each of them. They stood rail-straight as Ruby passed. On this approach to the gate, the street was new blacktop. Whether the structures lining it were homes or warehouses, Ruby could not be sure. They squatted, shuttered like crypts. Perhaps that was what they were.

At last, the gate was before them, rearing up atop a hill and pressed close against the southern edge of Lockwood. Here, cut into the low side of the hill, were lines of crude houses. Soldiers walked the mud shelf, looking into the occasional milky window, but they passed infrequently and seemed disinterested in their work. Though some lights burned in those windows, most of the Cholai were standing outside in the clay. Their wagons were crammed into a small space across the street, and rams and wisents milled about unfettered. There was little order. Ruby saw Benjamin and Moira moving through the crowds trying to bring their people together in one place. She and Arturus approached the dugouts, and two soldiers hurried to meet her.

"Your Majesty."

They bowed, and the larger of the two came forward.

"These *k'ēnan* arrived last night," he said, his face blank. "We're still trying to get them to stay in their homes. Most of them are unhappy with the lodging we've provided. Did the mayor send you, ma'am?"

"*K'ēnan*, eh?" Arturus said. His fur ruffled, he bellied up to the big one. "You use that kind of talk around them?"

Ruby put her hands on her hips.

"The mayor did not send me," she said, wearing a moue of disdain. "Let these Cholai go where they wish. They'll not stay here."

The soldiers looked at each other, wide eyes shining in the rain. The stocky one was black or brown beneath his heavy plate. Ruby thought he might be a wolverine. His partner on duty was unmistakably a moonrat. He looked positively miserable, his fur dripping wet on his wiry frame, and his armor was too large for him.

"You," Ruby turned to the rat. "You're not from Pearlwater."

"No, Empress," the rat stammered. "Driftgate. In Northover."

"But you were born on the fields. Butterbush, yes?"

"Well, I left the caravans at an early age. It was my choice, you know. We all got one. And I've been settled so long I barely remember my wandering days."

The wolverine made a face and Arturus looked at him with his brow raised.

"Free them," Ruby said.

Before she could go on, Benjamin appeared waving to her and shouting. He crossed the street and pushed between the two guards to greet her with an embrace, and Filwa was behind him.

"Look at you in your high collar and cape!" Benjamin said with a shining smile. "I can hardly believe this is the waif we found on the Silvermoor. You were sick and hungry, and you smelled like a drowned dog. Time has been funny lately, hasn't it? You're grown now. Queenly! The Empress, of course. Who else would be decked out like that?" He looked Arturus over with an approving eye, and Arturus made an exaggerated bow.

"Pleased to make your acquaintance, kind sir," he said.

Filwa had far less energy. Leaning on a black ash cane, she took Ruby's hand in her paw. She didn't need to speak to show her gratitude – it was all in her eyes.

"Please," said the rat, stepping forward. "Stay behind the lines. Empress, I apologize. They aren't used to being confined by boundaries."

"No respect for authority," the wolverine grumbled, and he stepped forward with his glaive to push Filwa and Benjamin aside. Arturus made a short charge forward, grabbing the polearm and shouldering the wolverine back with enough force to make the soldier stumble.

"Stop," Ruby barked, and again the guards were struck dumb.

"You'd herd them into the mud while their livestock walk in the streets?" Arturus growled. He pulled the wolverine's glaive from his paws and dropped it disdainfully onto the paving stones. Then he aimed a scowl at the rat. "Do you not see your face among them, soldier? You call them thieves, and you complain of their disrespect. Let them free."

Ruby put a steadying hand on Arturus's shoulder piece and searched the wolverine's face. He was trembling on the verge of fury.

"There's no need for a fight," she said. "No one's in trouble. I called for the Cholai; they're here to help. We are equals here."

The wolverine started to say something about the mayor, but the moonrat stopped him.

"We've not many places left to house them," he said, looking defeated, "unless they want to stay in the storehouses at the docks with the spiders."

"And they steal," the wolverine insisted. "Everyone knows that!"

"If we can't stick together," Ruby said, "then all is lost. There's no debating. The Cholai are our allies."

Now she knelt and spoke to Benjamin. He was harried and tired, but he had lost none of his warmth. He looked on her as a father might.

"Are your people safe here?" she asked. "Are you comfortable? I'll be going right to the mayor about finding a place for you, and I'm sending all the guards away."

"We were camped beside the Owof," Benjamin said. "We'd like to return there if we could." Ruby was amazed when he looked to the soldiers as if for permission. "City confines feel unnatural, see? Lockwood has its dangers, but we've come through worse territory. We'd prefer to risk camping to being cooped up."

An idea occurred to Ruby then, and she stood with a smile on her face. She patted Benjamin on the shoulder.

"This will be done," she told the soldiers. "Let them all out. And, Benjamin, I wonder if you would meet the mayor with me once you're all settled."

"Lots to be done," Benjamin replied. "New soldiers, yes. And hangers-on, I admit. Much hospitality has been shown us here, despite our numbers, comparatively speaking. I know how it looks, but we've seen worse." Now he addressed the soldiers. He seemed pleased with the opportunity to talk to them without being told to get back. "It can't have been easy to contain us. But then we dislike being contained. You see? So we'll hang on – it's what we do – and you'll see that we'll fight beside you when we must. Our captors, yes, bearing no ill will." Now he looked directly at the moonrat guard. "*And* our brothers."

Clearing the dugouts was a task that took all morning, and it was not made easier by scuffles between angry soldiers and indignant Cholai. The fog lifted, and the light rain became a downpour that churned the hill's soft clay to runny mud that sucked off boots and sank wagons. Ruby insisted upon staying until the whole great band was through the north gate and the business of reestablishing their camp near the quiet mouth of the Owof was finished. Arturus forbade her much muddy work, preferring to wade into the muck himself and shout orders. He was as strong as a wisent and proud to show it, and he seemed to see every streak of clay through his fur as a mark of honor akin to a war wound. By noon, the gates were closed and Sir Periwinkle was a matted mess of knots hung with gobs of dried mud and clay. He had a callus on his left paw that had been left bleeding from rope burn, and he showed it to Ruby laughing.

"It's no fang puncture," he said, "but now we're brother and sister in damaged paws!"

Michael arrived early, to the delight of Benjamin and Moira, and he immediately established himself as a mediator between the Cholai and the Pearlwater soldiers. Ruby was impressed by his unflappable gentleness, because of which he shone all the more in comparison to Arturus's combative approach to every problem regardless of its magnitude. He was clearly still tired, and his limp had taken an odd twist, though it seemed to be improving. As he stood between a fox marshal and a young Cholai hedgehog accused of cutting a soldier's purse, Ruby wondered if he would ever recover from the torment to which she'd left him at Owl's Head. Fearless, he put his paw on the fox's breastplate. This stopped the officer long enough for the hedgehog to place the purse he'd lifted into Michael's other paw. The Cholai boy went into the jailhouse at Pearlweather Hall instead of an unmarked pit in a potter's field.

At noon, they were on the wall looking over the palisade and the ill-kept bailey, beneath which the motte hill had partially collapsed years ago. All that remained of ancient Pearlwater Keep was a field of mossy stones. Beyond, the Owof flowed through a system of sluices and wound through the eastern city to the sea. Pressing her back to the bare, white points of the wall's timbers, Ruby saw the canals spreading south in a gleaming network, the banks studded with pearls harvested from the Owof's famous oysters. This was the oldest part of the city, and the structures sagged with a century's weight, dark with peeling paint, their windows warped. The streets were too narrow for carriages; traffic moved on the water.

Pearlwater's beaver gondoliers were renowned for their poetry. They poled their gondolas easily along the shallower routes, the best of them reciting from the works of the great northern poets. In deeper water, heavy craft carrying freight rowed out into the harbor, and those boatmen were fond of bawdier verse.

Michael must have seen something in Ruby as she stared toward the ocean. He propped himself against the iron rail before them and said, "You certainly do get yourself into some unusual situations early in the morning." Then he sent her an odd wink, and Ruby blushed.

"It wasn't even light out when Arturus came to get me," she said.

"You couldn't have woken me with a cannon shot," Michael replied. "You must have become a light sleeper." Now he was looking at her, searching her face for something. All of a sudden, Ruby didn't like the light in his eyes. "Or perhaps you weren't sleeping."

There was a cry down below. Arturus was pushing Pearlwater's chief healer out of the way to get to a Cholai woman who was trapped under a fallen ram.

"I told you that sleep was far from me," was Ruby's answer, and she hated it as it left her lips.

"Memnyr," Michael said, simply. "What has it shown you?"

"Nothing," Ruby lied. "Nothing that will help us in the coming days. My father's death. Moving across town with my mother. Arturus spoke of a man in his dreams. A man who opens a door. He watches me from the sword; his eyes are terrible. Wanting. He reaches out and he owns me. It's as simple as a touch...and I'm his."

"He can't tell you who you are."

"Neither can I tell him. He's a ghost. He doesn't listen." Ruby sighed and turned back to watch Arturus trying to lift the ram all by himself. It was easily seven feet tall – a Great Ram from Moonwood, where the Cholai stayed when they felt the need to stay somewhere.

"The sword doesn't think," Michael explained. "It just shows. You're the one who has to make sense of it. What happens when you stop watching it? When you stop listening?"

Ruby was about to tell him about Memnyr's voice in her head. She started to say that the Tidestone and the sword were part of the same terrible, whispering entity, but the deputy mayor called up to her from the wreck of the dugouts.

"Empress Ruby!" Alhagan was a young porcupine in a flat-collared frock and a silk hat that was much too big for him. He had been of little help during the move; he'd objected weakly to relocating the Cholai, and had rolled over without complaint when Ruby overrode him. Then he had disappeared into the mayor's manor to sulk. Now here he was shouting alarm, his long mat of quills quivering as he puffed at the bottom of a ladder. Ruby thought they might start to rattle against each other.

Michael frowned as Alhagan continued. "No word from the mayor. We're going to break down his door."

Warren had made no appearance at the gate, and messengers sent to his home and to his office reported neither sight nor sound of him in response to their calls. Ruby looked to Michael, embarrassed that she hadn't been more concerned before now. They descended the ladder, where Arturus met them.

"Let me handle that," said the guinea pig, barely recognizable now beneath a layer of drying mud. "No need to make things more difficult than they need to be."

"Tensions are high here, Alhagan," Michael agreed. "This morning has been difficult for most of the north guard as well as the Cholai. Some of the west guard were volunteering here, too. As complicated as this whole situation already is, I think it's best not to go ringing the alarm bells until we know exactly what's going on."

Alhagan nodded and looked sullen.

"His brother got into the house with a key," he said, nearly whispering now. "Warren wasn't there. I have his personal guard standing by at his office with a battering ram, but if we can do this more quietly, I suppose we should."

He led them past the guardhouses toward the square and added, with a growl, "He wouldn't approve of any of this, you know! Setting up that camp in Lockwood is inviting trouble. The wanderers have been sending patrols out well beyond our own. They're risking capture!" Alhagan said *wanderers* as if he was spitting out a bad bite of food.

"That's over and done with," Ruby said. "Good Alhagan, let's not snipe at each other. There are greater concerns now."

Alhagan flicked his whiskers and sniffed as if he had more to say, but he bit his tongue. The four continued down the main road at the fastest waddle Alhagan could manage without looking as if he was in a hurry to get anywhere. The group attracted some attention from a crowd of churchgoers who were headed to lunch after the morning service; Ruby heard them chattering amongst each other about the *k'ēnan* that were being moved out of the city.

"It will be good to have them out," said one. "We won't have to worry about having our homes burglarized! I bought a knife as soon as I heard they'd arrived."

"We should never have granted them asylum," another replied. "They certainly wouldn't have done the same for us!"

"But maybe they'll be of some use," a third laughed. "We could throw them in front of the South'nders' swords."

The door to Warren's office was made of white pine and had no keyhole on the outside. It stood inconspicuous outside a much larger office with elaborately carved double doors, beside which soldiers stood with pikes and high-crested helmets. The only thing to distinguish it from the other plain doors in the hall was the team of armored guards gathered outside it with a small ramming pole. They fell into formation as Ruby and the others approached, and Alhagan waved them away. He shuffled to the door and leaned against it almost lovingly, his spiny cheek and paw pressed to the wood.

"Mayor Warren," he crooned. "Are you there? It's Alhagan, sir." He tapped on the door with his knuckles. "Are you there? We're going to push the door in, sir. If you can hear me, please try to stand back."

There was no reply from inside. Alhagan shook his head and looked at Ruby with his beady eyes cast in shadow. The doubt and the pain on his face were striking; they made him look many years older than he must have been. His shoulders drooped, his tail curled up under his broad pile of white-striped quills. Alhagan pushed himself away from the door and motioned to Arturus, who strode to the door tossing his head as if he had a lion's mane.

Arturus tried the knob just to be sure, and when it did not turn he put both paws on the door and stepped back. His knees bent, his face suddenly twisting into a mask of terrible anger, Arturus lunged against the door, driving his shoulder into it just above the knob. For a moment, nothing happened. Arturus pumped his legs, biting his lip over a groan, and then the jamb splintered and he went charging into the room as the door flew open.

Warren's office was immaculate. The mortar and pestle were exactly as they had been, and his flying machines were lined up facing the desk's edge. The single hand of the grandfather clock was indicating *NEW MOON*. The silence as the four filed into the room seemed to be charged with some frigid energy. Ruby could almost see it coursing through the air, rippling into the wood surfaces and the carpet. She could see her breath here; the mayor's stove had been cold for some time. Alhagan rounded the desk and made a little noise from the pit of his throat. He backed away from Warren's supine body where it lay on the floor, eyes staring almost wistfully, his one lop ear pinned behind his head. There was a teacup on its side beside him, and what remained of its contents pooled into a black stain on the carpet. Ruby looked at him for a moment, briefly afraid that she might smile. He looked peaceful – happy even. His eyes twinkled, and she imagined him lying on a hillside looking up at the stars. Then Michael knelt over Warren and brushed his eyes closed, and Ruby had to look away.

"Warren," Alhagan was saying. "Oh, Warren."

"Poisoned," Arturus pointed out.

"A dreadful loss," Michael said, at once somber and strong. Ruby put her arms around him and pushed her face into his fur as she had on the Fields of Silver. "Our day has just begun."

Save for his aides and the occasional high-ranking soldier or official, no one had access to the mayor's office. He did most business in his larger office, and he only made appointments through his secretary. Alhagan deduced that it must have been one of Warren's aides that had poisoned him, and Michael agreed.

"Southunder has operatives here," he said. "We have to assume that much."

"That means we have to assume they know about our plan," Arturus added. "In that case, it won't be long before they're storming. It's how the Nixies took Southunder to begin with, I hear. We should brace for it."

"They'll be ready," Ruby said. "They'll fall on Pearlwater with all their force."

"I won't back down now," Alhagan huffed. He was pacing. "I won't give Pearlwater over. That's just what they want! It's what they've always wanted. It can't be over. Not like this." He stopped and thumped the floor with his tail. His jaw worked, but he couldn't speak for a moment. Then he puffed a breath through his twitching nose and said, "We'll arm up. Gate the sluices, send every available soldier to the north gate, and let the spiders out. The Cholai will have to fall in with us; or else they can form a front line before the gate, if they feel inclined to sacrifice themselves."

"Now wait," Ruby said. "We don't have to give up the plan just because they might know about it. We can change it. The Cholai have only just arrived. Let's think about this for a moment." She turned toward the door so she didn't have to see Warren's body. It was suddenly hot, but she remained in her large coat and cape; it didn't feel right to remove them here. "We could pretend to give up the plan. Turn ourselves over to Southunder, and let them install whatever puppet they intended to lead in…" she choked a bit, finding it difficult to speak his name, "…in Warren's stead." Would he rise, dead and angry? Would saying his name give him power to move his poison-burned corpse? Ruby waited silently for Warren to stand up from behind his desk.

"Yes," Arturus replied. Ruby was aghast to see him smiling. "Tell the soldiers to stand down. Pretend to give up; submit to Southunder and, while they're busy working out what to do with us, we send the Cholai in to cut their legs out from under them."

"There will be no working out," Alhagan said. "They'll throw us in prison and they'll storm in here and burn the mayoral manor down. Even if the Cholai were to follow my orders, they would be walking into their own deaths. And we haven't heard anything from William or Dimwood! The plan cannot continue, but I won't surrender. I…I'm the mayor now, as terrifying as that is to say. And I won't hand Pearlwater over to the South'nders under any circumstances."

"It's likely that whoever betrayed Warren was promised mayorship by Southunder," Michael said. "And if that individual is one of the aides, he may well have been ordered to assassinate you, too, Alhagan. We have to act quickly to take the reins in this situation, or we'll risk losing Pearlwater altogether, and then Dimwood is doomed whether they arrive to win the fight in Hawkport or not. If we stand and fight, we abandon Dimwood. But if we go ahead with the plan, we can still salvage this resistance."

"We have allies Southunder doesn't know about," Arturus said. "And we have to use what they don't know against them. You know it's the only way."

Alhagan couldn't decide. Minutes passed like hours, extended to hellish frontiers of tension by the slow disfigurement of time. The heat became stifling, and Ruby struggled to keep her breathing even. It had been cold when they broke in. She looked at the stove, expecting to see it burning, but its barrel was dark. A delicate filigree of frost was spreading across the outside of Warren's bay windows.

At last, Alhagan relented. Arturus assured him that he wouldn't really be surrendering. Michael sought to praise him for his bravery in his new position, but he would have none of that.

"I won't be half the mayor that Warren was," he said, nearly sobbing. "But I'll die for Pearlwater – it may be all I can do for her now. Tell the troops to stand down."

They called a meeting of the mayor's aides, and posted the captain of his personal guard outside Warren's office. It made Ruby heartsick to leave the poor rabbit lying on the knotted pile, but she agreed that he should not be removed until a decision had been made about the ramifications of carting him out in full sight of everyone.

The aides met in Alhagan's smaller office, and among them was the ermine Timothy, who had earned Warren's trust so quickly. With him came Castor and his brother, beavers from the east and representatives of the Gondolier's Guild. Finally, Roger, a mink, and a lame opossum named Henry crowded into the space around Alhagan's desk, which was plain and bare except for an inkwell and a gorgeous rilla quill pen. Michael closed the door and locked it, and Ruby thought she felt the air rush out of the room.

"We're faced with a crisis," Alhagan began. Then he took a deep breath. Ruby watched as he gathered his strength before he said, "The mayor – Warren – is dead."

This announcement was met with stunned silence. Roger's peg-toothed mouth dropped open. Castor leaned against the wall and shook his head.

"He was poisoned," Alhagan continued. "And our plan is scuttled. We have no choice but to submit." Amid protestation from the aides, Alhagan raised his paw. "This is my first and last act as your new mayor. You've all served with great dignity, and Pearlwater thanks you. Warren thanks you. I'm sure you understand the need to handle this situation with the greatest tact and decorum. Warren will be interred in the mayoral gardens tonight, and we will be going to Southunder tomorrow morning with the terms of our surrender."

"But Dimwood!" Henry wheezed. He was propped up on a heavy walking stick. Most of his whiskers were burned to his snout.

"Will we leave them at the mercy of the Empress?" asked Roger, in an elegiac tone.

"We've heard no word from Dimwood," Ruby interjected. "William never reached them, it seems. Our plan was doomed from the start."

"If Southunder suspects any trickery, they will crush us quickly and brutally," said Castor, and suspicious eyes fell on him immediately. Even his brother looked at him askance. Castor shifted on his feet. "Well, won't they? They'll expect collateral. We know they don't trust us, and they have to know what we were planning. What will we give them to prove that we truly mean to surrender?"

In Ruby's mind, Castor became a wicked figure. She saw guilt hanging around his neck like a noose, and now he was stepping onto a stool and throwing the rope over a rafter. In the instant it took for him to ask this question, she loathed him completely.

"Me," she said. "I will go before their Nixian lord. I'll give myself up. If that doesn't convince them, then I'm sure that nothing will."

Once, Lockwood Forest spanned the whole of the Eastfair from Halcya to the Pearlshores and from the Auburn Mountains to the Bay of Mirrors. The gnomes' three eastern kingdoms were failing in those days, and Southunder was the last great gnomish city. Then there was a long winter; snow fell for three seasons, and great mountains of ice carved down to mar the face of the east. Lockwood shrank, its green walls broken, and the gnomes were forced to retreat into Lampblack. Southunder froze, abandoned, and the dead lay preserved in its streets until the winter's end. Spring dawned, and Southunder sweltered in the new heat, and while gnomish bodies rotted in that city not even the darkest things would go near it. It fell under a curse of neglect, and it was eventually destroyed completely in Alamandra's apocalyptic campaign to cleanse Melidora of evil. A new capital was built upon the ruins, but the builders never completed it, and none remember who they were. They died out or went away, and for a long time the new Southunder lay silent.

In stillness, hope grew. People came out of the old woods and settled along the Owof. In time, they found the unfinished city, and they brought life to it where there had been only shadow and fear for so long.

They were beavers and minks and otter shrews, and when they had built Southunder into a place of deep peace and great beauty, they moved south to found the river city of Pearlwater.

Then the Nixies came, and they were without a leader, and they appeared benevolent at first. Southunder learned of steam and coal, and they learned to harness the dangerous power of electricity. The city became a hub of industry, but there were those who believed that the gifts of the Nixies stirred up old gnomish ghosts. The Nixies left Southunder suddenly, and in the days soon after there was a man born there who, with his son Dalon, would bring to the city the means to surpass all others. Building on Nixian knowledge, Martan Thorn Bratcher invented the first working flying machine.

Martan was a scholar, a warrior, and a mystic with a powerful influence over the lord of Southunder at the time. He made his first flying machines to deliver bombs, and he armed them with copper-barreled carbines. Envious and bitter for reasons he kept secret even from Dalon, Martan gave his flying machines away as weapons, demanding they be used to raze Pearlwater to the ground.

It was no surprise to most how Martan met his end. A cruel man, he was killed cruelly himself before he could see his war machines in use. But the war went on, and his evil persisted in the doom that came to Pearlwater. It was raked to bits and burned, as he had wanted. But the slaughter was too great. The flying machines were too effective. In the aftermath, the lord of Southunder walked through the ruins of Pearlwater grieving, for the massacre had been total and the canals ran dark with blood and ash. He forbade the use of flying machines for war ever again, and for a while this law held. Pearlwater was left empty, like the gnomish capital of Southunder, and it was a long time before anyone set foot beyond its shattered gates.

But memory fades. Darkness swallows all a bit at a time. Pearlwater was renewed, fresh with ghosts and a curse of its own to match Southunder's, and weapons returned to the wings of Martan Bratcher's flying machines until the rise of the Empress of Nix.

Warren Dallaxīm was buried with his collection of hand-designed model flying machines as well as his mortar and pestle and his mayoral seal in a public ceremony that lasted from dusk until midnight. The candle-lit service moved south in a procession from Warren's house and then looped through West Park to Canal Lodge, following the mayor's daily walk. There it became a party, as per Warren's wishes. There were bands and dancing songs, but the affair remained somber. Grief weighed spirits down, of course, but there was a shadow of fear moving among the crowd as well. Ruby watched it prowling for hearts, its shoulders low, leaving panic swelling perilously behind it. Alhagan gave three speeches, each more passionate than the last. He begged the people to keep hope alive in the city, but he didn't tell them of the plan. It had been decided that he shouldn't. Ruby addressed the crowd to a cool reception; she was nervous, and that impeded her demonstration of grief, and she thought she came away looking selfish.

Most of the Cholai remained in their large camp, but a few caravan leaders attended the funeral in a representative capacity. They were forced to stand at the back of the procession. Pearlwater's fear poured over them; they were easy targets, and they did not retaliate. They told none but Ruby and Michael that there was another funeral being held in the thick of the forest that night – a smaller one – for the fortuneteller Leora.

"She died in the Black Mountains, as many did," Benjamin had told Ruby early in the day, calm as a dove. "But she went sleeping, and she was peaceful. Quiet. Just resting. No pass through the Black Mountains they say, and it was true. We all know. But the east is sealed up tight; we had to make one, and you might call it Leora's Pass. We can put it on a map if you want to honor her. She would like that, probably. She will like that when she is born again."

The night deepened. The moon refused to show anything but her cold, silver crown. The snow fell as gray as ash; when Warren was in his crypt and the funeral party dispersed, it was whirling up into a blizzard. The canals began to frost over, and ice-cutter boats and salters were set afloat. Though Alhagan thought it was risky, Ruby and Michael spent the rest of the night in the Cholai camp. They honored Leora as best they could, for they hadn't known her well, offering songs and burning hemlock at her grave in the foothills of the Black Mountains. Moira gave Ruby a scabbard wrapped with strips of old cloth to hide the Mirrorblade. They disguised its long hilt with similar rags, and decorated the hanging tatters with beads of painted bone.

"Pretty sure only you could wield this sword," she said, "but that won't keep no one from trying to take it. Be sure of that."

In the morning, snow was piled knee-high. Wrapped in whale skin and blue-silver greatcoats, Ruby and Michael set out into Lockwood unescorted. The leafless aspens looked sick and frangible protruding from the snow. Their tops scraped up uselessly toward the copper-dim sky, rocking as if in prayer. They followed the ash-blond Owof as it pushed clots of leaves downstream, and deer moved in the hush far to the north, passing in and out of Lockwood from the Hearthemeade lawn. Ruby felt the deep force moving in her, and for a long time she was afraid of it. But there was something new in her mind, and as the morning went on, she grew accustomed to the burgeoning feeling of strength. Ruby felt not just old but depressingly mature.

"Not that I've known him for too long," Michael said as they trudged up a hill, "but I think William would disapprove of this plan. Too much of a gamble. Yes, Empress?"

"Yes," Ruby laughed. "Too many variables." She breathed a puff of dwindling mist. "I hope he's arrived safely at Hawkport."

"I have a feeling that he has," Michael replied.

"Do you?" Ruby was surprised by his optimism. "And what gives you that feeling?"

"The Halcyon doesn't fail," Michael said, simply. He shrugged, as if no further explanation was necessary. "Warren's death, while tragic, hasn't changed the plan he helped to develop. It has only sweetened it…perhaps that is an apt expression. It has increased the element of surprise. I trust completely, Empress. I trust you and I trust the Halcyon, which calms the seas. These are dark waters, and treacherous, but the Halcyon shall not fail. Do you doubt?"

"No," Ruby said. "Perhaps I have the same feeling about William. But if he has arrived, maybe it would be best to keep that the closest of secrets."

"Maybe indeed," said Michael, and he took a swig of coffee from his canteen.

The day warmed quickly. Light grew in the east, and then the sun was overhead. Clouds barred its disc, frustrating its efforts to melt the snow so that the ground would freeze when night fell. Southunder rose in the near distance, its towers decorated with mallow tiles and long, red-black shingles. They ascended the hill away from the river now, and the woods grew deep and thick with kettle-thorn, dogwood and lesser celandine where the snow was thin. It was here that the rangers found them.

A big pangolin came over a rise from the south, and then a large-eyed creature with the loose flaps of a patagium wrinkled beneath his arms. More appeared from the snow itself, or so it seemed, stepping like phantoms from among the naked trees. Ruby thought of the bearcat and the surprised expression he had worn as he cocked his head so long ago. She hadn't seen the arc of blood, but she had seen the life pour from his eyes before he collapsed. The warriors that approached to surround them now were no inexperienced scouts. The scars on their bodies, the notches on their light armor, and the deadly cold of their countenances marked them as career killers.

"Trespassing," said the wrist-winged ranger. He carried a gog's carbine. A web of complex reflections shimmered across its barrel as he leveled it at them. "Reach up. Turn around."

"Wait." An ocelot stepped forward. She was lithe and beautiful, with dawn fire lambent in her golden eyes. Crow feathers hung from a chain on her ear. Even in this cold, she wore very little. Ruby caught Michael staring at her.

"Empress Ruby," Ruby said, carefully, "And Lord Underbridge of Dimwood. We've come to discuss Pearlwater's surrender."

The rangers communicated with small moves and glances. An ear tipped back. Whiskers twitched. The pangolin gave a sniff and tossed his head.

"Turn around," the glider said again. He lowered his gun and brought out two pairs of manacles. "Cross your wrists behind you."

The rangers took Memnyr first. Ruby tensed as they turned it over briefly. The visions it had shown her spun in her mind, grinding together like cogs. She had seen this through a fog – she even recognized the pendant on the pangolin's necklace. But the sword toyed with her. It showed her disconnected scenes, ideas with tails trailing, and it was apparently incumbent upon her to assemble the pieces.

When no one drew the blade, Ruby felt a weight slip from her shoulders. She breathed a puff, but she was still tight as a cord. Next, they took her ornamental sword.

"A gift," she told them, "for your lord."

She had removed the Tidestone from its cord and hidden it in the front of her dress. The glider ran a paw over her lightly, clearly nervous about touching her. Even if she had been hiding another sword strapped to her thigh, he wouldn't have found it. The rangers said nothing as they put the sword in a bag with Memnyr. Michael had come unarmed. Alhagan had insisted that Ruby do so as well, but the Mirrorblade would not part with her. When she tried to leave it, it would not stay on its stand, and it had grown heavy when she tried to put it down. Now, the rangers zipped it up in a ram's hide duffel and latched a chain to Ruby's manacles. She listened, but the sword was silent. She thought she should have been relieved that it felt safe where it was, but that relief remained beyond her grasp. Ruby doubted that the sword knew as much as it seemed to know.

The rangers chained Ruby and Michael together in single file and pulled them up the hill past a watchtower and several tree stands, all of which were manned by archers and riflemen. They said very little, but when it was necessary for them to speak the rangers used an argot that Ruby couldn't follow. The ground dipped sharply toward the west road, which ran between sheltering banks of Highclere holly hedges. These rose above shoulder-height as they neared the city, and arches adorned with gnomish symbols spanned them. The masonry was chipped and old, friable in places, and one of them hung broken over the road, its north pillar missing. Guards in heavy plate armor glowered down at them, and two bears met them at the gate with swords drawn.

"Business," one of them growled. His helmet was too large even for his huge head. Ruby wondered what larger warriors than these Southunder might have.

"I want that reward in diamonds," the glider chuckled, and even when he laughed he sounded angry. "I'll be buying you all out. This is Ruby."

The bears came down to stare at her. One of them gaped. The other poked her arm as if he thought she might be made of paper.

"David said we were looking for someone younger."

"Well go get him," said the glider. "Let him know he was wrong."

There was a small commotion at the gate as more soldiers came to marvel at Ruby. They spoke of her as if she wasn't there, or they touched her hair and her gown with an almost worshipful affect. For every one that derided her, there were two more that practically fell at her feet. Michael was not ignored either; Lord Underbridge was well-known, albeit not by many friendly folk. Not here, at any rate. He was shoved a bit, and they laughed at his helplessness, but he remained calm and silent through it.

"Leave him be," Ruby attempted, and this sent a nervous snicker rippling through the gathered armor.

"You hold no sway here, miss," said one of the bears. "You abdicated. Or don't you remember that?"

Smiles appeared on whiskered faces. Ruby wondered how many of them remembered what they had done the day before yesterday or why they had pledged allegiance to the Empress of Nix. Many stayed near the back of the group, and Ruby saw the shadow of the Forgetting hanging over them. Their eyes were blank, and their bodies were limp. They laughed when it seemed appropriate, but they made no attempts to engage the crowd otherwise.

A horn sounded from within the city, and the gate groaned open on heavy chains. The glider led Michael and Ruby onto smooth, even streets that slid into the distance around graceful curves to circumnavigate old buildings and statues. Newer structures sprawled across whole blocks, their towers huge, and their high-domed windows paned with stained glass. A small crowd gathered as he helped them into a carriage hitched to a Nixian horse. He locked the doors, and a few paws went up to knock meaninglessly on the frosted glass windows. A thump on the roof must have been the bag containing Ruby's swords. The glider climbed into the seat to drive the carriage himself.

"I've seen this," Ruby said to Michael once they were alone.

"As have I," Michael replied. "But from far away. I dreamed of this last night. I nearly woke up time and again, trying to get it out of my head, but it's all I could think about in my sleep." He looked at the windows. It was impossible to see much through them. "Our moment has come. I don't know what I expected when I went into the east to find you, Empress. I was dim, then. Do you know how much light you've brought us? How much hope?"

"It doesn't feel like much," Ruby sighed.

"It never does," Michael said. "There's never any great green swell, flowers springing up where you step. Hope is a slow-growing thing. But you should know that you have brought it. The seed was there, and you set it germinating. Remember that, if you remember nothing else after all this is over."

"I suppose they shall make Castor mayor," Ruby mused as the carriage began to move. "At least until whatever shall happen has happened."

"Do you feel he's the one?"

"I can't help but feel it! Poor Warren." Ruby lifted her chained wrists as best she could and put her chin in her hand.

"He looked so peaceful there," Michael said. "Rarely do the dead look really at peace. There were a few large battles before you arrived. The Battle of Donchapel claimed the greatest toll of life. I saw friends fall screaming, lying on their backs with their faces frozen in horror. That was when we first saw the gogs and their carbine rifles, and I remember that first smell of their bitter smoke. Death is the last great fear, and many preserve that fear upon their faces when it takes them. But Warren looked almost starry-eyed. He died for something; he must have known that. He'll be remembered for great things, regardless of the legacy of his mayorship."

"That's the way of heroes," Ruby said. "They exist beyond death and beyond fear – beyond all the things that make us what we are."

"Perhaps it could be said that heroes represent not what we are but what we are *not*." Michael's ear twitched madly. He couldn't scratch behind it. Ruby saw him centering himself and was impressed that he could.

They rolled deeper into the city, and the crowds outside dispersed as the carriage picked up speed. Ruby stared at the window and the black shapes moving beyond it. She could feel a weight passing over her, a heat behind her ribs. They had moved into an older quarter; the road grew rougher, and the air tasted sour. Here, there was a steady pulse coming up through the floor of the carriage. It thrummed out of time with the beat of the wheels over the ancient cobbles and the whine of the Nixian horse's pistons. It was a deep and empty drumming, the rush of the blood of the earth; it was the rhythm of the restless dead as they rolled in their graves. The ghosts of gnomes were walking, looking into the carriage windows, sad-eyed and frozen. The Tidestone brightened beneath her gown, and she covered it with her hand instinctively. From far to the north, Ruby heard a dire-dog howling.

"I'm afraid," she said.

"Don't be," answered Michael. "Everything is going well."

"Who will we meet when we reach our destination?"

"Perhaps a Nixian lord," Michael said. "Perhaps only whatever Southn'der brought the poisoned cup."

"Why shouldn't I fear?" Ruby asked. "What if they know about the plan? What if it was Alhagan that killed Warren? They could kill you."

"If they know, we still have an army," Michael replied. "And heroes are beyond fear."

"In that case, I'm no hero."

Michael chuckled. It warmed Ruby's heart to see his smile.

"Then neither am I," he said.

At last, the carriage began to slow. Ruby wished she could watch through the windows as Southunder's capital tower came into view; she was not content with the smell of smoke and the roar of factory fires. They rolled to a stop in the midst of a crowd. The onlookers babbled like kittiwakes outside, and the glider engaged them for a moment. Michael smiled, his head against the window as if he could see what was going on. Then his dark eyelids fell, he pressed his snout to the milky glass, and he started to sing in Melidoran.

Into the sweet embrace of sleep,
The moon unclouded overhead,
And astral lamps in reaches deep
Of space, the ghosts of light long dead
Rest peacefully through balmy dawn
Dream happy journeys, long-lost friends
And lips to place your kiss upon
When your halcyon slumber ends

The song was low and tuneful, and it struck Ruby deeply enough that her eyes welled up with tears. The heat in her chest dissipated, the terrible thumping ceased beneath the carriage, and something akin to relaxation spread from the crown of Ruby's head to the seat of her stomach. She felt clean and renewed, if only for an instant, and when the shadow returned to claw at her she was able to push it away with greater strength. Michael turned with a smile, his whole face aglow with love, and Ruby was about to thank him for his song when the wrist-winged ranger threw open the chariot door and took up the chain that bound them together.

"Get out," he said brusquely. "Keep up and stay quiet."

Fourteen

The Cradle

Southunder's Lower Quarter sloped down into the pit of a shallow crater. Titan, snow-topped structures reared up along its walls. Round stone lodges brooded beneath copper roofs, their cupolas adorned with strange spires. Grass pushed up through the road where the snow lay thin. The forest was constantly intruding here, forcing roots and branches through the masonry. The lord's hall was at the top of a white marble ramp that flanked by towering pylons. Its stacks breathed ash. It looked like a new building. There was a dry fountain in the courtyard.

The glider led Michael and Ruby up the ramp, and guards in white hoods stepped aside for them. The little crowd stayed around the carriage and looked up past the pylons with fear. Their energetic chatter soon dwindled with distance. The glider went into the hall, under archways edged with precise scrollwork. They passed through a great vault with a coffered dome. Light slanted gem-blue through an opening many feet above the floor. Here, even the sound of Ruby swallowing was amplified. Open doors revealed bedchambers, kitchens, and an arboretum under steel-ribbed glass. Ruby was fascinated by a brief glimpse into a library; she couldn't help but tarry for a second to get a look, and this earned her a hard yank at her manacle chain.

"Nothing in there for you," the glider grumbled. "Keep pace with me."

At the end of a corridor hung with paintings, they came upon a huge set of gold and alabaster doors. More white hoods waited here, and, the glider tried to push past them.

"Wait outside," one of them said. The emptiness in her voice was awful.

"You know me," said the glider, sweetly. "I want Marcus to see who caught her."

"Wait," the hooded guard said again, and the glider stepped aside.

"It's my reward," he huffed as the guards took the chain from his paws. "You know it's my reward!"

The white hoods paid the glider no mind. They turned toward the door in unison and pushed it inward, and it creaked in mighty complaint as it opened into a columned chamber of profligate grandeur. The white-garbed soldiers moved as if they were made of wood. As they took Ruby by the arm and removed her manacles, she cried out under the power of their grip. Beneath their hoods were masses of motile darkness where their faces should have been.

The throne room was built around a dais of pure silver. Twelve steps ascended to it, and a carpet of blood-burgundy poured down them, smooth as water. There was an archway behind the throne. Now Marcus entered from under it to stand upon the dais as the hoods placed the glider's bag beside Ruby and forced her to kneel.

Marcus might have been an otter once. He was svelte and chocolate brown, with a honey-white face and long whiskers. But his head was unnaturally long, almost ophidian, and it was encased in black Nixian metal. A brace ran down his back, terminating in an articulated mechanical tail with spines along its top and barbules at its lashing tip. One arm had been replaced by a heavy prosthesis, leaving him asymmetrical, and his legs were little more than splay-footed hydraulic struts. Ruby's stomach turned and grimaced in disgust. Michael gasped as Marcus descended the stairs on the red velvet cataract.

"Empress Ruby," Marcus said, his voice deep and soft as a butterfly kiss. "And Lord Underbridge – Michael of Dimwood. It has been a long time since the Battle of Donchapel."

"What have you done to yourself, Marcus?" Michael spat. "What have you given them?"

"Don't be angry," Marcus said. He stepped past Ruby to take Michael's paw in his. His arm whirred as it moved. "I'm sorry for everything. I want you to know that I'm being honest, despite all that's happened. I'm sorry for Donchapel, and I'm sorry for poor old Warren." He was posing – preening like a bird. "It needn't have ended that way. He refused to hear any reason at all, and it broke my heart. Perhaps you think me false, but he threw even my most desperate attempts to dissuade him back in my face. Who would not have been concerned? Would not have been insulted? I never begrudged him his stubbornness; it was his ungratefulness that hurt the most. I saw him draw up his own order of execution, but I stayed my paw. Do you know that? Do you know that my generals have been barking for blood since the day I took the throne? Warren's blood, mind you. Well." He wiped his paws as if absolving himself of anything. "If Alhagan will see reason, some good can come of this. You are his gift to me?"

"A token of his submission," Ruby replied. "Given the tone of your recent dealings with Pearlwater, Alhagan worried that you wouldn't accept his surrender without a gesture."

"He sent two gifts," Marcus said. "He was wise. One for me and one for the Empress. The true Empress, Ruby. She who sits on the throne."

Marcus opened the glider's duffel and lifted the ornamental sword from it with his eyes wide. He drew it slowly from its jeweled scabbard, and ran his remaining paw over the flat of its shining blade.

"From the halls of Dimwood," he said, awed. "I'd recognize it anywhere. Forged in Lampblack by the gnomes, they say. Not meant for cutting, but I note that it's seen some use. That might diminish its value in the eyes of some, but this spot of oil here and this amber fluid drying above the crossguard show me that it has drawn Nixian blood. That makes it worth far more to me than it would have been unsullied."

"Another gift," Ruby said, trying to steady the tremor in her throat.

"And this?" Marcus took Memnyr from the duffel.

"Confiscated," said one of the white-hooded guards. "I must mention Oscar. It was his detachment that found her."

"Confiscated," Marcus repeated.

Ruby bit her lip. Surely he would draw the blade. Surely he could hear it calling. Its voice was all but deafening in Ruby's ears. The Tidestone responded, and then she was left nearly dizzy with the susurrus din. She put her hand to her breast and pretended to cough, but her throat was closed. Only a squeak came out.

"Well," Marcus continued. To her incalculable relief, he placed Memnyr before her without drawing it. She should have left it behind, but it had insisted; defiance had not been an option to her then. "You're going to need it where you're going, Miss Ruby."

Ruby pulled Memnyr to her chest and Marcus waved his mechanical paw dismissively. The white hoods surrounded her and put their hands upon her, pulling at her arms and her greatcoat, urging her back toward the alabaster door.

"Wait." She tried not to scream. "What is this?"

"You're not my gift," Marcus called after her. "Michael is the token of good faith. My gift is Pearlwater. You will go west to the Cradle, and Lord Underbridge will return to Alhagan. But not immediately."

Ruby struggled in vain against the monstrous strength of the white-hooded guards. No matter how hard she kicked, they gave not an inch. They marched inexorably toward the door, and Ruby finally resigned herself to clutching Memnyr close while they dragged her out. As the great doors groaned closed again, she saw Marcus approaching the manacled Michael and pressing his metal fist into his open paw.

NO, she wanted to cry. *We gave you all you wanted!* But Marcus clearly wanted more. She had seen this, yes, and she knew the lord of Southunder would give Michael little more than a good bruising, but seeing the truth laid bare before her left her gut twisting as if she'd swallowed a hook. She wept for Michael, and she tried to keep his song in her mind, but, to her increasing sorrow, she found she could not immediately remember anything but the tune. The door swung shut before she saw Marcus cock his fist back, and the white hoods dropped Ruby to her knees in the hall.

"Your reward," one of them said to the glider. "Now fetch a carriage."

The wrist-winged ranger disappeared down the hall at a shuffle, leaving Ruby alone before the great door. The hallway arched huge, but it was narrow. She knelt on the carpet for some time, the white hoods standing silent and still as statues on either side of her. She felt the deep force within her as a comfortable heat, a reassuring power that filled her with every heavy beat of her heart. Her pulse hammered in her throat for a few minutes. She took a few deep breaths and tried to focus on strapping Memnyr around her back again. When Ruby stood, the white hoods remained where they were; even when she went to the throne room doors and pressed her cheek against the cool stone, they simply watched. They were like patient birds of prey. The door would not move for her, and she could hear nothing through it. She pounded it with her palm, and it only towered, cold and still.

She had the Mirrorblade. Remarkably, neither the glider nor Marcus had seen it for what it was. For a moment her hand lingered upon its hilt. She would draw it out, and it would sing through the air and tear those hoods away from the faceless heads they covered. When the ranger came back, she would cleave him in twain. Twice at least, Ruby came close to releasing Memnyr, but she resisted. The sword wanted to cut. It urged her to destroy; it had a frightening hunger. But she was finding her strength. Here, in the heart of a mass gnomish grave, the hallway now shrinking around her, she centered herself, and her hand fell away from the Mirrorblade's handle. In the Cholai camp, she had known she would need it. She had seen herself carrying it. When it had called, she had given in. But now it was battle-lust she was defying – the sword's naked need to swing wide, to pierce and to separate – and that was the last thing Ruby wanted. It wasn't time yet.

Ruby pushed away from the door and moved off down the corridor. The glider seemed in no hurry to fetch a carriage. While he dallied, she wandered the manor, poking at last into the library she had seen before. No one stopped her as she entered it and began to peruse the shelves. The quiet was enormous, and she found herself compelled to look over her shoulder whenever her back was to the room. There were books in English and in Melidoran, and there were older works near the back written in a language she had never seen. Even with the

Forgetting having receded so far, Ruby couldn't imagine what the small, twisting symbols could mean. They ran from right to left and from top to bottom across scrolls that had gone yellow with age. Many of the scrolls were decorated with paintings as well. She stared at these for a long time, and it finally occurred to her that these writings might be gnomish. This realization sent a strange chill through her, and after a few more minutes she could stay no longer in that section of the library. She left the scrolls lying on the floor and walked the high shelves toward an alcove full of maps.

Straight away, she saw a copy of Warren's map on the wall. Below it was a collection of smaller maps suspended in cherry frames. One of them was very crude, and, though the outline of the Melidoran coast was virtually identical, there were names and features upon it that were wrong. The Black Mountains were gone, Lampblack was called Blackwarren, and Nirfang was in the north, separating Eastfair from West. She saw her own name on it.

Rubi

Below it, in surer script, the Melidoran letters practiced and well-formed, was her sister's name.

ßⱤ∂ℙℲℬⱤℬℙ

How Elizabeth had loved the sound of that word. Now it woke old and bleary memories. Ruby had called her sister *Uda* after that name. Their father had not understood, but their mother had encouraged it.

Ruby remembered her soaring joy when the horizons of her imagination began to expand. The world seeming vast, so many things imagined already, boundaries stretching beyond any limits Ruby could ever fully explore. She remembered now how her sister had fostered that. She remembered why she had loved Elizabeth, and why, in her adulthood, she had *been* Elizabeth. Melidora had been Elizabeth's world first. It was Ruby's now – only Elizabeth's in homage.

Games of pretend, drawing the maps of Elizabeth's secret worlds, learning to make symbols no one else could read. Days in the sun, and her sword had been a stick, and her cape had been her jacket tied around her shoulders. Running on the shore, or at the docks, and Melidora was there in the sand. In the water. The cries of the fishermen were hymns to the Halcyon, and Ruby remembered learning those ageless tunes and adding to them. She would sing at night in her bed in her house by the sea. She sang even after Elizabeth was gone.

She tugged the map from the wall and sat down with it in her lap, close to tears but unable to weep for the light of her smile. She traced the old roads, the wrong geography, and she must have been there for more than an hour before the glider came around the stacks and frightened her nearly to death.

"There you are," he cursed, and Ruby started. The map in its frame clattered to the floor. "I should have known to look here first! Your carriage is ready, 'Highness'. Come on." He laughed at that, and then came to take Ruby by the arm like a child.

Now, Memnyr would sing. She would slash his throat to the bone – open his chest like butterflies' wings. She was the Empress.

But the thought of blood spilling across the library floor made Ruby's vision blurry. She choked and swallowed, suddenly sick. The Tidestone was pulsing against her skin. Memnyr was singing in her head, rattling her conscience. She stood, tossed her hair, and smoothed her dress. The Mirrorblade stayed in its scabbard.

"No," she said, standing, and she suddenly realized how much taller than the glider she was. "You needn't lead me about. I can manage."

The glider accompanied Ruby out into the street, trailing her like a kicked dog. The carriage at the curb was small and storm-black, adorned with quartz and amethyst, and it sat bunched up like a hiding spider. There was no driver; Ruby assumed that the Nixian horse to which it was attached was capable of driving itself. The crowd remained, still loitering beyond the pylons, though it had dwindled a bit. Ruby helped herself into the carriage while the glider gawked.

"Leave this place, ranger," she said to the glider, her foot on the step and her gloved hand on the door sash. "When you receive your reward, take your men and head into the swamp." With this, she climbed in and shut the door while the glider stood on the curb wringing his paws and staring after her with eyes like pools of nectar. The horse sprung to life, kicking up a whirl of snow and grit as it made its way around the dry fountain and down toward the onlookers gathered at the mouth of the ramp.

Ruby took the Tidestone from her gown. She watched the Lower Quarter recede with a sigh of imperfect relief. The crater sank away to rot with its ice-trapped spirits and its cyclopean architecture. It was like a city of cemeteries, a living grave with its lord supervising its continuing excavation. She was glad to be out from under its oppressive shadow, but it broke her heart to leave Michael there. Her heart had been broken so many times – she wondered that it could still beat at all. Now she drew the curtain and sat in dim light, breathing deeply and trying to reach out to the world around her. Pearlwater with its canals, Hawkport at the Great Confluence, the Black Mountains with Leora's Pass cut hard through ceaseless snows. She expanded, straining to touch the waving hands of the trees on the Fields of Silver. Moonwood lay beyond, gray and cold, with Martan Thorn Bratcher moldering in a cage of roots. She felt the grass and the bark and the crystal pools. She imagined the water flowing over her. She tried to feel Elizabeth, but worry was an obstacle.

To the Cradle, she thought, *to meet the Empress.*

It was where she needed to be, of course. She had seen that. But she had also seen Michael and Arturus fighting alone. She had seen William kissing the black shaft of an arrow; when she slowed her breathing, she could almost hear him whispering, "Fly straight." Was all ordained? What did fate mean in this place?

Welcome back, the skeleton had said in that stone chamber beneath Thimblewand. *Welcome back, Elizabeth.*

And so, at last, Ruby drew the Mirrorblade. It thrummed with power, and burned with an inner light that danced across its blade like ball lightning. Now was the time; that is what it told her as she placed its tip between her feet and tilted it toward her face. She looked into it, past the old face there with its slack cheeks and ashen hair, past the light of its strange life and the silver swimming under its reflective surface, and she saw the void open beneath her feet again. The abyss was alive, and it breathed hard upon her, and her skin went cold. Her heart felt as if it was made of lead. Her blood was charcoal. She saw her hair redden. Her cheekbones rounded. Dimples appeared at the corners of her smile, where she knew there were only webs of wrinkles now. Her chin curved to a cute point. It was her face and Elizabeth's, because she had lived her life in homage. And now she was looking into the deep off the Bay of Mirrors, and as she descended with the storm raging at the surface, Memnyr burned its secrets into her.

Not all acts of creation are deliberate. Minds cast shadows, colors deepen, and new shades appear unintended. Once life is bestowed, it proliferates beyond the confines of will, if only in small ways at first. Novel forms arise, unconstrained even by death; from the graves of ideas rise chimeras that sow themselves with exotic influences. The creative impulse travels across a web, and one strand moves another, and before long the whole structure is vibrating.

It *was* about listening.

At first, the vision was the same. William arrived at Hawkport with an army from Dimwood. They were joined by King Nicolas of Eggplant and by two platoons of his knights and archers. They lay in wait for some days beneath Arane's shadow, and the City on the Water grew wary of the unnatural darkness beyond its borders. Hawkport scouts were allowed to pass through it unconfronted unless they were unlucky enough to spot a soldier; in that case, bodies were delivered onto the Hawk River Bridge wrapped in silver thread and exsanguinated.

Then Ruby saw Castor in Warren's office. This was a new aspect of the vision. It shimmered like a shower of gold, and she had to strain to see it. Castor tipped a vial into a teacup. Warren sipped, and Castor waited. Next came the funeral, and then her departure for Duskwood while Michael suffered in Marcus's custody. And then Ruby saw Castor going west under cover of night. He rode a white pony and tried in vain to hide himself beneath a dark cloak and a hood. He did not penetrate the black veil; William put an arrow between his ribs at seventy yards. She heard him murmuring with his arrow nocked.

"Fly straight and kill."

But this was yet to come. Ruby took a breath and turned away from the Mirrorblade to rest. The carriage was bouncing through Lockwood Forest now. She looked out the window to see the Owof curving south. It was frozen white here; she could feel the cold beneath its surface and the dark dreams of ancient trees as they slept along its bank. The wind in Duskwood was bitter and sickly warm. The ground was chipping like stone under the deepening frost. She had yet to cross the Golrace, but she would be there soon, suffocating in the Everdim. She sat back and tried to sleep for a while, but the howling of her breath in her ears kept her from drifting too far. She took up the blade again. Looking into Memnyr was something like sleep; the visions it showed slowly sucked the outside world away and forced her into a dreamlike focus. When she was done, she knew she would feel as close to rested as she was likely to get at this point.

Now, Ruby saw Michael in the Mirrorblade. He was battered and one of his teeth was missing, but his smile remained hopeful and bright. She didn't feel the tears running down her face; she didn't see her own smile reflected in the glass. Ruby was engrossed in the vision as Michael returned to Pearlwater with a military escort. Marcus had received word of Castor's untimely disappearance, and Ruby imagined that he might send another puppet to rule Pearlwater in his stead, but the sword did not show her who it was. Its surface shimmered strangely, and the vision changed.

She was lying on her back in a field of flowers. Elizabeth was dead, and Ruby was picking marigolds to make a crown.

"This is for you," Ruby said, and she placed the crown beside her. "And I'll wear a necklace."

There was the gray man standing in the doorway, backlit by the hall light, his eyes hooded. And there was his black blade. It had her named carved right on it: *Rubi*. And then Memnyr's mirror went black as oil. Ruby was under a weight. She couldn't move. Alhagan's face swirled up in a splash of silver and then was consumed again. Now she saw Warren's starry eyes in death, and William rushing over the Hawk River Bridge in a crowd of guinea pigs. Ruby sucked in a breath, but her lungs burned. Someone was tending to her, but what they did hurt. She was propped up in a bed. William's knife was in a Hawkport soldier's neck, pressed just between the high shoulder plate and the beautifully engraved left panel of the helmet. Now she saw the arc of blood. The Knights of Eggplant crushed the barricade at the end of the bridge to pour into town like a tidal wave, dragging down even the largest of magogs in their fury. She saw arrows in a swarm, black against the glow of the signal fire. Southunder was ablaze, but she was staring up at a gray ceiling and a ceiling fan that squeaked and couldn't be turned off.

"You need to keep air circulating," someone said, "or you'll burn up. It gets hot here in the summer."

The Cholai had sent patrols further into the forest than Pearlwater had deemed safe. It was a young hedgehog warden that spotted the squad of gogs coming down from the Black Mountains during the Battle of Southunder. Ruby heard the high whine and stammer of flying machines' engines. She saw their guns spitting fire, raking Southunder's High Street. Marcus fell, pierced by Michael's daggers. He bled on the white marble ramp and died between the pylons in his city of cemeteries. For a moment, the vision narrowed into a point on Memnyr's blade. Then it exploded, and the signal fire was set alight in Southunder.

The flame spread across a whole row of apartments. Alhagan and Roger ran across the street and up into the neighboring district, clinging to the shadows beneath manicured topiaries. They returned to the dugouts in which they had been forced to stay while talks for surrender were underway, and Ruby couldn't help but smirk at the irony. Michael followed close behind them, his face singed badly on one side. He packed snow into his hood to cool the burn, and his knife glittered in starlight as he stole through the bushes to escape the oncoming fire teams. William had been watching in the cold for two days. He had barely slept, but he seemed no worse off for it. Ruby felt his heart thumping and his lungs squeezing ragged breaths. She shivered as the hair on the back of William's neck went up. The fire was roaring out of control, fueled by a strange oil of Filwa's device.

All will heal, Filwa had said. Ruby remembered it clearly. The Forgetting was a bit of black on her growing strength, a mere discoloration when it had once been a great fog that obscured even the memory of her personhood. She looked briefly to the gem glittering upon her chest. She felt its light in her blood. Its warmth nestled along her spine. *Cholai medicine always works*.

Outside, the Golrace was thundering toward the sea. Hawkport waited where that river met the Hawk in the Great Confluence. The carriage was nearing the high Golrace Bridge. Ruby tugged her glove off one finger at a time. Then she used the Mirrorblade to split the bandage around her hand. She was careful, but the blade was thirsty. It bit into the side of her palm, drawing a pinprick's bead of blood. The drop soaked onto the reflective surface, and the images playing across it became dark. Vanreah's tooth had pierced Ruby's hand through and through, but the wound had healed completely. Ruby flexed her fingers, working the stiffness from her knuckles. Some of the feeling was gone from her fingertips. She touched the window, the curtains, and the violet sash. She touched her old face and felt only a prickling memory of touch – and this might have been a phantom. Sliding her hand back into the thick glove and leaving the bloodied bandage on the floor of the carriage, Ruby wondered again if her whole life had not been a dream. Perhaps she was the phantom – or a vessel for Elizabeth's ghost. *Welcome back, Elizabeth.*

She could look no more into the blade tonight; she needed to conserve her strength. Memnyr would not return to its sheath, so she left it lying on the seat before her and looked up into the dark. She did feel rested, albeit only in her mind. Her body felt a thousand years old.

"A thousand years ago," she told the underside of the folding head, "gnome mines spanned from Eastfair to Westfair. Their tunnels and excavations sent the Blue Mountains crumbling through the plains and drowned the lauded Haff of Swans, where it's said that the Alamandrians first appeared."

That was where the Thimbles had come from. She saw them now, dark at the mouth of the delta, domed rocks standing in the sea over a flooded gnomish cavern.

She sighed and closed her eyes. The carriage was on the covered bridge, and Ruby could just hear the roar of the Golrace River under the steady thunder of the Nixian horse's hoofbeats. Slowly, she retreated from the land. She drew herself in until she felt as though she was standing on the head of a pin. The sword was speaking to her, but she had found the strength to resist it. Listening to it fed the deep force within her, and she drew on that to shield herself from Memnyr's call.

"A thousand years ago," she said again, "my mother went around the house in black, covering all the mirrors. I remember how empty everything felt then. Everything in the house looked like dust."

Ruby crossed upper Donchapel as the last pink light of dusk was draining from the sky. A winter night settled on the highlands, clear and starry. The moon slid along her appointed ascent at last, piqued by the promise of fire and blood. By the time the horse was slowing at the head of the Great Road, Michael and Alhagan would be in a Southunder dugout discussing with Roger the plans for the next night's fire and the battle to follow.

"Time is a storm in which we are all lost."

Ruby heard William say this almost as if he was at her side, his lips against her ear as if it were the shaft of an arrow. She had not withdrawn completely. She felt herself compacted, back again in the prison of her mind, but she realized that there was another part of her she could no longer call in from wandering. Through those eyes, she saw the army waiting in the dark beside the river. With that discorporate mind, she knew that impatient fervor dwarfed the fear in Arthur's heart. Eager and distracted, he sharpened his sword in the Bratcher Hall barracks. Ruby wondered if she could reach out and touch him, but he shrank from her mind when she tried. She could collapse the pockets of her extended perception like bubbles, but whenever one disappeared another appeared to replace it.

She stepped from the carriage with Memnyr in her hand. The Great Road was an ill-paved gash through Duskwood. In the light of the Tidestone, it stretched out before her, grim and bloodstone-flecked. What trees were left growing along it were pale and injured. Red silk ribbons marked these for felling. The whole road spanned a great denudation, a ruin of miserable proportions that made Ruby's chest feel empty. But there were no Nixies. The road was as dead as the trees. For some time, she stood at the end of it, trying to gather the courage to proceed. The Everdim was merciless in its oppression of her spirit. She was stronger now, she could feel it; but in the gloom, she remained fragile as a doe.

All at once, she saw a light appear at the end of the road, where the Cradle Tower rose up out of the forest like a knife from the breast of a murdered bride. The light was coming from a torch, and as it bobbed toward her Ruby thought she saw a small civet beneath it. It drew nearer at a steady jog, and she saw that the civet's fur was black and spotted liberally with white. It was a skunk then, and only a kit. He approached with his torch high above his head, his face wrenched into a grimace of care and concentration. The light burning that oil-soaked bulb was all that mattered to him for the moment it took to reach her, and he held it aloft with such intrepid passion that she couldn't help but smile. She was still grinning when he arrived before her, bowed politely, and puffed out a greeting.

"Evening, miss," the little skunk wheezed. "A torch to light your path?"

Ruby nearly laughed. "Are you selling them then?" she asked.

"No, ma'am," the skunk replied, a little indignant. "I'm a link-boy. You know? I'll follow you up the road. You mustn't brave the dark alone! You know?"

"Well," said Ruby, kneeling to look him in the eye, "I have this gem. See? It shall light my way very well. I don't think I'll need a link-boy! But I do thank you. What's your name?" She showed him the Tidestone, and he looked utterly unimpressed.

"Begging your pardon, ma'am," the skunk replied, "but everybody needs somebody to hold a light for them in the dark. You know? That's why I'm here. I'm Michael – your link-boy! But you don't have to call me by my name, you know. I'm just here with the light."

"Michael," Ruby mused, "is a very nice name. And you're a good boy! Come then, Michael. Lead me. Help me find my way."

They proceeded forth through the Everdim. The Nixian horse stood motionless behind them, venting quietly, its motor singing a descending note. The desolation reached out for them, poisonous, but the young skunk was unafraid. His torch wasn't half as bright as the Tidestone, but the patter of his little boots was reassuring. He was beside Ruby, real and heavy, breathing quickly as he scooted over the stones. The torchlight danced along the Memnyr's blade. Faeries swirled around it, staying just beyond the lethal range of its heat. The canopy had been ripped open, and the moon and stars were visible in the darkling firmament. Leora's silver disk reminded her of the oculus in that Southunder manor, the light falling through it to fill the coffers with shadow. But the moonlight could not reach her now. The stars burned uselessly in the black. The Everdim surrounded them like a fog, and the scarring of the forest seemed to strengthen its dampening effect. Their footfalls barely traveled far enough to echo. The skunk's torch set a crown glowing above his head, but could not illuminate much more.

"Where do you get your energy?" Ruby asked, jokingly. "This gloom is like a pile of blankets covering me."

"I guess I don't think about it that way," was all Michael the skunk had to say about that.

The road angled slightly toward a set of low stairs. Ruby realized that the white marble ramp leading up to Southunder's capital hall was meant to be its twin. But that ramp was immaculate; the Great Road had clearly been abandoned long ago. It cracked upward as roots struggled up from beneath it. Here it was badly chipped, and it looked as if Duskwood had taken a bite out of it. Despite the ongoing deforestation, the forest was fighting to regain this ground. Perhaps that was why there were no Nixies along the road.

"Where is everyone?" Ruby asked. "Honestly, I'd expected a fight. This road looks like it hasn't seen any maintenance since the day it was laid."

"It was once well-kept," said Michael the link-boy. "Painted and tiled and everything. Guards all along it. But there's no real need anymore, I guess. Numbers are dwindling – the Nixies' numbers. You know? So there's a place here and a place there, but they don't come to meet anywhere specific like they did."

"The Nixies don't come here anymore?"

"Hardly anymore," explained the link-boy his tail bobbing behind him in an S shape. "They don't stay in any one location. No HQ, you see? Just the little places here and about. Well, not here much, but about. About and around."

Ruby couldn't help but be amused by the skunk's peculiar way of speaking, despite the fact that it was a little difficult to find an answer in it.

"But the Empress," she began.

"I don't know much else. Just that this place used to be sort of the main place, but now it's not, and there is no real main place anymore. The bands rove around, operating from a camp here and there. The patrols have tightened. Empress is still here though. Some are still here." Michael he looked up at her, though he seemed ashamed to do so. His eyes were ocean-blue.

"Why are *you* here?" he asked, and then he started with a little cry.

There was a loud bang from the base of the tower. They were no more than a few paces from the stairwell now. The snow-blanketed earth dropped into a ditch with oleaginous fluid sitting inches above a bed of reedy mud. The ditch was clogged with discarded machine parts as well as broken weapons and armor. There was a body near the stairs, its legs dangling into the ditch, as if it had died climbing out. The door at the top of the stairs was nothing more than a broad plank of pine that had been cut to roughly match its frame. It banged open, and a pair of starlings took flight from the roof of a low-hung bartizan. Pale light fell onto the steps, and a figure stepped out into the doorway.

"Thank you, Michael," said a voice near the silhouetted figure. "You can go now. That's a good boy."

Michael the skunk turned to leave, but tarried for an instant, looking up at Ruby.

"Take care, ma'am," he said, and she knelt to put her hand on his arm.

"Michael of Duskwood," she began.

"I'm from Heddlegard, miss," the skunk corrected her. "The faerie town. In Thimblewand."

"Right," Ruby smiled. "Michael of Heddlegard, you are the light of this world. Do you know that?"

Michael of Heddlegard stared blankly at Ruby.

"Well, whether you know it or not, you are. There are many lights, but I can see that you're part of the Greater Light. The Deep Light. That's a good thing, Michael. You've helped me in an inhospitable darkness, and for that I free you. Go south again. Follow the river to Thimblewand. Go to Heddlegard in the carriage that brought me here – go as fast as you can – and raise up as much of an army as will join you."

"An army? That won't be much, ma'am. Heddlegard's not anything like a proper town what with mayors and lords and sheriffs and the like. Just a hole, really, where people live that don't want to take part in much."

"Take as many as will follow you," Ruby said, trying to be sure and positive with the Everdim slowly crushing her. "Go to the town of Hawkport. Find William, the archer cat. He will need your help."

The skunk kit looked up at Ruby with his gem-blue eyes soft and baffled. At first, Ruby thought he might frown; his expression grew so dark and his brow strained down into deep furrows of worry. But then a little laugh bubbled out of him, and he bowed again, as if he didn't know what else to do.

"OK, miss," he said. "I'll try to do you some good."

Ruby looked up at the figure in the doorway, but no one spoke to stop the link-boy as he hurried off toward the waiting carriage. His torchlight bobbed away, and darkness followed him.

The figure in the doorway was large and lean. Ruby saw the hard, angular shapes of armor on its hips and shoulders. There was a masculine authority in its posture, and the voice she had heard had been barrel-deep, fearless, and decisive. As that voice spoke again, the figure came forward to descend the stairs and set a heavy boot onto the Great Road.

"Young Ruby," it said.

The light of the Tidestone revealed a narrow face, a tapering muzzle, and tall ears tipped with black. Argent fur spread out from deep cheekbones to form a mane that fluttered in passionate revolt against a hair binder. She saw the dark blade of a sword, the glint of a plate mail cuirass, and ember eyes that danced with rapacious fire. It was a wolf, and she had known it would be.

"I came to see the Empress. I'd hoped I wouldn't have to fight," she said. She heard the carriage pulling away behind her. The mechanical pounding of the Nixian horse's limbs tore horribly through the silence.

"You don't have to do anything you don't want to do," said the wolf. His words dripped out like sap. She could almost see them on his tongue. "But this is what you want. You wouldn't be here if it wasn't."

The wolf took a step closer. His breastplate was decorated with incredibly fine etching. He wore a symbol she didn't recognize.

"You always wanted it, Ruby," he continued, a tincture of malediction hardening his voice. "I saw it in your eyes. That little sparkle. The way your mouth tips down, people said it looked like you were always frowning. But you just hide your smile. It's underneath like a vein of silver. You just have to dig deep. You have to be close – very close – to find it."

He was close indeed. Ruby could smell him. Heather, sage, bog mud and deer piss. His breath was Vanreah's – the toxic reek of a carrion feeder's. He was a killer. And now he was reaching for her face, one finger out, as if to trace the line of her mouth with his onyx claw. Ruby trembled. She frowned deeply, trying to ward him away with her anger – to poison him if he should touch her. But his paw dropped, and suddenly he grasped the Tidestone and was pulling on it.

Memnyr flew from her side, singing triumphantly, and it was all she could do to hang onto it as it struck out at the wolf. The wolf kept hold of the Tidestone and continued trying to tug it from its cord even as he rolled into a dodge and batted Memnyr away with his char-black blade. Ruby took two quick steps back.

"Let go!" she cried, but the wolf only pulled harder.

He lunged at her with his shoulder, knocking her off balance, and raised his sword to swing for her neck. Ruby tilted her head reflexively, pressing her chin against her shoulder. She blocked the strike with Memnyr ringing mutely. The Everdim softened every sound. No one could hear her. The wolf pushed his knee between her legs and forced her backward over his heel. She fell hard and bit her tongue, and the wolf knelt upon her with his grin spreading wide. He was yanking at the cord, trying to break it. The Tidestone was burning bright, casting his leering face in shadow. For a long moment, Ruby could only scream and writhe. She beat her heels on the ground, furious at being rendered powerless. And then the deep force moved tremendously within her.

Ruby felt her stomach flip. Her mouth opened, her lungs compressed, and she was sure that she was about to throw up. What surged out of her next was power, and the Tidestone seemed to explode with light. With one hand on the wolf's sinewy throat, she thrust up desperately. She briefly saw the flash of her soul shield as the Tidestone's cord snapped and the wolf fell backward onto the paving stones, yelping in pain.

She got to her feet, her dress torn, panting and wracked with tremor. The wolf rolled easily into a crouch and regained his footing with a mad cackle riding out of him. It was like a howl stuttering from the flaming barrel of a flying machine. He held up the rose-pink gem as if he and it were the only things in the world, and he stared unafraid into its searing light as the fur and flesh on his face began to char. Ruby charged. There was a sound like a train whistle coming from her mouth.

Her throat felt like molten steel. She hauled the Mirrorblade through the air with both hands, and the wolf got his dark sword up in time to see its blade cleft in half. He looked down at the useless hilt in his paw, and then Ruby brought Memnyr down upon his arm. She watched his howling face smoke in the reflection on the blade. Burning ash whirled up from his singed fur like a demon's crown. The wolf's paw dropped to the ground with the Tidestone in it. The wolf fell backward, clutching the stump as it poured blood. Ruby saw that the blood was gold, like the ichor of the gods.

She stooped to take the Tidestone from the wolf's lifeless paw. The wolf was struggling to tie his belt around his bleeding arm. For a moment, she was all blood and fire, and a profane need for mortal violence twisted in her gut. A throbbing ache in her loins demanded death, and she very nearly gave in.

"Dog!" She spit at the wolf as he thrashed. "You were wrong. You were wrong about what I wanted. I can't have what I want. Do you see that? And that's saving your life."

Ruby jogged toward the steps and the open door before her. She shut the door behind her and closed the ancient lock, though she was skeptical that it would hold. Beyond the door were more stairs, and she climbed them as quickly as she could with her strength draining away. After three flights, she stopped on a landing to try to tie the Tidestone around her neck again. The tower rose beyond her sight; the stairs curved around a central column that was stained with oil and amber liquid. Crude signs had been drawn on the column and the walls: Melidoran symbols corrupted with base designs and spelling out slurs in rust-red stains. And here was the Sign of the Blotch – the crimson mark the Nixies had worn in the early days of the emergence. Ruby didn't spend much time examining this graffiti once she managed to get the cord tied. She cast off her greatcoat, cinched up the hem of her dress as best she could, and started to leap up the stairs by twos. It wasn't long before she heard the wolf at the door below, pounding to break the lock. The door gave with a battered shriek, and then the wolf's voice came wafting up the spiral staircase like the smell of rot.

"Lyall's coming," he announced. "You should have killed me, Ruby."

Ruby charged up the stairs, fighting the soreness starting in her calves and thighs. When the stairwell opened up into a hallway lined with doors, Ruby fell into the first one she found unlocked, locked it, and waited behind it. She cowered against the wall, knees against her chest, the Mirrorblade's hilt in her sweating hand. She could not help but stare into the blade then, and as Lyall's prowling footsteps echoed up the stairwell she took refuge in the scenes that opened like lilies across its surface.

Pearlwater's harbor warehouses yawned, cavernous in a wet winter night's mist, and from their mouths crept a living darkness. The quay was deserted. Black tendrils spread over gates and guard towers left abandoned by terrified soldiers. With Ruby gone, there was no one to deal with the Weavers.

The dark washed north across the canals and spread through Lockwood Forest, guided by subtle chemical impulses. All within a certain distance of the masking cloud were stricken with a lingering dread. The colony moved up the hill at speed, leaving silver draped upon the trees, whispering like storm winds warring over gable roofs. It had been a century or more since the Weavers had moved in the southern woods, but the colony was old, and Weavers do not easily die. They remembered the trees and the animals of the forest. They remembered strange routes far from the track of the Owof, and they reached Southunder's lower walls without alerting the rangers to their approach.

The fire started in the east. It spread from a basement corner, lambent upon walls splashed with Cholai oil. It burned intensely hot, and its heart was like a jade crystal as it climbed through the floors and swallowed the stairwells. Smoke rose into a snowstorm, the burning air carrying screams. Michael the weasel had been led to believe that the apartments were empty, but he had not had time to do thorough enough research.

The tenants burned, and Ruby could not watch. She turned away, and Lyall was very close. He must have been dizzy. He must have been in pain, but something was driving him that was stronger than will. He was nosing at the doors like a dog. Ruby heard his hobbled steps slapping in the hall and held Memnyr's hilt as though she thought she might fall into Lyall's waiting jaws if she let go.

The Cholai were leaning ladders against pine timbers when William saw the signal. He turned to whisper to a guinea pig praetor and to Malcolm, the captain of the Dimwood regiment. Their horses were well-fed on pearl milk. Arane wove her shadows tirelessly, circling the waiting army for days, her strength old and unnatural. Ruby felt Arane's connection to her children, saw the clouds of chemicals drifting along impossible eddies to reach them, and felt the silver thread closed tight around her chest again. She wheezed, and she was sure that Lyall would hear her. It was all she could do to regain herself.

Southunder was caught completely by surprise. Marcus had proven as shortsighted as he was arrogant. The Cholai stole over the walls of the hangar, and South'nders fell bleeding into the snow in terrible silence. The flying machines had been left ready for battle. Marcus had intended to use them, of course, and now the sword showed Ruby his darker intentions. Marcus had a mind full of blood. Once he had taken the south, he would turn on the Nixies. He knew they were weak and scattered, but that knowledge would go to waste. It sickened Ruby to think of all the lives that would spill out onto the snow and amount to nothing.

The surprise attack and the subsequent emptying of Southunder's forces into Pearlwater unfurled grimly across Memnyr's blade. The flying machines beat their wings like birds; she saw them as if from below, vulture shadows against walls of flame. In wedge formation, they circled Southunder on strafing runs, and arrows were useless against them.

Then they were over Hawkport. The two battles merged on the marsh of Thimblewand, and many guinea pigs were cut down in a catastrophic charge against a gauntlet of magogs. Many more emerged unscathed, and she saw them tear machines apart with their small, bare paws. Hawkport's bridges collapsed in flames, and woody refuse choked the Golrace.

Scenes of terrifying finality – glimpses of bleeding faces, tears mixed with blood, and fire burning ravenously – twined one into the other with no one thread connecting them all. She saw bodies wrapped in silver silk and hung from the trees of Lockwood. She saw Arturus at the high gate, where the mud had frozen slick and the dugouts were strewn with bodies. He was killing in a gleeful frenzy, leaving South'nders much larger than him at his feet. And now it was Nixian blood flowing down his blade, thick as ink. The black seemed to wash over Memnyr as well, and the vision died out in a whimper. After a moment of taut silence, Ruby realized that she was the one sobbing.

"You can't think we're done," Lyall was saying in a singsong voice. "I hear you."

The door shook as Lyall rushed against it. Ruby screamed and covered her head. The wolf rammed the door again, and now it was hanging on one hinge. She rose to her knees with the Mirrorblade ready, her face dark with tear tracks and the deep force rumbling within her. *The creative force*, Michael had called it, and now she was seeing it divide into something more. It stormed in her, gut-wrenching, and she gritted her teeth as if to prevent it from rushing out of her mouth.

The door broke, and Lyall toppled into the room. He fell over a desk, howling in pain, and Ruby put up her shield against the shattered door. Lyall writhed on the cold stone, twisted in a tangle of furniture, and Ruby crossed the room to address him with all the calm she could muster. This was not much. Her tongue felt fat in her throat; she sounded slow as she tried to talk around it.

"Who are you?" she demanded.

Lyall wretched and bled.

"Who?" Ruby said again. She was on the verge of screaming.

Lyall began to laugh. The sound was like metal tearing.

"The wolf at the door," he said, and then he mentioned something about guarding the Empress.

"What?" Ruby took a difficult step forward. Memnyr's point hovered above the broken wolf in the heap of chairs. Its blade reflected nothing now. Ruby sagged like a puppet, controlled remotely, her consciousness perched on the edge of the sword.

"Can't remember anymore," Lyall managed. "Here for you. Doing it or not? Don't. Let me suffer, Ruby. I'm Lyall – the wolf at the door. I'm here for you to break. Go away. Leave me alone."

Ruby watched, bewildered, as Lyall stopped thrashing. Blood was pouring from his arm despite the tourniquet. It spread toward her feet like a sentient thing. Disgusted, she backed away from it.

"So long I waited," Lyall muttered. "You made me wait. Here I am now, RubyElizabeth. I'm here."

With that, he fell silent. A chill caressed Ruby's heart. The room became horribly still. The fire in Lyall's eyes died away. His etched cuirass was cracked. One shoulder pad was splintered. His silence was pregnant with violent promise. The air seemed to squirm with menace – to prick along Ruby's back like needle fingers. Worse than any of his bizarre taunting, Lyall's last breath puffed out in an ash-white cloud. The Tidestone's light guttered, and for an instant the darkness was total. Heartsick and appalled, Ruby left Lyall lying in the cold, the last of his blood stretching out the door in a thread of perfect gold.

It was only by the light of the Tidestone that Ruby could continue up the spiral stairs. The stairwell was irregular, and the steps varied greatly in height and breadth. The further she climbed, the deeper into a monstrous darkness she progressed, and for quite some way she had to crawl up the stairs on her hands and knees. There were bundles wrapped in silver thread attached to the walls and to the column itself, and she saw more hanging from the ceilings in further rooms. Some of the bundles were leaking oil and amber fluid. In others she saw the shapes of weasels, badgers, or guinea pigs. Occasionally she would hear a whisper or a scuttling sound, but she saw no Weavers on the stairs or anywhere else. She ascended at last into the pinnacle spire with the darkness crawling on her skin. It tugged at her gown and her hair, and by the time she reached the last step she was fordone by the weight of horror.

Ruby pushed through a trapdoor at the top of the staircase and climbed into a plank-floored room with a low ceiling. The wind was sighing around the structure. The room rocked a bit in heavy gusts, and Ruby sat down against the floor to rest and steady herself. The sword called to her, and she couldn't resist. Even after all she had seen upon its blade, it was the only refuge she knew anymore. She dearly wished Michael the link-boy was with her to hold a light for her in the dark. *But,* she thought, *Michael of Dimwood would be better.*

Ruby looked into Memnyr. It showed her green lands rolling toward a shining sea. Hills rose up, and the sunlight played across their verdant shoulders, and then trees were swaying all around her. They were oaks and elms, hickories and ash. Here was a stand of alders, and there was an aspen grove falling gently toward a shady valley. Trees were old, and they spoke in a windy language. She had always wondered what they were saying – what they had seen in their long lives.

The vision was bright but brief. She held onto its beauty, certain it was something she had seen before. The landscape of her memory was open, boundless, the Forgetting now no more than a memory itself. Ruby found the strength to stand up.

Sometimes, no matter what he learns, no matter what he gains or loses, a man doesn't change.

Michael's voice was in her head.

We make ourselves, and if we want to be different, it has to come from inside.

She had left him in Southunder. She had gone without protest, putting the battle to come behind her. But she had needed to be here. This was where she would make herself. Michael had known.

Ruby sheathed Memnyr. The room she was in was only a few paces wide. Its ceiling was hung with silver strands, and all along the walls were lucent sacs. In the center of the room was a short ladder. She crossed to the ladder and put her hand on a rung, feeling certain and full of purpose. *She* was going to be why none of this had been in vain. She hauled herself up the ladder, barely feeling the burn in her legs, and emerged in the pinnacle chamber.

Ruby blinked in the light of midday. The pinnacle chamber was open under its roof spire. Ruby put her hand on the rough edge of a long window and looked out over Duskwood and the southern coast. The sky was icy blue and cloudless. To the west, she could see Southunder burning beneath a pillar of smoke. Thimblewand was crawling with dark bodies; they smashed into each other and separated, circling, and curled inward to collide again. Time had raced away from her. The climb had seemed eternal, but now she felt eternity condensed into a pinpoint. She had been gone for far too long.

Ruby turned from the light. In the center of the room was a rude throne. She straightened her spine and approached it, and the wind tossed her clothes about her. The pinnacle chamber swayed sickeningly, and load-bearing structures groaned beneath the floor.

There was no dais. The throne sat upon the bare planks, and it looked to have been made out of machine parts. It sloped on one side, as if melting. Mechanical arms were arrayed in a fan behind it, hands splayed to present the Empress of Nix in all her glory. The effect was less regal than it was sad, as the arms were all askew and most of the hands were badly burned and missing fingers.

At first, Ruby didn't see the Empress. She was thin and given to fading, and at certain angles she appeared to vanish altogether. At a distance, with her head tilted in one way, Ruby thought she looked like a frog. But as she drew nearer she saw that the Empress was only a tow-headed girl in an orange dress that was far too big and a crown of tarnished silver that drooped upon her brow. Ruby went to one knee before her, as if genuflecting, and looked into her sleepy, violet eyes.

"Your Majesty," Ruby said.

The Empress of Nix rolled her head up as if her chin were a lead weight.

"Yes?" she asked. After a slow blink, she seemed to have the strength to continue. "What is it?"

Ruby looked at the bulbous nose and the ruddy cheeks. The Empress breathed between bee-stung lips that drooped open and were constantly wet. She was built rather like a tree stump, with a round body and short limbs. She wore a corundum gem of pigeon-blood-red on one willowy finger. Ruby touched her bare arm and found her skin was like soft bark.

"You," Ruby stuttered, "you're a gnome!" And of course she was.

The gnome Empress formed a frown that was as thick as honey.

"And you're from the Heff, aren't you? Or the Haff." The Empress spoke as if she had just woken up from a deep sleep. "The lagoon, anyway. Where the swans go. Or where they live. Where they come from. Yes?"

"I'm Ruby," said Ruby. She put her hand on a woody cheek and tried to keep the Empress from dropping her head again. "Ruby Fisher."

"You don't look like a fisher," the Empress said. Then she fell silent, and Ruby could see that she was trying very hard to remember. A ripple of color spread across her skin, and she went very pale for a moment. Then her eyes opened wide, and she managed something in the family of smiles. "Ruby! Yes. I think you mean Elizabeth. It has been a very long time, dear. Don't worry. We're all forgetting nowadays."

"Elizabeth is dead," Ruby said, and her eyes stung with tears that would not fall. "That's been a long time. I'm Ruby. What's happened to Nixieland? What's happened to you?"

"No," said the Empress, ignoring her. Something sinister crept into her voice, and Ruby backed away instinctively. "No, you were always Elizabeth. Don't you remember? Something inside you died, and you gave it a name."

"I do remember," Ruby said. "But I don't remember that."

"You can't trust your memory then, can you?"

Now, Ruby saw the real power in the Empress. It was something huge and dark reaching in from outside. In the presence of such abject wickedness, Ruby nearly quailed. Behind her eyes, the Empress was Vanreah and Lyall. She was the man in the gray room, standing in the doorway with light spilling in behind him – Arthur's nightmare, and her own.

"But the boy rose from the shade of the sycamores," the Empress continued. "He left the rushes beckoning and the dark water running into the heart of the earth. Torrilelei."

"It's you," Ruby whispered, without really knowing what she meant.

"No. It's *you*." The Empress climbed out of her throne with some effort. Her crown slipped down over the bridge of her nose, and she adjusted it with a scowl. The huge dress dragged behind her. Ruby wondered if even a woman of the usual size would fit into it. She felt a giddy laugh coming and stifled it with one hand.

"It's always been you," the Empress continued. "You're the one losing her memories. Erasing pain."

"You don't belong here," Ruby said. She stood her ground as the Empress put a finger in her face.

"You invited me in," the Empress scolded her. "There were things you wanted to scrub out. There always are. Memory is pain, isn't it? But now look! It's gotten out of hand. It always gets out of hand. You invited me in," she repeated, her face scrunching into a frustrated grimace, "to deal with *him*, and now everything is falling apart."

Ruby felt anger and despair break over her. The Empress crossed her arms, and her eyes grew dark. The hand moving her slipped away for a moment, and then she sagged like a doll.

"What have you come to do?" the Empress demanded, weaker now. "Will you kill me? You left the wolf to die on his own. You pushed him away, but you didn't wipe him out. That's why you needed me in the first place: to show you who you could be without him."

"No," Ruby replied. She slid Memnyr from its sheath at her back. "No one can tell me who I am." The sword thrummed, feeding on the daylight, its mirrored surface alive again and blossoming with visions. Ruby put the tip of the sword on the boards and turned the flat of its reflective blade toward the Empress. "Look."

"No." The Empress squeezed her eyes shut. "The sword lies."

"This is my world, Your Majesty. Look."

The purple eyes flew open. The wolfish darkness squirmed behind them; Ruby could feel its enormous fear rolling out of the Empress's small body. She stared into the Mirrorblade and went rigid. Ruby saw only herself in the other side of the blade. Her hair was as white as snow. Her skin was loose and seemed as thin as paper. She frowned at first, but then tipped her head to one side. She had been in bad light; her hair wasn't white after all. It was auburn, and it fell in thick locks down to her shoulders. Her face was fair and freckled, and what she had thought were bags under her eyes were her long, dark lashes.

Now the blade became translucent. Ruby could see the Empress of Nix through it, her wet lips parted in a half-gape, her eyelids drooping. She made a dizzy puling sound, there was a dim flash, and then the Empress collapsed into her voluminous dress. Ruby rose and sheathed the Mirrorblade. Memnyr glowed, sated at last, and now it felt as light as air on Ruby's back. She knelt over the Empress of Nix and stroked her cheek with a finger. She was sleeping, her breathing deep and easy, and the dress was spread out beneath her like a marigold's bloom.

"Torrilelei," Ruby said, and the little gnome stirred and smiled as if having a happy dream. Ruby patted her arm and then, on a whim, she removed the Empress's crimson ring. She slipped it on as she crossed back to the wide window, where she stood for a while watching the smoke billow up from Southunder.

Fifteen

Fading

On a clear night in August, Leora descended to the Wood of Thorns in a pale chariot, and stars accompanied her. They came to the Moon Pools, and Leora cast a spell upon the girding hedges so that none but her stars could penetrate them. Then she and her celestial host disrobed and slid into the warm water to soak.

Among all the wonders in Melidora at that time, Leora found the Moon Pools to be the most beautiful. The gnomes had dug the moon pools many centuries ago, searching for alabaster. Gnomish devices left in those mines heated them, and their bowls were tiled with the white stone. Leora slipped into the water, which was so clear as to appear invisible, and she bathed herself with starlight. She and her stars had peace and privacy long into the night, until an Alamandrian came upon the hedges and the magical barrier.

This was Martan, an exile from Southunder, and he had come a long way with a grievous injury hoping to heal himself in the Moon Pools. When he could not pass the hedges or even see over them, he whistled, and a bird within the barrier heard him. Martan asked the bird what it could see, and it described to him Leora in her glory. She was well known to be buxom and fair, with gray eyes and dark curls falling about her shoulders. This the bird confirmed in his report, and Martan was filled with desire for her. He waited by the hedges, and he asked the bird to report to him when one of the stars came through.

Soon enough, one of Leora's sidereal courtiers opened a door in the magical barrier and came out to pick black berries, and at the bird's whistle Martan slipped through it. He saw Leora, who was even more beautiful than the bird had relayed, and with her were a dozen or more starmaidens bathing in pale splendor. Leora spotted Martan standing at the door, the light of the errant star pouring through from behind him, and she sank immediately into the water until only her head remained above it. She cried out, and the starmaids fell upon Martan. They stabbed him with their silver daggers until he was dead, and they buried him in the mines under the pools.

Leora and her stars were hurt and violated. They left in haste and never returned. They abandoned the starmaid who had let Martan in, and what happened to her is not told. She may have wandered until she faded, or she may have drowned herself in the sea. It is often said that she became an empress of the Cradle Tower, though few have ever believed so.

But not all dead things remain buried. For some, death is only a first step. Ruby knew this much even if she wasn't certain about anything else. Martan walks to this day, looking for Leora, the moon, and her stars. He has taken another name, and he changes his form, but there is one secret aspect that can give him away. What that might be depends upon the storyteller, of course.

"His eyes," Elizabeth used to say. "His eyes are like pools of gold."

They had run through the fields and they had walked through the forests, and in the rich world of their minds they had lain on the shore hand in hand while the water slipped over them like silk. Elizabeth's life had been a bulwark against chaos. She had stood guard at the dark gates, and when she died they had been torn open. Chaos sucked Ruby down, drowned everything, and ruin became Elizabeth's legacy. A mile marker on the road to decline, Elizabeth became the last good thing Ruby remembered. So she had built Elizabeth a new legacy. It was the least she could do.

For a long time, Ruby stared over the marsh of Thimblewand and the fields of Donchapel, and as the sun set she realized that Melidora didn't belong to anyone anymore. The pillar of smoke blew away, and only a few white streams were threading into the sky. The sea pounded the Pearlshores, rocking boats in the harbor, and the canals swelled to flood some of the lower districts. Docks sank, and angry waves pulled a vendor's cart or two into the deep. Leora rose shyly, and the lands in view of the Cradle Tower lit up with campfires in a loose network.

Ruby left the Empress of Nix sleeping in the center of the room, her crown tangled in her lank, blond curls, and found a ladder up to the spire itself. She tried it, but the door above was locked tight. *A good measure*, she supposed, *lest any gods try to ascend from here again.* She went back to the window and climbed the sill to swing her legs out over the edge. She kicked her feet for a while, the wind clutching violently at her. She was in its territory now: the upper points of the world, where clouds passed thin under her swinging feet. It was angry, and she allowed it to buffet her. The Great Road was just a scratch in the forest from this height. Humming Leora's song, Ruby gathered the deep force – the creative force – a final time. She thought briefly that it had always been Elizabeth's, but that her sister had given it to her.

If she hadn't died, I would never have learned to use it.

After one more look back at the little gnome girl curled up in the blossom of her dress, Ruby slipped out the window and into a quiet plummet toward Duskwood Forest. The Cradle Spire rushed up behind her at terrific speed. Perhaps she would be caught up in the air. Perhaps she would vanish and wake up again coughing and choking in the Bay of Mirrors. She didn't much care what would happen; she simply spread her arms into the rushing wind and closed her eyes.

Ruby was awakened by a terrible smell. She sucked it deep into her throat and then turned to cough and spit. Her legs ached. Her back felt twisted. Moving her neck sent pulses of fire scorching over her left shoulder. On her hands and knees, she stuck out her tongue and hacked the bad smell onto the paving stones. She rolled over, still gagging, only to have that stench blown into her face again. Now she sat bolt upright, and doing so brought so much pain that her vision went black around the edges. At first, the face in front of her was just a dark blob. Strange, hard shapes curled off it, and it opened to breathe upon her again. She put her hand on the blob and lifted herself to her knees, blinking. There were shapes moving toward her. They were just far enough away that they seemed to materialize from nothing. She blinked again and rubbed her eyes. The blob nudged her, and as her vision finally cleared she saw it was Rachel.

"Maa," Rachel said, and Ruby threw her arms around the ram's neck. His wool was flecked with bog mud and his breath smelled terrible, but Rachel's warmth and softness of his body filled Ruby with a young and simple joy she hadn't felt in a long time. Now she stood and pushed her hand into Rachel's woolly flank.

"Gokhud," she said, and her throat went dry. "I thought the dog had gotten you."

"They return to the last one who paid for them," said a voice. "That's the way the Northers breed them."

Ketha emerged from the Everdim, armored in black and gold. He had a cast on his arm and a deep scar across the inside of his hood, and Michael the link-boy followed close behind him with a faerie crystal torch.

"You said there was a light in the sky," Ruby said, breathless. "You felt it in Lockwood Forest."

"I never lost hope," Ketha replied with a bow. "Now the sky is afire, and the shadow of Nixeland is burning away."

Michael arrived on his own ram, smiling through a grim shadow. Behind these two followed an army, a guinea pig leading them on Arturus's Junie. William stepped from the woods like a ghost, unharmed and alert, his smile for Ruby cold and taciturn even now. The whole of the Dimwood militia marched up the Great Road, and the knights of Eggplant came from among them to surround Ruby. They gave her hard bread and butterbush sap, and though she had grown quite tired of trail food, she ate and drank as if new to the experience. Last of all came the armies of Pearlwater, and they filled the forest with drums and piped hymns. Flags waved in the desolation.

Michael dismounted and approached Ruby. He bowed before her, and he would not hear her requests for him to rise.

"The Empress," he said, taking Ruby's hand reverently and placing a light kiss behind her ring. "We felt her die. The Forgetting broke all at once, and we were free. The tide was turning, and hope was failing. Then an army arrived from Heddlegar." Here, he patted Michael the skunk on his dark head, and the link-boy beamed unabashedly. "And then the darkness lifted at last."

"I didn't kill her," Ruby said, blushing. "She's sleeping in the spire. I only showed her the blade."

"Memnyr," William said, and Ruby nodded.

"You do not fail," Michael said, bowing his head again. "And we won't accept your humility now! You're a bit outnumbered, Empress. You'll have to submit to our adulation."

Then Michael laughed, and Ruby embraced him. She pressed her face into his fur and closed her eyes, and for a moment she was as free and happy as him. Finally, despite her protests, Ruby was lifted into a sedan chair and carried down the Great Road. She clung to the arms of the chair and looked out over a river of clanking armor. It poured into Donchapel and turned west toward Dimwood, and it glittered in the sunlight as if scattered with stars.

It was the first day of December, and snow lay thick on the fields. The knights of Pearlwater turned away at Donchapel Hill, and there were many fond goodbyes. Ruby moved among them, thanking them for their service, and they wrapped her in fine pelts from their own backs.

"You have won your freedom," she told the captain of the Pearlwater guard, "but at a great cost. I'm sorry for what you face at home – the funerals of friends and the consolation of mothers and children."

"It must be worth the price," the captain replied. "Warren believed it was, and so did Alhagan. Before he died, he gave this to one of our soldiers to give to you." He pressed a large, silver button into Ruby's hand. "It's from his coat. The only thing he had to give at the end, I suppose."

"I shall remember him by it," Ruby said, and she folded the button into her hands and held it against her breast.

"Thanks to you," the Pearlwater captain smiled, "we will all remember."

Halved, the armies continued on to Dimwood. Much to Ruby's relief, the knights of Pearlwater took the sedan chair with them. She mounted Rachel, and spent long minutes with her arms around his neck and her cheek against his musky wool. Riding near the head of the column with Michael and Ketha and with William walking beside them, Ruby listened to Ketha describe his betrayal at Lampblack and his escape from servitude in the north. There were arms of William's painstakingly established network that still functioned, despite increased pressure from the Nixies.

"But there is a heavy machine presence in Driftgate," Ketha warned. "I imagine that it will be some time before it is fully dismantled."

Two guinea pigs introduced themselves as Antonia and Theodorus. Ruby recognized them as captains of Eggplant; she had seen them in Mirrorblade, rushing behind their king in the charge into Hawkport. They told her of their home and their father, who had died in the North Wars, and they gave her a silver band to wear on her wrist.

"Made of Butterbush steel," Antonia said, proudly. "No steel is stronger."

Ruby was surprised at how little they had to say about their brother, who had been injured at some point and was recuperating in Pearlwater. She started to tell them that she knew him, but they seemed disinterested.

"Arturus is too brave for his own good," Antonia said.

"'Brave' is one word," Theodorus laughed. "But 'foolish' may be a better one."

They reached Dimwood in a howling blizzard, and there they found a few Cholai wagons waiting at the gate. They were blasted black and broken apart, lying upon the snow in various stages of reconstruction. Filwa was overseeing the repairs; she hunched through the snow under a great hood, pointing with her cane when she wasn't leaning on it. A number of weasels aided the Cholai's efforts, and two of them came to meet the returning soldiers. One of them was Andrew, Michael's aid at the House of Underbridge. With him was the wolf cub Ruby had helped rescue from Owl's Head Peak. He was decked out in heavy armor beneath which he was constrained to waddle a bit, and he wore a notched axe over his shoulder. He bowed, trying to look as knightly as possible.

"There's to be a reception tonight," he told Ruby and Michael in a low voice. "And the minister is waiting to meet you now. Everyone's all a-twitter! Especially the birds."

Ruby went to meet Filwa, but a hedgehog in a long coat and a scarf stopped her before she could get close to the damaged wagons.

"There will be a better time," he said. "Best to wait. She's mourning. Even getting up to help with this work was a hard thing; she should be resting, but most of the others have moved on. We do what we have to do, but she won't see guests right now."

"Mourning?" Ruby asked, aghast. "What happened?"

The hedgehog looked over each shoulder twice before answering.

"Death in the family," he nearly whispered. Ruby strained to hear him over the wind. "She is not so good right now. Angry, as you should expect." Ruby was about to ask if it was Benjamin or Moira who had died, but the hedgehog held up his paw. "We don't say the names of the dead, please. Not this soon. We've talked too much about it already. Just move on, and the mistress will come to you when the grieving is all done with."

Ruby stood at Dimwood's gates with the crowd, whipped by the cold, listening to them. Her heart fluttered, soft in her throat, dancing along the pulse of their cheers. They paid little mind to the Cholai. As they entered Dimwood, the crush swelled, desperate to meet their heroes, and Ruby followed. Husbands, wives, and young ones were returning from the field of battle to meet a new world of vanishing grief – a world on the edge of fear. They would be a long time healing. Ruby looked at Filwa as she passed through the gate, but she avoided Ruby's gaze and ducked into a tent as the company passed.

Once within the bounds of Dimwood proper, the crowd spread out. The streets were choked with knots of folk welcoming their loved ones or listening to war stories from the knights of Eggplant. Michael and William helped Ruby sneak away along backstreets. Her coat over her head, she trailed them through allies and gardens beneath arched pergolas covered with bougainvillea. Her legs still ached, and she limped occasionally. Their escape took quite a while, and by the time they reached Michael's beech tree, Ruby was panting and sore.

The beech was on firm, sandy soil, and its great roots formed a kind of cage to support the walls of Michael's burrow. A finger of the Charl ran nearby, and further north was the white bridge beneath which Ruby had found Michael fishing so long ago. Within, the burrow was close and warm, and it went back quite a way into the ground. It was sparsely furnished; the den had only rugs to sit on, and the table in the dining room was cut very short.

Michael lit a large faerie crystal with a touch, and then he sat back on his heels with his tail curling around him. William leaned against the wall, uncomfortable, while Ruby lay on her back on a luxurious rug and put her arms out. It felt like falling from the Cradle Spire all over again, and she closed her eyes.

"Arturus has requested to be taken to Robinegg as soon as he's fit to travel," Michael announced.

He lit a long-stemmed pipe. Ruby could smell sage and heather burning.

"Is he that bad off?" she asked.

"Worse off than he'll let on," William replied. "I hear the ball went through and through, so that's lucky, but it nearly hit his heart. While he might describe that particular organ of his as invincible, he'd have bled out like so many others if it had been pierced. He has some fluid on his lungs, and I believe they pumped him of it. Whether he'll need that procedure done again is something I don't know." William coughed daintily. "He was a damn fool, but I suppose that's no surprise."

"Tell me again how it happened," Ruby said. She tried to smile. The wind was rushing up beneath her. She was falling ever more slowly, but the wind was busy trying to strip her back of skin. "Was he part of the charge across Thimblewand – that horrible run through the gauntlet?"

"A good run, I'd call it," Michael replied. The air stirred. He was fanning smoke away from the center of the room. "It won the swamp for us. It'd have been worse if not for the troops from Heddlegard."

Ruby's frown wilted. She had seen many die in the blade of her sword. Perhaps that had been a future she had prevented. William began to speak, but Ruby interrupted him.

"Both of Hawkport's bridges fell. Right?" she asked.

She opened her eyes and saw William and Michael looking at each other.

"Only the north bridge," William replied. "We stopped the Nixies from burning the other."

"Hmm," Ruby said. Then she tugged her knees up to her chest and pried open her worry for her friends to see. "That's good. What I saw in the Mirrorblade was awful. Fire and death, horrors blending into each other. I imagined what you were going through seeing it firsthand."

"Some of us can handle it better than others," William said, and he licked his paw and slicked back the fur between his ears. "And I imagine the blade exaggerates a bit. It's not exactly an oracle, you know. It only reflects – if you get my meaning."

"But that's not to diminish the impact of the battles," Michael said, looking at bit irritated with William. "This will be a marker by which all of us will judge time – the Battles of Pearlwater and Hawkport. We lost so many, and I saw some of them fall. There are things I won't soon forget, don't doubt it."

"Perhaps now we will wish for the Forgetting," William purred. "It is only those who have neither fired a shot nor heard the shrieks and groans of the wounded who cry aloud for blood, more vengeance, more desolation."

"I saw knights of Eggplant fall in a massacre," Ruby said, distant now. She stared in no particular direction. "And I saw both of Hawkport's bridges burn."

"The battles could not have gone better, if you ask me," William said. "There was no such massacre of knights from any company. And, as I've already said, only the north bridge burned."

"Perhaps you only saw what you feared." Michael put out his pipe and went to sit beside Ruby. "But there's no reason to fear anymore. Sorrow I can understand. No matter how many died, even one death is too much for me. Some would say that freedom must be worth the price, but I would take back every death if I could."

"That would be a gruesome sight," William said under his breath.

"Would you give back freedom?" Ruby asked as Michael put his arm around her. "Would you put the Empress of Nix back on her throne?"

"To give life back to the dead?" Michael squared his jaw. His paw was on her shoulder, squeezing her against him. "I'm thankful that I'll never be burdened with that choice, Empress."

Michael had hoped they would have time for a meal before the crowds arrived, but he was barely able to open his pantry before Ketha's hooded face appeared in the opening of the burrow.

"You can't hide here, Lord Underbridge," he said. Ruby was surprised to see pain on his face. "The hero-worshippers know where you live. You'll have five minutes to slip away if you plan on running, but I can't imagine you'll get far unless you jump in the creek."

"No," Michael sighed through a smile. "We'll meet them here." He stooped to pick up his coat and then turned to Ruby. "Are you prepared, Empress? I could say that you're too tired to appear. That would be completely understandable."

"It's likely true," William added. "Won't you rest awhile? You might have to find a better place than a sandy hole under a tree, but you deserve some time to recuperate."

Michael sent William a playful frown. Ruby stood and pulled on her Pearlwater coat. She buckled it tight and tugged the hood up. Her face sank behind the shadow.

"Thank you both, but if you shan't rest," she said, "then neither shall I."

Ruby spent the next week in conferences. She saw hope growing anew in some, and in others she saw it in ruins. Roger, the new mayor of Pearlwater, was in Dimwood for several days to talk with her about the reestablishment of trade routes across the delta and the housing of freed slaves who were now filtering in from the Black Mountains and Northover. At night, her head swam with the enormity of the issues she was expected to face. She laid on her back in an imperial suite above High Street, and in the dark, the faces of widowers and wounded children burned behind her eyelids. By the time the fervor died down and work was underway, she felt ancient and boneless.

But repairs were in motion. Whole contingents of soldiers and craftsmen crossed the marshes to help rebuild. Pearlwater and Southunder merged to form a commonwealth, and Roger was installed as lord mayor over both cities. Dimwood fell into grim determination, and Ruby was proud to have set some of the parts of that machine in motion. She kept her pride a secret even from herself for a long time; it seemed like the worst kind of blasphemy. But contentment crept in. Pride bloomed in mockery of her shame, and she finally saw her self-deprecation for the waste of time that it was.

The new mayor of Hawkport refused to integrate, even after long talks and a promise of aid to construct a new bridge to the north. Ruby went with William to the Great Confluence to meet with the mayor, and she spent many days walking the harbors. She watched the water falling over limestone escarpments, the Hawk pouring into the Golrace with

Hawkport straddling both, and rainbows forming in the constant spray. She was welcomed among the shrews there; only the great, golden fisher cats that worked the Golrace below the falls refused to receive her, and the city's new leader had been elected from among them.

You don't look like a fisher, the Empress of Nix had said, and Ruby supposed she didn't.

Even after he signed the new trade agreement she had helped to draw up, the cats regarded her coolly. Being rejected was refreshing, and when she returned to Dimwood she kept their scorn like a levee against the returning flood of praise.

"Hate may keep us humble," William said as they crossed the south bridge and put Hawkport behind them, "but I'd keep an eye out. There is never any shortage of trouble."

They turned east then, where the first stones of a new road were being laid in the swamp. It would come down from the fields of Donchapel, and a bridge would span the Thimblewand delta, and from the other side it would continue toward the Pearlshores. It was an ambitious project, especially with the majority of Heddlegard opposing it. Ruby feared the camp would split and ultimately disintegrate; many had already moved south to haunted Argomanse. But the bridge would be built, one way or the other, and the road would slash through open country that had endured since the gnomes had vanished.

In Pearlwater, Ruby met with Roger and presided over the inauguration of Southunder's new mayoress. She was a young, pregnant possum with hazel coronas within otherwise gem-blue eyes.

"Ruby," the new mayoress smiled, her paw upon the high hump under her dress, "if she's a girl."

Ruby had tarried a long time in the possum's new office, fascinated by the curve of her belly and the light that seemed to spark from the tips of her every white follicle. She seemed to wear an aura, and the Tidestone responded to it enthusiastically. It glowed and pulsed, warm on Ruby's skin, and when she put her head against the muskrat's swell it almost seemed to sing. It whispered to her, and she smiled, and before she departed Ruby put the Tidestone around the mayoress's neck.

"Michael," she said, "if he's a boy."

She left for Pearlwater's West End House hospital complex with William, and there was a great weight gone from her shoulders. Her heart thumped in her chest, beating like a bird uncaged, and William looked at her strangely.

"Could it be that you're blossoming at last?" he asked with a sly smile. "You've been under a cloud since that day on the Great Road. You seem almost glad to be rid of that Halcyon's gem."

"I've found my way," she said, "that's all. Now someone else can find hers. Or his."

William only nodded and stuffed his paws into his shallow pockets.

"Well," he said. "It's a bright day that brings out the adder."

All her official duties attended to, Ruby hurried toward West End House as the sun was slipping to rest. The night opened in blues and purples, regal and cold and clear, and the stars seemed close enough to pluck from their spreading fabric. The moon rose high now – Leora in her ageless splendor. She was creeping toward midnight as Ruby and William entered the marble square.

A beaver in marshal's livery showed them to the lobby of the main building, where Arturus was sitting alone in a wheelchair. There was a splint on his leg, and his chest was bound with layers of gauze and cotton pads. He sagged like a sack of mud, his eyes were milky, and there was a pail beside him with long sticks of incense burning in it. Ruby called out, "Arthur," and the guinea pig looked up with such sad hope that Ruby felt like laughing and crying at the same time. The tired smile that spread across his face showed her that his expectations had been dashed and rebuilt more than once before.

"Empress?" He turned his chair gingerly. Ruby realized he was missing a finger. "Bill?"

William's eyes brightened. A warmth came over him that puffed up his fur and set his tail shivering. He stepped past Ruby in a casual hurry, his throat rolling with a lively purr, and went to one knee to take Arturus's paw.

"Birds have bills," William said. "You only have me."

They embraced as best they could, and Ruby saw the corners of Arturus's eyes shimmering. She hadn't realized they hadn't seen each other since the Fall of Nix. In the whirlwind of her imperial business, she had missed it. She went to Arturus's side to pet his head, but he pulled her into an embrace as well. His weakness was heartbreaking.

"They said you were coming!" He shouted. "I know you've been busy. I wanted to be in Dimwood last week, but they won't let me up out of this damned chair!"

"Why have they got your leg splinted up if you were hit in the chest?" William said. He beamed, and his incisors flashed in the starlight pouring through the window. Even in his elation, William looked predatory.

"I don't take well to being held down," Arturus explained. "They say I was in a terrible fury when they wheeled me in. They put restraints on me, and I started thrashing. Banged my leg, got a nice bruise and a blood clot, they say. *I* say it's their fault for trying to pin down a knight of Eggplant!"

"They should have taken the saw to you right there on the field," William laughed.

"Damn right!" Arturus raised his fist and then broke into a wheezing cackle. "Now they say I have to be off it most of the time. Oh, please say you've come to take me away."

"They won't order me around," Ruby said, and now she took a knee as well. There was a minor commotion in the lobby as she did; passersby tried in vain to watch inconspicuously as the Empress knelt before a commoner. "There's a carriage coming up from Canal Street. We'll take you home tonight. I'm sorry we left you here, Arthur, after all you gave."

"Duty first," Arturus said, with a wave of his three-fingered paw. "I take no offense. But you certainly took your sweet time with your duty, didn't you?"

He laughed again, but Ruby saw through him.

"Do you know I missed you, Bill?" Arturus went on, patting William on the shoulder. "I saw that young possum we got up from Cutcheon Mud. He's a regular military man now – grown to five times the size! Ratty tail and twitchy whiskers."

"Andrew," William said. "From Morton."

"The same. He sends his thanks, friend. It was a prize to see him again."

The staff made no complaints as they wheeled Arturus out into the winter evening. As soon as they were over the threshold, he insisted on walking. William draped his coat around Arturus's shoulders as they waited for the carriage.

"What will I do now?" Arturus wondered. He held Ruby's arm to support himself on his stiff leg. "I can finally remember how long it's been."

"Time is a storm in which all are lost," said William. "But there are ports now. There's land. We can put in. It's what we've fought for."

"We can put in," Arturus repeated. "But I think I might like to stay at sea a while."

At William's behest, the three crossed the marsh with a military escort. Ruby had given out no formal honors, but it was apparently assumed that her close friends held rank above even mayors. When she returned to Dimwood, she would arrange a ceremony to confer proper titles. She smiled at this; it made her think of Elizabeth.

I'll be the queen, she thought as they pushed through mud that was thick with ice runoff from upriver. *I'll be the queen, and you can lead the army.*

She could hear Elizabeth's voice in her head, but it was dim. It seemed to come from a long way off – a feeling more than a sound. William told her that time was tonic, but her years had dulled her mind. The Forgetting had been a powerful and stifling weight; now it was lifted, but the common erosion of memory remained. She watched William change Arturus's bandages and briefly wondered if there might be some to whom age was kinder.

Twice, they smelled bugganes, and the horses started at hooting wails far off in the forest. Duskwood remained gloom-cast and troubled, and reports of a large Nixian machine moving through it persisted. It was digging under the Cradle Spire, some said, but others had it moving north in a cloud of mist. Yet others insisted that it was no Nixie at all.

"They bored open ancient chambers," William opined, "and horrors will continue to crawl from them until they are all filled in."

En route to Dimwood, the driver of Arturus's carriage steered ever closer to the wet shores through Thimblewand, and the going was slow for a day. Ruby listened to stories of the storming of Hawkport and of the battle at Pearlwater's gates when the flying machines had been making their first runs. Arturus was a loud and enthusiastic storyteller, and his vivid descriptions of gore and death made Ruby feel ill, but she didn't have the heart to stop him once he got going. He remembered himself as fearless and unstoppable, and carrying on about his exploits seemed cathartic for him. He poured out his valor and his vitriol, oblivious to William's corrections, and when he finally began to tell of his fall he was a titan with the heads of his enemies on a cord around his waist.

"The wanderers saw the last of the Nixies coming," he said in a histrionic whisper. "We knew where they would be and when, and we cut them off quick as we could! One got lucky, but not for long. I brought that pile down with me, and I chewed on his wires as they came out with the stretcher. You know?"

By this time, William's objections had ceased. He allowed Arturus his grandiosity as well; it seemed to be doing him far more good than any medicine had done in recent weeks.

There were no Cholai wagons at Eastgate when they finally arrived. Ruby sent the chariot on into Dimwood with Arturus sleeping inside it while she spoke with the guards. The wagons had left early the previous day, their long repairs finally done, and they had left none behind when they had departed. Downcast, Ruby walked the thinning woods and the fields just outside Dimwood in search of any tracks or, at best, a Cholai encampment. By nightfall, she turned back, and as she surmounted a hill heading south, she walked into a new hanging of silver thread from the scant canopy.

Arane descended amid a chorus of whispers. Her six spinnerets worked beneath the point of her bulbous, black-striped abdomen. Four of her legs were wrapped around the human proxy beneath her true head, protecting it with an embrace that was not quite maternal. Ruby stood in the snow and dropped her hood to address the queen Weaver, but Arane spoke first.

"Your gem," she said, and Ruby could not stop a chill spreading up her spine. Her arms broke out in gooseflesh.

"I've given it away," she replied.

Arane was quiet for a moment, but she remained motile. Her huge mass shuddered and twitched, her legs making constant, quick adjustments along the extruding strand, her false mouth working on its wax-pale face. Ruby tried not to be repulsed; she knew Arane as an ally. But perhaps this was a natural reaction to such a creature. Arane must have known how she affected bipeds; she didn't seem offended when Ruby took a step back.

"You know the road ahead then," said the spider with two voices. "That is a good thing. It is what we hoped for. We've returned to pay our respects."

"I'm not sure I know what you mean," Ruby said. This was true on several levels.

"Follow," was Arane's only response.

Ruby followed the Weavers further into Duskwood than she imagined was wise. Tall, somber trees shrank into dense thickets hung with kudzu and dead blankets of climbing rose. Ruby pushed through, feeling much too old for such adventures anymore, until the thicket opened into a clearing on a little hill. Here, moonlight fell unimpeded by the Everdim. The Weavers gathered in the trees; branches swayed with strange weight, as if complaining, and silver thread fell over everything.

On top of the hill, a mound lay at the foot of a wooden plank. Arane moved over the hill to bend herself oddly about the mound and the marker, and then she turned to Ruby.

"Come," she motioned with three legs. "The wanderers bury their honored dead alone in deep woods. It is what all elders wish. Look upon her."

Ruby felt a lump in her throat the size of a fist. She went to kneel before the grave, and she was not surprised to see the name upon the plank.

"We know a little about everyone," Arane said quietly. "We make knowing our business."

"When?" Ruby whispered, and her voice seemed to disappear into the Weavers' constant muttering.

"'That we do not know," Arane replied. "Her kind paid off a debt to ours. That is why we came. She was the payee."

Ruby put her hand flat upon Filwa's grave. She was skewered on an icicle. The new day had brought out its first adder.

"I was gone," she said. "Off playing empress. I'm so sorry."

She sobbed, but tears would not come. Something in her wouldn't let her feel truly guilty – some bright spot that burned in spite of her. She hated that bright place for a moment, wishing it would become as dark and angry as she wanted to be. Her hand was whole again, as Filwa had promised it would be. Ruby felt she had broken a promise, but the bright spot refused to submit to guilt's corruption. Arane spoke as if she knew Ruby's mind.

"Do not grieve," she said. "You waste yourself. Offer respect instead. Honor yourself and her alike."

Ruby nodded, "She has my respect," she replied. "I hope she knew that."

"Whether she did or not is no longer of any concern," Arane said, coldly. "Know it yourself and be comforted – she lives only within you now, Empress."

Ruby spent a few more bitter moments on the little hill. The Weavers chattered about her, their joined voices like a black tide of whispers pulsing over her head. They spoke hymns and poems, and they told of the ancient deeds of Cholai kings. When her hands and cheeks turned red with cold, Ruby had to stand and pull up her hood.

"We offer respect to you, as well, Empress," Arane said. "We shall return to our mountain, and you are welcome there, though I do not expect to see much of you."

Ruby smiled and allowed herself a small laugh.

"You don't owe me that," she said.

"We give it nonetheless."

Ruby offered Arane a short bow. The Weavers' gratitude is not wisely refused.

"Return home with my thanks. Any who kill Weavers or attempt entrance into your valley unbidden will answer to me. It's the least I can do for all you've done. I would have looked for her for days. I was afraid she'd left angry."

It was impossible to guess how Arane felt. She replied without feeling, and her human face simply stared, dead.

"The Halcyon guides," she intoned. "We have kept our own borders, but we see your thanks. You are a friend to the Weavers."

Now the tide of whispers was ebbing. The Weavers withdrew into Duskwood. They passed away north leaving silver behind them, a creep of masking dark through the Everdim. Arane raised her front legs and dipped her huge body low. Then she was gone into the moonlight, the last of the elder spiders, no more than a shadow spreading like blood through the trees before distance and the Everdim swallowed her.

Ruby looked over Filwa's grave a while longer, knowing that Arane was right but fighting the urge to believe her. If Filwa had been angry with her at the end, Ruby couldn't blame her. Perhaps it was the way of spiders to let the dead rest. It seemed so easy for them to move on in their glassy quiet. Ruby finally turned and made her way back, following the trail of silver threads, and as much as she turned the thought over in her mind she could not bring herself to the spiders' level. She was mired in memory and sadness, and the guards at Eastgate saw her troubled expression.

They came to her aid, and she dismissed them kindly. Dimwood slept beyond the gate; the roads were quiet and gently lit with a few faerie lamps. Ruby made her way to High Street, where a Heddlegard link-boy rushed to meet her. He entertained her with fantasies about the winter festival to come; he was sincerely expecting all sorts of unlikely surprises, and he had many guesses about what might happen based on circulating gossip. He had a nose for the truth, or so he claimed, and could not be fooled by any exaggerations. He stayed with Ruby until she opened the door to the lobby space below her apartments, and then she gave him a kiss on the forehead and sent him jogging away blushing.

The lobby was mostly dark, and the single attendant was asleep at his large cherry desk. She made her way toward the stairs, and was startled when a figure appeared at the entrance to the stairwell. Her blood froze – blue faerie light spilled from behind him, leaving him in deep shadow. And then he stepped forward, and of course it was only Michael carrying a parcel.

"Ah, Empress!" He approached at a happy trot, and Ruby let out a long breath of relief.

"You startled me," she said, disappointed in herself. The light part within her had not allowed her to cry at Filwa's grave, and it had foolishly believed that her fear was over and gone. She cursed time, which erased her youthful joy and left trauma behind, fresh as dew.

"I'm sorry," Michael said. He bowed and presented the parcel. "This was delivered to my home. I saw William and Sir Periwinkle return, and I thought you were with them, but they said you'd gone roaming in Duskwood. I'd imagined you'd be back by now, so I've been waiting for you in your room."

Ruby took the package. It was small and heavy and wrapped in layers of bark and brown poplar leaves that had been treated with some aromatic oil. She hesitated to pull the blue silk ribbon on top – the wrapping had been done with such care.

"Who left it?" she asked.

"A Cholai boy," Michael replied, digging into his waistcoat pockets. "Ah! This was attached."

He produced a folded card, flipped it open, and held it out for Ruby to read as she finally began unwrapping the parcel. The handwriting inside was thick and large, and it faltered as it progressed across the paper. It was in a form of Melidoran that she only dimly remembered, and she struggled to read at first. Then the letters melted into meaning, and the words seemed to rise from the grain of the paper like bubbles to the surface of the sea.

I won't waste my time blaming you for a few deaths when I should thank you for many lives. A token of forgiveness.

The note was signed *Filwa*. Now the tears came; Ruby sniffed hard and passed the note to Michael who smiled as he read it.

"She must have had this delivered before the wagons left yesterday morning," he said. "I'm sorry you didn't get to speak with her before then. She stayed outside the gates; I didn't want to bother her."

Ruby didn't have the voice to tell Michael what the Weavers had shown her. Instead, she concentrated on opening the package carefully, peeling back the soft layers and setting them aside to reveal a simple box with a hinged lid. Ruby took a big breath and lifted the lid. Inside was a brooch with a purple gem set in silver.

"This was Moira's," Ruby gasped, holding the box open.

Michael gripped the bottom of the box, and Ruby lifted the brooch out. Then he helped her fasten it about her neck. It lay low on her chest; the chain was longer than it had looked when Ruby first saw it. Touching it, she remembered the wonderful smells that had convinced Michael to approach the Cholai wagons and the advice Leora had given about listening and believing. She hoped she had used it well.

We believe first and listen last. Ruby couldn't help but smile.

"It was always about listening," Ruby said, and Michael looked confused. "Listening first and believing last. I owe her this. And my hand."

Now she told him about Filwa's grave in Duskwood and about how the Weavers had found her wandering in the snow as the moon rose. She repeated what Arane had said about the dead, and Michael agreed.

"The Weavers are wise," he told her, and she stepped in to hug him close. "Filwa forgave you. Leave the burden of guilt behind. You saved all of us, Empress. You saved yourself."

The theme of departure was common to every Halcyon tale, but promises of return were an indulgence attributed to priests. There was an invisible horizon, and no one knew how to achieve it, but it would certainly be achieved one day. Beyond that was nothing – or an endless expanse of one thing, which isn't much different. They offered this covenant to the faithful, because faith is built upon unrealized expectation. Once faith is affirmed with proof, it doesn't need to be faith anymore. It becomes knowledge. So the Halcyon was ever returning in her temples; outside of them, there was less certainty.

Michael returned to preaching not long after Arturus arrived in Robinegg. William came to see his friend every day, and at the end of the week he would bring Michael with him. There was no shortage of belief among the three. Ruby sat in on extensive talks about truth, wisdom, and virtue. How was patience attained? What brought the most happiness? What was moral? She found the topic of freedom most fascinating, but it was not much discussed. Among the three, it seemed to be obvious that freedom was worth strife. Ruby thought that there had to be a line somewhere, but she never said so. She didn't know where the line was. Who was she to say?

The Cradle Spire had been leaning lately. Ketha reported cracks spreading across its base. There had been no Nixie movement through Duskwood for weeks. The horrors she'd seen on Memnyr's blade continued to plague Ruby. They played on a screen in the back of her mind, and she could not control them. She relived her plunge from the Cradle Spire whenever she lay on her back; the sensation was at once terrifying and an affirmation of her substance. *The sword lies*, the Empress of Nix had said, and she had flickered as if flat and tilting on an edge. On some nights, she woke feeling just as insubstantial. Some days before the winter festival, with Dimwood's banners hanging between linden trunks like spiders' silk, Ruby met Michael in his home and gave him Memnyr.

It was noon, and winter was trailing into an early thaw. Ruby was wearing Filwa's brooch – a gem to replace a gem, and this one neither glowed nor spoke. The long coat the knights of Pearlwater had given her was draped over one of Michael's few chairs. Her greatcoat, she remembered, was still in the Cradle Spire's haunted stairwell. Ruby laid the sword in Michael's paws, and he looked down at its blade. Ruby looked only at him.

"Why give me this?" he asked her.

"It's the Halcyon's blade," she replied. "I don't need it anymore."

He ran a paw over its surface, traced the edge with one black claw. Ruby stepped past him briefly to pull a tray of muffins out of the oven before they burned. He turned to her, holding the sword in one paw now, its blade up, as she set the tray on the counter to cool.

"It showed the future," he said, as if to himself. "Did it also show the past?"

"I'm not sure what it showed anymore," Ruby said, and there was more sadness in this admission than she'd realized there would be. "The Empress said that it lies."

"What's a lie? I'm sure William's explanation was better: it reflects. Maybe you saw what you wanted or what you feared. Maybe you saw what you already believed."

Ruby smiled and thought of Leora the shrew.

"That's possible," she said. "I've been thinking that memories are mostly lies we tell ourselves."

Michael swung the sword once in a slow circle, careful of the low ceiling, and then he found a place on the sandy wall to hang it. He looked at it for a minute, and Ruby worried that he would become entranced. His eyes went wide, his jaw loosened; but then he turned and smiled at her and crossed to the counter to poke at the tray.

"Muffins are ready, eh?" he said. "You know, I don't know so much about lies, Empress. If my memories are lies, then I'm a lie. You're a lie. This home, this land, this world. Everything I believe."

"Maybe not everything," Ruby interrupted.

"Perhaps not everything," Michael went on, "but many things. Memories are tools just like anything else. Like swords. Sometimes we use them, and sometimes they use us."

Ruby only nodded at this. After a moment of silence, Michael caught her staring.

"You're fading," he said, and Ruby started. "Arturus will be out in a day. The north bridge is rebuilt, and Hawkport is fully open again. The fisheries are running. Southunder's stacks are blowing. The beavers are singing again; Pearlwater's recovered from the flood. Everything is returning to normal, as they say. And you're fading. I've seen you, Empress."

"I don't understand it," Ruby said, frowning.

"It's normal. That's my point," Michael laid his paw over her hand. "You're the Empress, and you will always be. You were the day I found you in the Mirrorwood – the day you washed up in the bay, coughing. Do you remember?"

"I do," Ruby replied.

"I knew when I found you that you would have to leave. You've seen us through, as I knew you would, and you've stayed to watch us collect ourselves. We'll go to Thimblewand."

"I wanted to do this without saying it," Ruby thought aloud. She was just realizing this. "I thought it might be better that way."

"I suppose I've ruined that," Michael said. "But if you fear, you can tell me. This is your world, Ruby, and I'm here for you. We all are."

"It was your world first," Ruby said, a muffin steaming in her hand. "All I did was find it. Remember what Dallie Bratcher said."

"I remember," Michael smiled. "Because of you."

It was still dark. They rode through the gates unchallenged, Michael and Ruby on their rams and William mounted high on a tall, sooty mare. Arturus sat carefully astride Junie, who picked her way over the rocky fields of Donchapel as though she knew to be mindful of his injury. They went south past the hill, to which arthewags were finally returning, and there was the Cradle Spire withering in Duskwood. Seer's Knob reared black in the north, the Auburns a ruddy hump of jagged peaks beyond. Southunder smoked, Lockwood Forest butted up against the Hearthemeade, and Ruby thought of the Cholai wagons trundling toward Driftgate or Morton. Perhaps they would return to Moonwood and the pools of mystery there. Melidora was emerging from a long sleep. Ruby could tour it in her mind – she could stretch herself from Lampblack and Nirfang to the blue peaks of Halcya and Northover's icy wastes – and from Eastfair to Westfair the land was resplendent in its awakening. She felt light upon its face, the shadow shrinking, and its pulse thrumming in the rivers.

They reached the mouth of the delta with dawn growing across the sky. Just east of them, the Golrace spilled through sawgrass marshes that sank slowly into the sea. This far south, a line of rough pine rocklands separated Thimblewand from the Pearlmire. Ruby looked across the delta toward Pearlwater, and she could just see the top of the Tower Imperial over the hardwood hummocks. They rode onto the beach, taking their time, talking and laughing as the mud turned to sand and rushes. Then they dismounted, and William spread two great blankets on the ground.

Ruby had made muffins. Michael had brought two silver thermoses of coffee. William and Arturus opened a box of meat sandwiches. They warmed the coffee as they needed over a fire, and put bacon in pans to fry. Ruby had expected a cloud this morning, but the sky warmed to a flawless blue as the sun rose across it.

Arturus told of his knighting ceremony, and then of his father's heroism during the North War.

"I was only a lad, but I remember how much my mother loved him," he said. "It means a lot in hindsight. That's what a pup should see, I think. Antonia and Theodorus grew up and moved on, and they missed out on a lot of that. Perhaps that's why they think me such a fool."

He laughed at that, and then he recited a poem about his mother, extolling her beauty and her bravery in raising him after the death of Feodor.

William would say very little about himself except that he had been born in Gowspin and that his father lived somewhere on the Veldt of Skies.

"We never missed him," he said, chewing on bacon and dabbing his mouth carefully with a white cloth. "I did some work as a courier in my youth, and then branched out from there, if you take my meaning. From 'carrying to' to 'carrying away.' I learned the bow from a bird, and he's dead now."

"That hardly befits the occasion!" Arturus laughed, slapping William on the back. "Go on and tell something interesting. The story about the fish!"

William rolled his eyes in his feline way. The tip of his tail lashed the air.

"It was a simple affair," he sighed, "and not very interesting. I was fishing in Pinwale. Something caught my line and dragged me for a little bit. I recovered, cut the line, and then went to market to buy some more."

"It was a mermaid," Arturus said. "I saw her! The water's clear as glass in the harbor. She was seven feet long with green hair, circling above the mud at the bottom. She caught his hook and pulled him in, and I dived in after him."

"I'm quite sure it was a grouper," William asserted. "A large one, yes. Larger than any I had seen before or have seen since, but certainly only a fish. Green hair! Pinwale sits above a kelp forest that is thickest in the north. That's what you thought was hair, no doubt. The water is clear, but to compare it to glass is misleading. A grouper took my bait, a powerful one, and I didn't want to let go of my pole. It was bamboo, and it had been made for me by a friend – it had great sentimental value. I was determined to save it. Sir Periwinkle dove in quite unnecessarily; I cut my line and had to save *him* from drowning. Everyone knows guinea pigs can't swim."

"You never tell interesting stories," Arturus joked. William bristled, though he could not keep a smile from his eyes.

"Perhaps because I prefer to tell stories that are true."

Michael smoked his pipe and was quiet while the others talked and sang songs. He looked out at the Thimbles standing black in the sea, hunching like hierophants. When he spoke at last, he told of his journey east to find Ruby, a story that Ruby herself had never heard.

"It's only now that I can remember," he began. "It was a jay that told me you were coming – or that you had come. I left as soon as I could, and that was before Hawkport had been taken. The Nixies were leaning hard upon it, and its strength was failing. I crossed the south bridge into the city and was making my way out just as the last of the defenders fell. I saw the Nixies rush in, but I could not stay. I left them, but there was nothing I could have done even if I had stayed. The damage had been done. I suppose I should have seen the doors to the west closing behind me, but that was when the Forgetting was sitting heavy on everyone."

He went on to tell a rambling tale of near calamities. Kobolds had attacked him at Seer's Knob, and Ketha had saved him. There had been dire-dogs on the Fields of Silver, and then he had been diverted north during a storm by Nixie patrols in the Eastfair. He spoke until the last of the muffins were gone, and when he was finished, Arturus applauded.

"*That* is an interesting story," he said to William.

"And true," Michael replied with a broad smile.

"Perhaps, but it had no mermaids," William purred. "It was quite a trek, in all seriousness, and one for which you deserve to be honored as a hero."

"But I should dislike that," Michael confessed. He stood with the others and began to fold the blankets. "This whole journey, I did only what I needed to do, and I did it as safely as I could. If I had listened to you, Ruby, when you wanted to go north, we might never have been caught in the Valley of Silk."

"There's no use thinking like that," Ruby said. "For every one thing that might have been better, we could find any number of things that might have been worse."

"Acceptance of what has happened is the first step to overcoming the consequences of any misfortune," William said. "And I assert that what has happened could not have happened in a better way. No matter what your frailties may be, you were willing to risk death – what's more, you faced it heroically. That fact consecrates you forever, as far as I'm concerned."

"Tee-whit!" Junie added. She was bouncing from foot to foot on the sand and bobbing at the shadows of wheeling birds. "Tee-whit-willow!"

"Junie agrees," Arturus laughed. "That's good enough a philosophical argument for me."

They went down to the water. The sun was very high, but it still had a way to go before it reached the ultimate crest of noon. Kittiwakes nested on the Thimbles, and shearwaters pestered them. The beach was dark with rails, and as they descended toward the strandline the birds scattered on legs like willow switches. Ruby embraced each of her friends in turn and kissed each on the cheek as she said her goodbyes. In a story, Luna had climbed the Cradle Spire in hopes of finding the Halcyon's ring, but had not been there when she had reached the pinnacle. Now Ruby slipped off the ring she had taken from the Empress of Nix and pressed it into William's paw.

"This is for all of you," she said. "A relic to replenish your faith when darkness comes."

"You do not fail," William replied, bowing to her.

"Nor do you." she addressed all of them. "From the bottom of my heart: thank you all."

She had expected to be bitterly sad and had brought a handkerchief. But she was filled with a rush as she stepped into the tide. Her friends looked on her with smiles bright and certain, waving, and beauty swelled up in her heart until she felt as though she was glowing. Arturus blew her a kiss, and she made a show of catching it. It didn't feel like leaving. She felt loved and whole. Junie was still bobbing on the sand. Ruby blew a kiss back to all of them, waved a final time, and then closed her eyes and fell back into the southern sea.

The dark closed around her. The water sucked her down, pressed her to the sand, and then pulled her out past the Thimble rocks. She held her breath, her arms out at her sides, and then she was falling. The wind rushed up against her back, and the water pulsed above her. She felt the weight of the whole ocean upon her; her lungs burned, her stomach felt like a pit opening into an eternity of pressure. She opened her eyes in a brief panic, coughed and choked and brought her hands to her throat, and then she was calm. She drifted in the black and became thin. She guttered like a flame. It might have been a moment before she came to – it might have been a million years.

She awoke in her bed, warm and still and breathing. The walls were a flat, gray-blue. A ceiling fan rocked above her, and a blue gem hung from its chain. She heard a voice that seemed to come from another world. It was soft and muddled, bleeding into itself. Then she turned her head and saw her son sitting beside her.

He was in the same chair he sat in every week, his back to the window. It was summer behind him; the world shone green and gold, and heat poured in through the open pane. There were linden trees on the lawn.

"'Outside, the north wind, coming and passing, swelling and dying, lifts the frozen sands, drives it a-rattle against the lidless windows and we my dear sit stroking the cat stroking the cat and smiling sleepily, prrrr.'" Her son looked at her and smiled. He seemed so young. He had finally shaved and gotten a haircut. "I always liked that one," he said, seeming distracted.

Then he saw that her eyes were open. He took her hand and leaned over her, gaping in disbelief.

"Ma?" he managed. "Ma, can you hear me?"

Ruby nodded, and her heart was like a flutter of butterflies. She squeezed her son's hand and reached over to stroke his strong fingers. She glanced briefly toward the door and saw it was open. There was no one there.

She looked at the young man she had raised, proud of how handsome and loving he was. She saw a light in him that she had forgotten. He had saved her, but she knew now, finally, that she had saved him, too. Now she found her voice, and she held his hands in both of hers and looked into his gem-blue eyes. With her fluttering heart overflowing, she greeted him at last.

"Michael."

The William Quotes

"Reasoning at every step he treads, Man yet mistakes his way, Whilst meaner things, whom instinct leads, Are rarely known to stray."

-William Cowper

"He must teach himself that the basest of all things is to be afraid; and, teaching himself that, forget it forever, leaving no room in his workshop for anything but the old verities and truths of the heart, the old universal truths lacking which any story is ephemeral and doomed - love and honor and pity and pride and compassion and sacrifice."

-William Faulkner

"Time is a storm in which we are all lost."

-William Carlos Williams

"It is only those who have neither fired a shot nor heard the shrieks and groans of the wounded and lacerated who cry aloud or blood, more vengeance, more desolation."

-William Tecumseh Sherman

"Wise are they who have learned these truths: Trouble is temporary. Time is tonic. Tribulation is a test tube."

- William Arthur Ward

"Acceptance of what has happened is the first step to overcoming the consequences of any misfortune"

-William James

"Outside, the north wind, coming and passing, swelling and dying, lifts the frozen sand drives it a-rattle against the lidless windows and we may dear sit stroking the cat stroking the cat and smiling sleepily, prrrr."

- William Carlos Williams